The Synchronicity
By Dietmar Arthur Wehr

MW00954474

Amazon Edition

Copyright 2013 by Dietmar Arthur Wehr

http://www.dwehrsfwriter.com/
The Synchronicity War Part 1 paperback version
The Synchronicity War Part 2 paperback version

Acknowledgements: I wish to express my most heartfelt thanks to Jill Linkert for her diligent editing and suggestions. Jill has made me a better author.

Notes to Edition 4: This novel has been completely re-edited by someone who knows what they're doing. The formatting is substantially different from Edition 3. It also now includes a Cast of Characters section and a Glossary of Terms. As of this writing (March 11th), Parts 1,2 & 3 are now available with the final installment (Part 4) expected to be published some time during the summer of 2014. However, prior to that, I plan on publishing a short prequel (Part 0?), which I will try to get Amazon to give away for free. If you happen to be a fan of H. Beam Piper's works, then check out my website for new material based on two of his books.

Cast of Characters:

Human:
Senior Space Force Officers:
Admiral Sam Howard, Chief of Space Operations
Rear Admiral Sepp Dietrich, Chief of Personnel
Rear Admiral Sergei Kutuzov, Chief of Logistics

Base Commanders:
Sen. Cmdr. Korolev

Squadron Leaders:
Sen. Cmdr. Torres
Sen. Cmdr. Yakamura
Cmdr. Shiloh
Cmdr. Cabrera
Cmdr. Dejanus
Cmdr. LaRoche
Cmdr. Mbutu
Cmdr. Bettencourt
Cmdr. Rolen

Other Space Force Officers:
Cmdr. Adams (Exploration Frigate Commander)
Cmdr. Caru (Exploration Frigate Commander)
Lt. Cmdr. Angela Johansen (XO, FE 344)
Lt. Cmdr. Amanda Kelly (Team Leader, Strategic Planning Group)
Lt. Cmdr. Svetlana Chenko (XO, FE 344)
Lt. Cmdr. Brad Falkenberg (Deputy CAG, CVL Defiant)
Lt. Cmdr. Michaels (2nd Officer, FE 344)
Lt. Cmdr. Farnsworth (2nd Officer, FE 344)
Sen. Lt. Sykes (Weapons Officer, FE 344)
Lt. Rodriguez (Astrogator, CVL Defiant)
Lt. Verlander (Helm Officer, FE 344)

A.I.s: (In Alphabetical Order)
Bulldog
Cyrano
Firefox
Hammer
Hunter
Iceman

Glossary of Terms:

CSO   Chief of Space Operations
CAG   Commander, Autonomous Group
TF   Task Force
KPS   Kilometers Per Second
Klicks   slang expression for kilometers
A.U.   Astronomical Unit equal to the average distance between the Earth and its Sun.
A.I.   Artificial Intelligence
SL   Squadron Leader
C.O.   Commanding Officer
X.O.   Executive Officer
W.O.   Weapons Officer
E.O.   Engineering Officer

Chapter 1 At The Edge Of The Abyss

Cmdr. Victor Shiloh noticed that the usual Bridge chatter had died down to almost nothing as the Squadron emerged from Jumpspace. Everyone knew the stakes. One of their own was missing, and they were here to find her. FE 319 – Frigates didn't rate names – had not reported back to base, and it hadn't sent a message drone. This was very worrisome. If the ship had been able to return, it would have. If it had malfunctioned or there was some other reason for a delayed return, such as a major discovery of some kind, it would have sent the drone back. The entire squadron, seven Frigates under the command of Squadron Leader Torres, had been sent to investigate. FE 344, under Cmdr. Shiloh, was designated as the rear guard, staying behind at the point where the Squadron emerged so that it could jump back into Jumpspace with a warning for HQ if something nasty happened to the other six ships of the squadron. FE 344 decelerated to a crawl, relatively speaking, while it changed its orientation to enable it to jump away from this star system instead of closer to it. With that maneuver done, Shiloh relaxed just a little bit. They could now jump at a moment's notice if they had to.

"Now we wait," he said, loud enough for the rest of the Bridge crew to hear him. He switched his command station's main viewer to show the long range Tactical display. He saw his ship, at the center of the display, as a green triangle, with six other green triangles slowly moving to the top of the screen, spreading out as they did so towards the inner part of this star system. As he watched, the display showed clusters of smaller green dots moving away from the green triangles. The Squadron had launched reconnaissance drones for long range snooping. A star system was a big place for one small ship to hide in. By comparison, a needle in a haystack was trivial. Without the recon drones, it could take weeks to find the missing ship.

Nothing of significance was occurring to engage Shiloh's attention, and he began to ponder how the nature of faster-than-light travel determined Humanity's expansion into the rest of the galaxy. The rate at which ships traveled through Jumpspace was determined by how fast they were moving when they entered Jumpspace. The more velocity a ship had, the faster the transit through Jumpspace, although the relationship was logarithmic rather than linear. If you wanted to go twice as fast in Jumpspace, you had to build a velocity that was ten times as fast in normal space. Entering and moving through Jumpspace required energy that was generated by the fusion of heavy hydrogen. The contra-gravity engines that moved a ship through normal space also required lots of energy. So when a ship's limited supply of heavy hydrogen was low enough to be a factor in a planned transit between two star systems, the Astrogator calculated the optimum combination of normal space acceleration, Jumpspace duration and normal space deceleration at the other end, to minimize the total consumption of fuel. What irked Shiloh, and most of the other exploration frigates commanders, was the fact that their ships hadn't been designed to be able to refuel themselves by skimming the atmospheres of gas giants, separating the tiny amounts of heavy hydrogen from the more abundant normal hydrogen. For some reason, which no one seemed to understand, the designers had traded the self-refueling capability for a larger fuel capacity. This meant that the frigates could operate for longer periods of time before having to rendezvous with tankers, but they still had a limited range of operation. That meant that explorations squadrons were tied to tankers, which themselves could only move forward if they were certain that the destination star system contained at least one gas giant, and not all star systems did. SFE144 was operating at the limit of its internal fuel supply. Regardless of what they did or didn't find here, the squadron's frigates had just enough fuel to make it back to their assigned tanker.

It was an hour later when things started to happen. By that time, the rest of the Squadron was far enough away that there was an appreciable time lag in two-way communications. The other six ships kept in constant contact with 344 by tight beam, low-powered lasers, and 344 acted as a relay station, keeping each ship in the squadron in contact with the rest, albeit with an even bigger time lag. It was easier for them to stay in contact with one fixed location – 344 – than it would have been with multiple moving locations. The relay ship kept track of the moving ships by the direction of the incoming laser beams and by the navigational data that each ship provided about its speed and course. Computers onboard the relay ship aimed the return laser where the target ship would be by the time the laser beam arrived there. Theoretically, two ships could communicate from opposite sides of a star system, but the time lag of many hours made it not worth the effort. Shiloh became aware that his Executive Officer had arrived on the Bridge to relieve him.

"You're relieved, Skipper," said Lt. Commander Angela Johansen.

Shiloh nodded and swiveled his command chair around to face her. After getting up, he waited while she sat down and adjusted the command chair to better fit her body's smaller dimensions. A properly adjusted chair made a four-hour duty shift a lot more tolerable. As she did so, he couldn't help noticing – once again – that she had a very attractive figure. Not that he was actually tempted to do anything with that fact. While physical relationships between officers were not prohibited, they were 'discouraged' on the theory that anything other than a professional relationship might result in biased performance reviews. When she was finished, he leaned over so that their conversation wouldn't distract the rest of the Bridge crew who were also in the process of being relieved.

"No sign of 319 yet, or of anything else for that matter. The ship's in stealth mode. Maintain the status quo. I'm going to hit the sack, but I want you to call me if there's any new development."

"Understood. I'll pass that on to Michaels when he relieves me. What do you think happened to the 319, Skipper?"

Shiloh shrugged. "There's no distress beacon, no message drone beacon. That's not a good sign. It suggests to me that whatever happened to the 319, it happened so fast that they didn't have time to launch a message drone, or else the message drone was destroyed or disabled." He paused while both of them pondered the implications of that. "Listen, stay sharp and make sure everyone else stays sharp too. I don't want us to be surprised, right?"

The XO nodded. "Right."

Shiloh gave her an encouraging pat on the shoulder as he moved away, heading down to his cabin. He was surprised how tired he was. This mission was a lot more stressful than the survey missions the exploration frigate squadrons normally engaged in, and it wasn't the first time an FE had gone missing. That first ship had belonged to another squadron exploring a different sector of space, and no sign of it had yet been found. When 319 was declared overdue, their nearest forward base had ordered their squadron to search for her under the rules of engagement that had been designed for war but never used – until now. Hence the ship was operating in stealth mode. There were no running lights and no energy emissions of any kind, except for the tightly focused communication beams that were impossible to detect unless another ship happened to pass exactly between the sender and the receiver.

By the time Shiloh reached his cabin, he was too tired to think about their situation anymore. He didn't even bother to remove his uniform as he let himself fall face down on his bunk. Sleep came almost instantly … and when his wakeup alarm sounded, he immediately woke up. For a few seconds he thought he must have set it to the wrong time. He checked it and realized that he had slept seven hours, which gave him one hour to shower, dress and grab something to eat in the Officer's Mess before heading back to the Bridge for his duty shift. While he got ready to take a shower, he decided to check with the Bridge.

"Intercom," he said, activating the two com implants, one in his ear and one adjacent to his voice box. "Bridge …"

"Bridge here, Skipper."

"Status report, Michaels."

"No sign of the 319. The Squadron is continuing its sweep pattern. No change in ship's status."

"Acknowledged."

By the time he had showered, dressed and began drinking a coffee in the Officers' Mess, he was feeling much more alert. Just as he started to eat his breakfast, the Bridge called him.

"Shiloh here."

"Skipper, 301 reports that one of their recon drones has detected a vessel at long range. It seems to be drifting.

As far as they can tell at that range, the ship is the right size to be the 319. The SL has ordered 323 and 299 to rendezvous with her at the drifting ship. It'll take them approximately five and a half hours to intercept the drifting vessel with zero velocity. The drone is being vectored for a flyby, and 301 expects to have a positive ID in approximately 34 minutes. With the time lag in transmission, we should know about 9 minutes after that. "

"Did the Squadron Leader have any instructions for us?"

"No Sir."

"Very well then. We'll wait until there's a positive ID before I inform the crew. Anything else, Commander?"

"No Sir."

"I'll be up to the Bridge shortly then. End message."

Shiloh pondered the information he'd just received. If that really was the 319, then perhaps it was just a malfunction of some kind. Anxious to get back to the Bridge, he finished his breakfast quickly and headed up. Even though he was almost 15 minutes early for his duty shift, he decided to relieve the Second Officer now. After relieving Lt. Commander Michaels, he did a quick check of the ship's systems and status, and then settled in to await word of the drifting ship's identity.

The time-lagged word came through the comlink just about right on schedule. It WAS the 319. Squadron Leader Torres had ordered the drone flyby video feed to be retransmitted to the relay ship and then to the other ships of the squadron. Shiloh watched the video in real time and then replayed it in slow motion with maximum zoom. The drone got to within one klick of the 319, and the video clearly showed that the 319 had suffered some kind of damage to its hull. Shiloh could see in its hull what appeared to be a long straight gash that cut diagonally from the Bridge almost all the way back to the Engineering Section. He couldn't imagine any kind of malfunction that would cause that particular kind of damage. What he could imagine was an attack by an energy weapon like a laser. He decided to keep his suspicions to himself for now, but the crew deserved to know that their sister ship had been found.

"Intercom … ship-wide … Attention all hands. We've just received confirmation that one of 301's drones has positively identified a drifting ship as the 319. No contact with her crew has been achieved, so there's no way to know at this time what the status of her crew is. As soon as we get additional information, it will be passed on to all of you. Let's hope the news is good. That's all for now. End message."

Now that he'd gotten that duty out of the way, Shiloh checked the incoming data feed from Torres. The Squadron Leader hadn't expressed an opinion as to the cause of 301's situation either. However good the drones' optics were, the definitive answer would have to wait until human eyes got up close and personal. What the SL had done, though, was to order the recon drone to swing around for another slower – and closer – pass. The drone would still make it back to the 319 before the 301, 323 and 299 arrived in the vicinity with zero remaining velocity. But once there, Torres would send over a ship's boat with a boarding party that included not only medical and engineering personnel, but also an inspection team to look closely at the exterior damage. Until then, they just had to wait and see.

The remainder of Shiloh's shift went surprisingly fast. After being relieved by Lt. Cmdr Johansen once again, he went back to the Officers Mess for lunch. He was alone, as usual, since his eight hour 'day' just happened to coincide with most officers' eight hour 'night'.

His lunch finished, Shiloh leaned back in his chair and lingered over his coffee. Even though he wasn't tired, he felt the urge to close his eyes. Then something happened that had not happened to him since he was in his teens. He felt an unusual, yet strangely familiar sensation come over him. When he opened his eyes, he saw himself standing in front of Admiral Howard's desk back at U.E.S.F. HQ. He heard the Admiral speak.

'It's a good thing you launched those recon drones when you did, Commander. The mission would have ended very differently if you hadn't.'

Then he felt that same urge to close his eyes for a few seconds.

When he opened them again, he was back in the Officers' Mess on board the 344. The last time he had a 'vision' like that was when he and some friends were climbing in the rugged wilderness of the Rocky Mountains. In that vision, he saw and heard a rescue paramedic congratulate him on having the foresight to attach a second safety line to his friend before climbing the cliff they had planned to ascend. So he did, in fact, attach a second safety line. Halfway up the cliff the first line snapped, and his friend only suffered a painful gash instead of a fatal plunge to his death. At the time he thought the vision must have been just his imagination, and yet here he was having another one.

After pondering this situation for a few minutes, he took a deep breath and said, "Intercom … Bridge."

The XO responded almost immediately. "Bridge here."

Shiloh said nothing for a few seconds, and then said, "Angela, how many recon drones are we carrying this trip?"

There was a slight pause as the XO checked. "We have four type seven drones, Skipper."

Shiloh said nothing while he pondered whether to follow his vision.

"Was there something else, Sir?" Johansen asked with a puzzled tone to her voice.

Shiloh came to a decision. "XO, I want you to program two recon drones for a circular track around the ship at a range of … 100,000 klicks, with minimal overlapping coverage. What's the maximum duration we can get with that?"

He waited while she asked the computer for the answer.

"Approximately 48 hours, which means the drones will complete three trips around the ship. If you were thinking of extending our sensor coverage, then I would recommend using three drones with circular tracks in three dimensions, with one complete circle every eight hours. That would mean the drones would exhaust their power supply in twelve hours, but if we recover them prior to shutdown, we can recharge them. With four drones, we can have three on the go all the time if we launch one every four hours."

Shiloh shook his head. "But that would mean only partial coverage for the first eight hours, correct?"

"Affirmative."

"No good. I want complete coverage from the get go."

The XO pondered that requirement. "Okay. Here's how we do it. We launch three drones now, then retrieve and refuel one every four hours when we've replaced it with a fresh one."

"Okay. That works for me. Implement it right away and maintain until further notice."

"Aye, aye, Sir. Anything else, Sir?"

"No that's it. Shiloh clear."

Shiloh felt better for having taken that action, even as he wondered how he would justify it in his log. Somehow he didn't think the brass back at HQ would think much of his admission to having a 'vision'. Senior Officers tended to get nervous when the Commander of a 20,000-ton Frigate started 'seeing things'. Shiloh decided not to mention his vision in his log. He went back to his cabin and sat down to go over the daily reports and the other administrative tasks that a Commanding Officer regularly needed to attend to during his free time between duty shifts. Halfway through the pile of paperwork, the Bridge called.

"Bridge to Shiloh."

"Shiloh here."

"Skipper, we just received the video feed from the drone's second pass. The level of detail is much higher. Maybe I'm just being paranoid, but the hull damage looks like what you would expect from laser fire. Torres hasn't expressed an opinion, but if you ask me it's obvious as hell."

Shiloh felt a shiver go down his spine. "Based on what I saw from the first flyby, that doesn't surprise me." He pondered the situation for a few seconds before adding, "Okay, I'm coming to the Bridge. End message."

When Shiloh got to the Bridge, the XO started to get up from the Command Station, but Shiloh waived her back down. "Just pretend I'm not here," he told her.

Johansen just snorted in reply as Shiloh went to the Com Station and asked the Com Tech to replay the drone's second flyby video. The XO hadn't exaggerated. The video feed clearly showed a deep, straight gash with blistering around the edges. Laser fire was the only possible explanation.

"Com. Is a message drone being updated with the data from the Squadron?"

"Affirmative Sir."

"Intercom … ship-wide … Attention all hands, this is the CO. I've just seen evidence from the 301's recon drone flyby that our sister ship, the 319, was attacked by unknown forces. The 301 will be sending over a boarding party to search for survivors. As soon as I hear what they find, I'll pass it along. In the meantime, we have to be vigilant for whoever did this. If we need to go to General Quarters, you have to be ready to act instantly. If you hear the GQ alarm, it'll be the real thing. I'm suspending drills for the duration of this mission. That is all for now. End message."

Shiloh was just about to walk away from the Com Station when the Com Tech turned to him and said, "Skipper, there's a message for you from Cmdr Torres."

With the 9-minute time lag, it was going to be a one-way message.

"Okay. Replay it from the beginning, Chen."

"Aye, aye, Sir. Switching now."

One of the screens at the Com Station suddenly showed the face of Commander Juanita Torres, who began speaking immediately.

"Shiloh, by now you've probably seen the evidence that 319 was attacked. The chances of finding survivors seem slim based on the exterior damage that we can see from here. 323 and 299 will be rendezvousing with us soon. I have a nagging suspicion that 319 is being used as bait. If that's correct, then we may also be attacked at any moment. If you haven't already done so, I want you to launch a message drone with all of the data collected so far. If my hunch is correct and we are attacked, you are ordered to immediately, repeat immediately jump back to our staging point and make sure the Base knows what happened. Do NOT under any circumstances come to our aide. I'm instructing the remainder of the Squadron to come together and join us asap. It's my intention to leave this system as soon as we've finished recovering survivors, if any, and have downloaded 319's datalogs. Your primary mission is to get word back to Base. If you're attacked, you have permission to jump out of here as quickly as you can. Good luck to us all. Torres out."

Shiloh didn't hesitate. "Com. Launch the message drone now and acknowledge the SL's message."

The response was immediate. "Message drone launched, Sir, Squadron Leader's message has been acknowledged."

"Understood."

He walked over to the Command Station and met the XO's gaze. "You heard?"

She nodded and was just about to say something when they heard the phrase that Shiloh had been dreading.

"Sensor contact bearing 089 by 022!"

Johansen switched one of her Command Station screens to the same display as the sensor tech was watching.

"Can you determine distance, course and speed?" asked the XO.

"Not yet, Sir. Only one of our recon drones has detected a faint reflection of sunlight off a metallic surface, and we'd need at least two drones to triangulate an approximate distance, course and speed. The other two drones are scanning the general direction of the reflection. We may have a better fix momentarily, Sir."

Johansen looked at her Boss. "Skipper, I recommend we go to General Quarters," she said quietly.

He didn't hesitate before nodding. After the XO sent the ship to General Quarters, Shiloh said, "XO, I'll take the Con."

As she turned to get up, she said for the benefit of the Bridge crew, "Skipper has the Con!"

When Shiloh sat down in the Command Chair, he took the precaution to strap himself in, just in case the ship had to maneuver more violently than the inertial compensators could handle. He took a good look at the screen displaying the sensor contact. It showed the three recon drones – one in the center and the other two in the upper and lower right corners, a green triangle that was equidistant from the three drones representing the 344, and a red flashing line extending from one drone to the upper left side of the screen. The alien vessel was somewhere along that line. If one of the other two drones could also detect a reflection, the screen would show a second line from that other drone, and the intersection of the two lines would indicate the position of the alien vessel. Without that approximate position, there was nothing that 344 could do. The screen also showed the message drone gradually moving away from the ship on a course that could take it dangerously close to the alien vessel, depending on where that ship might be. If the alien detected the message drone and tracked its course backwards, it would have a pretty good idea that another ship was lurking in the vicinity. While he was waiting for a second drone to get a fix on the alien, Shiloh realized that he should inform Squadron Leader Torres of their situation.

"Com, I'm recording a message for SL Torres and the Squadron. Transmit it as soon as I'm done."

"Aye, aye, Sir."

"Commander Torres, we have detected an unknown and presumably hostile vessel. The bogey's range, course and speed have not yet been determined. I don't believe that we've been spotted yet. It's my intention to attack the bogey as soon as we have a better fix on its position. A message drone has been launched but may be detected, which is why I'm going to distract the bogey with our own attack. 344 may have to maneuver without warning. I recommend that the rest of the Squadron establish a new com link with you, using your recon drone near the 319 as a temporary relay. If my attack is successful, I will follow your previous instructions and head back to our staging point without further delay. End message."

There was still no second sighting. Shiloh wished he could attack now with the 344's lasers, but the faintness of the reflection was too imprecise to allow for much chance of a direct hit. A near miss would only alert the enemy vessel to 344's presence. He had to have at least two sensor sightings to have a realistic chance for a laser hit. Three sightings would improve the odds even more. The fact that neither the 344 nor the other two drones had seen any reflection suggested that the alien vessel's hull was at an angle relative to the sun such that no reflections were being bounced in the general direction of the other drones or the frigate. That implied that the alien wasn't maneuvering and therefore hadn't detected them. If it detected something, it might change its course and/or speed and perhaps even its orientation relative to the sun.

Shiloh suddenly had an idea. He decided to take over direct control of the recon drone that was farthest from the bogey. He ordered its onboard A.I. pilot to broadcast an omni-directional signal lasting a fraction of a second, hoping it would be just enough to get the alien's attention and cause it to begin maneuvering. The ploy worked. No sooner had the drone transmitted the signal than the bogey began to maneuver AND rotate its hull orientation. Its hull's irregular surfaces caused sunlight to bounce in new directions, and both the frigate and one of the other drones caught the reflection. Sensor data was quickly analyzed by the tactical A.I. The range to the bogey was now determined to be 144,000 klicks away. Speed was only about 13 kilometers per second, but it was accelerating at a very respectable 1.1 kps squared in the direction of the signal from the drone. Shiloh glanced at the screen showing the Tactical Officer's primary display. The Tactical A.I. was projecting a laser hit probability of 61.8% but as more sensor data came in, the hit probability was getting better. At the rate it was changing, it would reach 90% in a few seconds. Shiloh had another idea. He asked the Tactical A.I. to plot possible intercept courses for the recon drones versus the bogey. Only two of the drones were close enough

AND fast enough to intercept the alien ship if it maintained its present course and acceleration. One of the two drones had been the one that sent the signal. Shiloh ordered all three drones to attempt to intercept and ram the alien ship. Even though the third drone would not be able to catch up to the alien ship if it continued its acceleration, it provided insurance against the chance of the bogey reducing its speed. Shiloh looked at the hit probability display. It was approaching 90%, but the rate of increase was slowing as the law of diminishing marginal returns kicked in. Theoretically it would eventually hit 100% if enough sensor data was accumulated or the target got close enough, but at this distance, the best probability that Shiloh could hope for in a reasonable length of time was in the low 90's. 344 had two standard laser turrets, designed primarily for use against unarmored pirate and smuggler vessels. If that alien ship had any kind of hull armor, his lasers might need multiple hits to penetrate it. That was another good reason to try to ram the bastard. Even hull armor would have difficulty in mitigating the damage caused by the kinetic energy from a collision at the kind of speeds that both the bogey and the drones would be traveling. The effect would be similar to what happened when tanks fired armor-piercing, kinetic energy shells at other tanks. The kinetic energy at the point of impact was so great that the impacting metal rod instantly turned to a jet of super hot gases that punched through even the densest armor like a hot knife through butter. If 344's lasers didn't cripple that ship, then Shiloh hoped the ramming drones would.

Without turning his head, Shiloh called to his Weapons Officer. "Weapons!"

"Sir?" replied the officer with a tense voice.

"When I give you the word to open fire, I want you to keep firing until I order you to stop or until the target is destroyed. "

"Understood, Sir!"

Shiloh monitored both the hit probability screen and the Tactical display screen. The bogey's vector was up to 55 kps and still climbing. The range hadn't dropped that much, but as the speed increased, the range would start dropping faster and faster. At least the message drone seemed to be undetected. Its speed was increasing quickly too. Another two and a half minutes and the message drone would reach the optimum speed for a least time jump to the star system where the support ships were waiting for the squadron to return. Shiloh wanted to wait as long as possible so that the hit probability would be as high as possible. On the other hand, the longer he waited, the greater the chance that the message drone would be detected. The 344 could make a microjump right now and get away from that alien ship, but then they would need to spend time accelerating fast enough to reach their departure system quickly. The message drone could get back faster and was therefore worth protecting. Since it was being constantly updated with data from the ship up to the point when it entered Jumpspace, the support ships would know what was happening. The hit probability indicator reached 90%. With two lasers firing, the odds of both missing were one chance in a hundred. The chances of both hitting on the first shot were slightly better than four out of five. Shiloh decided not to wait any longer.

"Helm, go to maximum acceleration now! Weapons … open fire!"

"Opening fire now, Sir!" Almost immediately he continued, "Two hits! We got two hits! Lasers recharging. Ready to fire again in … five … four … three …"

Shiloh watched the Tactical display. The bogey had changed course. Its heading was swinging towards his ship. 344 hadn't been hit by return fire yet. Shiloh assumed that the bogey had fired and missed, or else they couldn't fire due to damage from 344's initial shot. 344 fired again. It was time for his ship to change course.

"Helm, pull up 90 degrees! Go vertical then commence evasive action!"

The Helm's response mingled with the Weapon's officer's reporting of two more hits. Still no hits from the enemy vessel. Shiloh didn't think their luck would continue for much longer. He checked the status of the message drone. It was still accelerating and apparently undetected. He checked the range to the bogey again. Still dropping, and the rate of decline was increasing. 344 was pulling a higher acceleration than the bogey, but its initial velocity might as well have been zero for all the good it did them. The bogey had a lot more velocity to begin with, so even though 344 was gaining speed at a faster rate, the bogey was still moving faster due to its initial head start. The only thing that was working in their favor was the fact that by going vertical relative to the system's plane, 344 was beginning a whole new vector. The bogey was moving fast 'horizontally' but not 'vertically'. At some point the 3-dimensional geometry would start to work in their favor, and the range would start to widen again. A part of Shiloh's mind took note of the fact that the bogey's rate of acceleration was still 1.1 kps squared. 344 was piling on the velocity at almost twice that rate. One possible explanation for that discrepancy would be that their hull had a lot of armor on it. The extra mass would degrade acceleration performance. It would also explain why the four hits achieved thus far didn't seem to have any effect on the alien vessel's ability to maneuver. If that ship did have enough hull armor to reduce its maximum acceleration by half, then 344 was in big trouble.

Shiloh checked the relative positions and time to impact of the recon drones. The drone that would reach the target first was still a minute and a half away from contact. The good news was that by following the 344's vertical course change, the bogey was no longer accelerating horizontally, and that meant that drone #3 had a viable intercept solution. A flashing red indicator on one of his screens caught Shiloh's attention. The Sensor Tech confirmed it.

"We've got active scanning! The bogey's gone to active scanning!"

That was both good and bad news for Shiloh's ship. Active scanning meant that the bogey's return fire was bound to be more accurate. The good news was that the active scanning itself gave away their position even more precisely than tracking it by reflected sunlight had done. There was no way that 344's two lasers would miss now, and in fact they would be able to aim both lasers at exactly the same point, thereby doubling the energy trying to penetrate the hull at a specific spot. Shiloh turned his attention to trying to keep his ship from getting hit.

"Helm! Redline the engines and go to max evasion!"

Shiloh dimly heard the Helm Officer acknowledge his orders. 344 started to maneuver so violently that its crew began to feel it. Shiloh was glad he was strapped in. Just then the ship took its first hit. The extreme maneuvering saved the ship from taking the full brunt of the enemy laser. Instead, they got a glancing blow that cut through the ship's minimal armor as if it wasn't there and knocked out one of the maneuvering engine assemblies. 344's acceleration dropped by eight per cent and the severity of the evasive maneuvers declined slightly, but that meant the chances of getting hit again had just increased.

"Two more hits!" shouted the Weapons Officer, his voice beginning to get hoarse. "We did it! We got through their hull! Reading atmosphere venting! Ready to fire again in three … two … one … Firing! Two more hits! More hull penetration!"

The Tactical display showed the bogey's acceleration dropping for the first time by almost 0.2 kps squared. Shiloh also noticed that 344 seemed to be firing more frequently than the alien ship. If their weapons were far more powerful, then it would take a lot more energy to recharge it after every shot. So it was a race to see if the strategy of multiple shots with less power could damage the alien vessel severely enough before their more powerful but less frequent return fire crippled his ship. To his surprise, another full minute went by without another hit from the enemy vessel. During that interval, 344's lasers penetrated the alien hull three times, the results showing in reduced acceleration. Just as Shiloh started to hope that they might get through this with only minor damage, 344 took a direct hit. Both laser turrets were knocked out as the beam slashed along the ship's spine. Multiple compartments experienced explosive decompression with instant death for the occupants. Collateral damage included the severing of key control linkages between the Bridge and the rear half of the ship, which meant they could no longer maneuver the ship from the Bridge. 344 continued to accelerate but now only in a straight line. This meant that the next enemy shot would hit her again for sure. Shiloh's Command Station screens lit up like a Christmas tree with multiple red and yellow damage lights. He heard his Helm Officer call out.

"I've lost helm control! We can't evade!"

The Com Officer said, "All com channels with the rear half of the ship have been cut!"

Shiloh had to find a way to get the ship maneuvering again. It was their only hope of evading another devastating blow. He thought fast.

He called out the Weapons Officer's name, "Sykes! Get down to engineering and tell the XO to take over Helm functions from there. Tell her we need to start evading again, fast!"

To his credit, Sykes didn't even waste time acknowledging the order. He was already on his way by the time Shiloh had finished speaking. Shiloh didn't know how long it would take the alien vessel to recharge its weapon. Sykes would have to detour around damaged areas of the ship and might not get to Engineering fast enough, but he couldn't think of anything else to try. Conning the ship from Engineering was their only hope. He checked the status of the drones again. The closest one was only seconds from ramming the enemy. Those few seconds seemed to take forever, but eventually they passed and the Sensor Tech gave an exultant cry.

"Direct hit! Major hull penetration! ... sensors picking up secondary explosions from inside the hull ... acceleration has dropped to zero! We plastered her good, by God!"

The whole Bridge erupted with shouts of joy. Shiloh grinned but said nothing. He understood their need to vent their feelings, but he felt it was premature to declare victory just yet. There was no way of knowing if that ship could still fire its weapon. With both ships apparently heavily damaged, the winner would be the one able to get in one final, good hit. He checked the drone status again. Drone #2 was about 34 seconds from impact. As the cheering died down, the Helm Officer shouted out.

"We're evading again! Sykes must have gotten the word to the XO!"

That brought another round of cheering. Shiloh watched the seconds count down to the second drone intercept, desperately hoping that the alien ship wouldn't fire for just a little bit longer. As the last few seconds fell away, he looked at the direct video view of the enemy ship. It was too far to see the ship itself, but the sudden burst of light in the distance at the moment of impact was all he needed, to know that drone #2 had hit the target dead on. Even the Sensor Tech's report was more subdued than before.

"Drone #2 made a direct hit … I'm reading major pieces of debris scattering in all directions … energy emissions are now zero." He looked over at his CO. "I think we've killed that ship, Skipper."

Shiloh nodded. "Yes. I'm inclined to agree with you. We'll let drone #3 impact the wreck, anyway. Helm? I want you to transfer to Engineering and take over helm functions from there. Tell the XO we can stop evading, and I want us on a course for a jump back to our departure system. Also tell her to send a complete damage report to the Bridge by runner if the com system isn't repaired by then. Com! Any word on casualties yet?"

The responding voice was heavy with regret. "Preliminary reports say 13 dead and 8 more injured. Repair teams are working on the damage. No estimate yet of when we'll get com links back up with the other half of the ship. There may be more casualties that haven't been reported yet. I've asked Chief Watson to send a runner to check on casualties from the areas we can't contact, Sir."

"Good thinking. Send a signal to any of our ships you can reach, telling them that we appear to have won the battle and are leaving the system as soon as possible. Wish them luck."

The Com tech acknowledged the order.

"I'll address the crew now ... Intercom ... ship-wide."

"Attention all hands. This is the CO. I know that only some of the crew can hear my voice, but I wanted you to know that even though we've taken damage and casualties, the alien vessel that we engaged appears to be in far worse shape and is currently drifting in space, apparently unable to maneuver or fight. We're going to hit it one more time with a recon drone set to ram. I doubt there'll be any survivors on that ship after that happens. We're not going to stick around to find out. We've been ordered by the Squadron Leader to make sure that HQ knows what happened to the 319 and to us. We're going home asap. First stop will be at our departure point where we'll top up our fuel from the supply ships waiting there, and then we'll resume our journey home. The rest of the Squadron will hopefully follow us by a few hours. I'm keeping the ship at General Quarters for now. As soon as we enter Jumpspace, we'll stand down from General Quarters. You all deserve to pat yourselves on the back for your efforts in getting us through this. I'm proud of this ship and its crew. That's all for now. End message."

He settled back in his Command Chair and felt the adrenaline fatigue begin to hit. Even the impact of the final drone was anti-climatic. There was less visible light from impact #3 versus #2. When he asked the Sensor

Tech if there were any signs of life on board the alien vessel, the answer was a definitive 'No, Sir.' The message drone entered Jumpspace a few seconds later. It would arrive near where the support ships should be and notify them that 344 was on its way back.

Just over 10 minutes later, the ship entered Jumpspace. With the com channel links restored to the rest of the ship, Shiloh ordered the crew to stand down from General Quarters. When the XO arrived back on the Bridge to finish what remained of her duty shift, Shiloh said, "Your duty shift will be over soon. I'll cover the rest of your shift for you until Michaels takes over."

The XO looked at him with sadness in her expression. "Commander Michaels was killed by that laser hit we took, Sir."

Shiloh sighed and said nothing for a few seconds. Finally he spoke, "Michaels was a promising officer. The kind of officer I have a feeling we're going to need very badly before this is all over. Okay, Angela. You take over now and cover the first half of Michaels duty shift. I'll take the second half in addition to my own. By the time you relieve me again, we'll have reassigned personnel to cover the gaps. Do you need a few minutes break before you take over here?"

She thought about it briefly before nodding.

"Then go ahead and take a break. Have a coffee and a bite to eat, and I'll see you back here in a little while."

"Thank you, Sir."

She left, and Shiloh was alone with his thoughts. The more he thought about their close brush with death, the more worried he became. He doubted that this would be the last time Humanity encountered that alien race. He had a terrible feeling come over him that this had been just the opening skirmish of a much larger conflict, Humanity's first interstellar war.

Chapter 2 To Fallen Comrades

While the 344 was accelerating in preparation for entering Jumpspace, Shiloh realized that the energy drain from the multiple laser shots fired at the alien vessel had used up a significant amount of their remaining fuel. In fact, the ship had barely enough heavy hydrogen remaining to reach the refueling tankers waiting for them at the other end. The only workable combination of acceleration and jump time, followed by deceleration, required them to enter Jumpspace at a slower than normal speed. That meant that not only would the 344 arrive at the exploration mission staging system with very low fuel reserves, but also that it would likely arrive after the other ships of the squadron. This in spite of the fact that those ships would have entered Jumpspace after the 344 did, as a result of passing them while in there. Unfortunately the means to communicate while in Jumpspace hadn't been invented yet.

The extra trip time filled him with frustration. He wanted to get his injured personnel back ASAP! He knew that in their destination star system, the Squadron had left behind a collection of support ships including two small tankers, a supply freighter and a Command/Support ship containing various support staff like medical personnel, scientists, engineers, etc. The Command ship could handle most kinds of routine maintenance in order to keep the Exploration Frigates in the Field as long as possible. Medical facilities were capable of handling all but the most extreme emergencies. In any case, the support ship had better medical facilities than did a Frigate, and some of the 344 crew injuries were serious.

Upon arriving back in normal space after a jump transit of almost 42 hours – versus the usual time of 36 hours for the same distance – Shiloh was again on the Bridge. He quickly fired off a message to the last known station of the support ships in the expectation that they still would be there. Because 344 had emerged from Jumpspace at the outer edge of the star system, the signal would take hours to reach the gas giant where the tankers skimmed for heavy hydrogen when necessary to top up their tanks. And since the ship emerged from Jumpspace with the same velocity that it had entered Jumpspace, the 344 was moving towards the inner part of the system less quickly than normal. In order not to fly past the gas giant, the ship would have to decelerate. That would require pretty much all their remaining fuel, and the possibility that the tankers might not be where Shiloh had last seen them made him sweat. They SHOULD be there. But the Demon God Murphy sometimes reached down to muddy the waters, or as someone else long ago once said, 'shit happens'. So it was with great relief that almost 13 hours after dropping back into normal space, 344 received acknowledgement from the support ships that they were ready to refuel the 344 and take care of the wounded.

Shiloh received some other news as well. The message drone had arrived. As expected, some but not all of the rest of the Squadron had arrived ahead of 344. They were about to rendezvous with the support ships. The bad news was that the 301 and 299 had been ambushed by at least three other alien ships, roughly fifteen minutes after 344's short, violent clash with her opponent. Squadron Leader Torres had explicitly ordered the other four frigates not to come to 301 and 299's aid, because active scanning had confirmed the fact that there were even more alien ships waiting to pounce once the other frigates got within range. She ordered the rest of the Squadron to retreat to the staging system. Communications with both the 301 and the 299 were lost while they were still fighting for their lives. No one knew what the ultimate outcome was, but the odds for survival were not good. Torres had also communicated her belief that the ambush had been triggered early as a response to 344's confrontation with the alien vessel. Had it not been for that, Torres believed that the entire Squadron would have been attacked once they had regrouped. Her recorded message praised Shiloh for deploying the recon drones and, as a result, springing the trap early enough that half the Squadron could get away unharmed. The tone of that recording, combined with the unknown fate of both ships, made the message particularly poignant. After sharing it with the crew, Shiloh asked all off-duty officers and NCOs to assemble in the Officers' Mess where they raised a solemn toast to fallen comrades. Shiloh was absolutely certain that it would not be the last such toast he would participate in.

By the time that 344 entered orbit around the gas giant and rendezvoused with the support ships and the rest of the Squadron, the other frigates had already been refueled. Carrying all of the data from each of the surviving frigates, another fresh message drone was already in Jumpspace on its way back to a forward Space Force base. There the data would be further disseminated via another drone, and so on. Shortly before commencing refueling operations, Shiloh participated in a video conference with the other Frigate skippers and support ship COs. They wanted to hear about 344's battle first hand and then compare notes. The general consensus was that all the alien ships were more heavily armored, and armed with more powerful laser cannon, than their Space Force counterparts. 323's Skipper, Cmdr. Omar, in his capacity as acting Squadron Leader – being the most senior officer present – had declared his intention to wait another six hours. Then, if neither missing ship showed up during that time, the four combat capable frigates would return to the battle system to search for survivors. Omar had told Shiloh that since the 344 had a damaged hull and crew casualties, with no operational laser turrets left, he would order it to head back to Sol System for repairs. Shiloh thought going back to the battle system was a mistake and respectfully said so, but Omar was adamant. Since there was no point in 344 waiting to find out if the 301 or the 299 showed up before heading home, Shiloh ordered the now fully refueled ship to leave orbit as soon as her more seriously injured crewmembers had been transferred to the Command/Support ship for further treatment. With that task accomplished, and with plenty of fuel to burn, 344 left orbit at maximum acceleration. Her destination was the same Space Force base that the message drone was headed for. The message drone was not a waste of effort. Standard operating procedure was that important data/communications were to be sent by more than one method to create a redundancy that would minimize the loss of the information due to unforeseen circumstances such as a malfunction.

It was with a wistful sigh that Shiloh examined their intended jump route back to the Sol star system. Exploration Frigates had enough fuel capacity to travel up to 12 light years in a series of short jumps, or a maximum of 18 light years in a single jump. The Sol system was just under 90 light years away, but places where they could refuel weren't spaced out evenly enough to permit the ship to make the trip in just five jumps. It would take a total of seven, and almost 440 hours of transit time. That was almost 18 days, a long time to ponder recent events ... and the future.

Though his duty shift was over before the ship reached the specified pre-jump velocity, Shiloh stayed on the Bridge until 344 was safely in Jumpspace. He then spent some quiet time in the Officers' Mess, which he had to himself. Soon he was thinking about the vision that had led to his deployment of the recon drones. Had he not had the vision, he doubted he would have taken the action on his own initiative. Shiloh had never considered himself a spiritual person. If he looked deep within himself, he supposed that at the most basic level he believed in some kind of higher power. Most Space Force personnel eventually came to believe in one version of God or another. The universe had so many awe-inspiring vistas that it was hard not to feel at some emotional level that it had to have been planned that way. In Shiloh's case, he also had a thirst for knowledge about the sciences. The order that he had seen and heard about, ranging all the way from the inner structure of atoms up through the mind-boggling complexity of human DNA and the marvelously perfect functioning of a human body, all led him to the conclusion that it was just too complex and too perfect to have been the work of mindless random forces. From that deep basic belief in a higher power, he now wondered if that higher power had intervened, and if so, why? Was it to save him personally? He didn't think that likely. Maybe it was someone in the crew whom God or an angel was looking out for. As he often did when he was pondering a mystery, he started making a list. At the top he wrote 'Possible explanations for the vision'. Under that he wrote the following.

It was a hallucination
It was a use of unsuspected pre-cognitive esp talents
It was the result of external intervention
intervention by God
intervention by aliens
intervention by humans
from within the ship
from within the squadron
from the future
from some other source

He looked at the list and couldn't think of anything else to add. The only possibility that seemed to be halfway plausible was the use of unsuspected pre-cognitive esp talents. He remembered scoring above average when he was a student in a university lab experiment testing for esp ability, but it wasn't above average by enough to be considered significant. Even if he did have some unsuspected esp ability, he was at a loss as to how to turn it on or off. If he couldn't control it, then what good was it? Would it happen again? And if so, when? He discounted the other possible explanations, mainly because of the similar experience as a teenager, long before he joined the Space Force. It seemed unlikely that aliens would intervene at that stage in his life to help him save a friend who, this far at least, had no obvious connection to the Space Force or any human colony. And intervention from humans, whether from the future or from within the squadron, was unlikely for the same reason. That left intervention by God, or a hallucination. In both those cases he would have expected to experience an auditory sensation, such as a voice instructing him to deploy recon drones. Instead he'd had what appeared to have been an out of body experience. He had actually watched himself standing in front of Admiral Howard's desk. The key was to see if the Admiral actually did compliment him on coming up with the recon drone deployment idea. If he did, then hallucinations or divine intervention would also appear less likely than a spontaneous instance of precognition.

Satisfied that he wasn't crazy – for the time being at least – he decided to turn his thoughts to other matters. HQ would obviously want a detailed report on the whole mission. He had plenty of travel time in which to write it, and he was probably going to need every spare moment for that task. Having served for a year on the staff at HQ, he knew they would be expecting more than just a dry, factual, minute-by-minute account of what happened. They would also want some analysis, even if only guesswork, about the nature and capabilities of the unknown enemy and, even more importantly, recommendations on what should be done next. Shiloh already could think of quite a few recommendations, but he wanted to get some input from his XO too.

Shortly before Johansen's duty shift ended, Shiloh called her and asked her to stop by his cabin for a short chat as soon as she was free.

When she arrived he said, "The Powers That Be will want a detailed report from both of us, XO. You can bet your last credit they'll be asking us for analysis and recommendations. I suggest you start giving that some serious thought, and have something ready for them by the time we arrive."

Johansen nodded and said, "I've already thought about that. Can I bounce some thoughts off you?"

Shiloh nodded in return, and she began to speak.

"I've been trying to figure out WHY those aliens attacked us without attempting to make contact. I can see them being angry or trigger-happy if we had stumbled into an inhabited system, but from the brief time we were in that system, there was no data to indicate any kind of colony, station or resource extraction facility. If that was an uninhabited system, why the big panic? The fact that they had multiple ships in that system suggests to me they were military vessels, and the nature of their response to us tells me they were either defending a border against incursion, or they were engaged in, for lack of a better phrase, reconnaissance in force. If Space Force had stationed ships at our borders to guard against alien incursion, wouldn't it be reasonable to expect that we would at least try to make peaceful contact with any 'visitors'. Why piss off somebody if you don't have to? So the only thing I can figure out that would explain their actions is that their psychological makeup as a race has made them either extremely aggressive or extremely paranoid. Both of those alternatives give me the shivers. They may come after us, even if we don't move any further in their direction, assuming that we find out what that direction is." She paused, waiting for a response.

Shiloh nodded again as he began to reply. "Your analysis makes a lot of sense. I hadn't gotten that far in my thinking, but now I have to believe that we've stirred up a hornet's nest, and we better get ready to deal with them fast. Any other thoughts you want my reaction to?"

Johansen shook her head. "Not now."

"Okay. We can talk more at a later time. I don't want to take any more of your sleep time."

After the XO left, Shiloh looked at the partially written report on his computer screen. The blow-by-blow account was essentially complete. It was time to move on to the more important part of the report.

"Start new section entitled Analysis. First paragraph ..." He started to talk. Over the following days, he did a lot of talking.

***

The short refueling stop was uneventful. Shiloh did his best to answer the barrage of questions that the base commander fired at him. Space Force bases were not especially well armored or armed as a rule. Pirates and smugglers tended to keep well away from them, for obvious reasons. Humanity hadn't come in contact with another space faring race until now, so there wasn't a perceived need for heavy – and expensive – defenses at fixed stations. The shock of the station personnel at hearing the news of the battle brought home to Shiloh just how unprepared Humanity was for this encounter.

By the time 344 emerged from Jumpspace beyond the orbit of Jupiter, he and his Executive Officer had discussed the implications of the alien encounter in considerable depth, and they both agreed that the Space Force had to plan for a major war. What worried Shiloh was whether the civilian Oversight Committee members to whom Space Force answered would see the urgency. The Human Race had to mobilize for war, and that might be just too much for the committee members to accept and authorize since they had their own agendas to consider.

By the time the ship received a reply to its warning message, 344 was considerably closer. HQ had ordered them to head for one of the asteroid shipyards for repairs, with a fast transport tasked with bringing Shiloh and his crew back to Earth asap. When 344 was safely snuggled within the deep recesses of the hollowed out asteroid that served as a shipyard, Shiloh took a few minutes to fly over the damaged sections in a small craft used by shipyard workers. He was shocked by the transformation of his beautiful, sleek ship into an ugly, wounded lump of metal. It wasn't unusual for crewmembers to form a bond with their ships, of a kind that had started back in the days of sailing ships. Seeing his ship damaged like this evoked the same emotions he had felt when he visited his injured crew on the way home. The notion that an inanimate object had a personality and could feel pain was completely irrational, but quite common nonetheless. It was with great reluctance that he boarded the fast transport ship along with the rest of the ship's crew. Because of the relative orbital positions of the asteroid and Earth, the trip would last another 10 hours. Many of the crew took the opportunity to sleep. Even though he was desperately tired after being awake for almost 20 hours, another 4 hours passed before he fell into a deep and dreamless sleep.

It was early morning at Headquarters, located in Geneva, Switzerland, when they arrived at Earthdock. There was a shuttle waiting to take them to the surface. The trip down was just long enough for Shiloh and his people to eat a hasty meal. Shiloh knew that HQ already had all of the data, logs, messages and reports that had been transmitted when 344 emerged from Jumpspace, but he couldn't rid himself of the feeling that he had forgotten to bring something.

When the shuttle landed, there was quite the delegation waiting to greet them. Shiloh and his crew had been told what would happen next. All personnel would be debriefed separately. The debriefing would be short for most of them, since they hadn't been on the Bridge or at any key station during the battle. Bridge personnel and all Officers and NCOs would go through a more thorough debriefing. As his crew were sorted and directed to a waiting convoy of ground transport, Shiloh was busy saluting and shaking hands with more Space Force brass than he had ever seen in one place at the same time during his entire career. The greetings were positive but somber in tone. There were congratulations on his victory and his bringing his damaged ship home, but he could tell they didn't feel he'd won a glorious victory, but rather some kind of consolation prize. It was as if they were saying 'you started a war, but at least you won the first battle'.

Shiloh was asked to accompany a Senior Lieutenant to a waiting limo that was flying the flag of a three star Admiral. After settling into its very comfortable interior, he waited alone for what seemed like a long time. The door was still open and he could hear voices coming closer. He was able to catch the last few phrases.

"—yes, I know it's a goddamn mess, but we have to keep acting as if it's a victory so the public won't panic."

"Just wait until the Council hears that we're in an interstellar war with an enemy we know nothing about. One that can outgun us! God! What a mess!"

"Okay. Okay. Let's hope it's not as bad as it sounds. I'll go with Shiloh. You ride with his XO. We'll compare notes after the debrief."

With that, Admiral Howard, Chief of Space Operations for the United Earth Space Force, entered the limo, nodded to Shiloh, and rapped on the transparent partition separating the passenger section from the driver. The door hissed shut, and the limo accelerated smoothly. Howard said nothing for a few seconds while he looked at Shiloh. Then he opened a compartment in the middle of the seat, a compartment that Shiloh hadn't even known was there, and took out two cigars. Without saying a word, he offered one to Shiloh, who took it with a curt, 'Thank you, Sir.' Howard grunted acknowledgement and lit his cigar with the limo's cigarette lighter. He handed Shiloh the still hot device and the Commander did the same.

After taking a deep puff of his cigar, the Admiral said, "Well, Commander. You've had an interesting trip. I've seen the preliminary data you transmitted, so I know the overall sequence of events. It's too bad we don't know the fate of the 301 and 299, but I expect we'll get some news sooner or later." The Admiral shook his head in obvious disapproval before adding, "I can't believe Omar would take his undamaged ships back there after Torres ordered him to retreat. That was a damned reckless thing to do!"

Shiloh said nothing.

Howard took another puff and then said in a calmer tone, "I've read your report. Very well thought out by the way. I was particularly impressed with your analysis of the overall implications of the encounter and battle. How convinced are you that a crash mobilization is needed to defend against these aliens?"

"Admiral, I've given this a LOT of thought on the way back. The more I think about it, the more convinced I am that we need to start building ships immediately. Lots of ships, and I don't just mean more frigates. We are going to need ships that are far better armored, with more powerful weapons, and plenty of them. That means bigger ships. MUCH bigger ships. These aliens will come looking for us, and we need to be ready for them when that time comes."

Howard sighed and nodded. "Based on what I've learned so far, I'm reluctantly forced to agree with your assessment. The problem I foresee is that the kind of response you're talking about will costs thousands of billions of credits, and government revenues still haven't returned to the level they were before the Depression hit. It's going to be tough to convince the politicians that we need to do this. There's an election within sight, and emergency-spending programs of this magnitude will have to be financed with increased taxes. I'm sure you know what that means?"

Shiloh nodded. Howard went on.

"Finding the money to build a fleet of big ships is one thing. But it also takes time to build ships like that. Do we have that time?"

Shiloh considered his answer carefully. "I just don't know, Admiral. The system where the battle took place is over 28 parsecs from Earth. That's almost 100 light years away. If they know which direction to go, they'll find us soon. But if they don't, they'll have a lot of stars to explore. That will take time, especially if they explore each system with large groups of ships."

Shiloh was about to say more, but the Admiral interjected. "What if they were able to download navigational data from the 319 or 301? Any idea what the chances of that happening are?"

"Well, Sir, with the security features that our ships have to prevent unauthorized accessing of data, I'd say there's only a remote chance that they would be able to figure out how to access any data without triggering the self-erase program. In the case of the 319, the video showed the ship had taken a slashing hit across her Bridge section. From the external damage, I would guess that there wasn't much left of the Bridge computer equipment after that hit. As far as the 301 is concerned, it's my impression that SL Torres would understand the necessity to keep the enemy from gaining access to any information and would take whatever steps were necessary to prevent that. I'm sure she would have ordered the 299 to take the same precautions."

"I see," was all the Admiral said.

Neither of the men said anything else until they arrived at the underground entrance to Space Force Headquarters. Howard asked Shiloh to accompany two junior officers to a debriefing room, which he did. After they got him a coffee, the debriefing session started. Two hours later they brought in lunch and continued the session while he ate. He answered a barrage of questions, looked at computer screens showing data that 344 or one of the other frigates had collected, and tried to explain to them what the data meant. After another four hours they were done, and Shiloh was exhausted. One of his debriefers told him that he and all of his officers would be taken to an isolated but comfortable hotel for the night. Their personal belongings, which they had brought with them on the shuttle, had been transferred there already. He went on to explain that while the official debriefing sessions were over, the Brass wanted to have the opportunity to talk unofficially with at least some of them the next day. After that they would be given time off to go home and visit family, or do whatever else they chose.

Shiloh was escorted to the underground garage again, where he found a Space Force bus waiting for him. Apparently he was the last of the group to finish the debriefing. He climbed aboard the bus and found all his officers, as promised, waiting for him. The bus left as soon as he sat down. Forty-five minutes later they arrived at the hotel. It was comfortable enough and certainly isolated. As far as he could tell the Space Force group were the only guests. The staff seemed perfectly at ease, and Shiloh guessed that this hotel was actually run by the Space Force to take care of the U.E. government officials and politicos who frequently visited Space Force HQ. That would make sense from the point of view of securing the safety of the visitors, as well as allowing them the flexibility to discuss classified information amongst themselves, without worrying about being overheard by members of the general public.

That evening he and his officers were finally able to relax. Several got drunk, and most went to bed early. The next morning at breakfast, Shiloh got a call from one of Admiral Howard's aides, informing him that the four ships under Cmdr. Omar had returned safely from the battle system, and were en route to Sol via the same base at which 344 had refueled. Their return would take longer due to the fact that the support ships were coming with them. The base, known as SFB Bradley, had dispatched a message drone to HQ as soon as the frigates and support ships had emerged from Jumpspace. Shiloh wanted to know what Omar's force had found in the battle system. The aide didn't know. She passed on the Admiral's request, an order really, that Shiloh and Johansen come to the Headquarters by

0900 hrs. When the aide terminated the call, Shiloh turned to his XO, who was seated at the same table.

"The CSO wants us back at HQ by 0900. Omar's ships are on their way back."

Johansen's eyes widened at the mention of the frigates. "Any word on what happened to them?"

"The Admiral's aide didn't know, or wouldn't say. I'm hoping we'll find out when we get there. Let's finish eating. I don't want to be late."

The XO nodded. *So much for lingering over another cup of coffee.*

Chapter 3 Now What Do We Do?

Shiloh and Johansen arrived at HQ by 0900, as requested, and then they were kept waiting in the conference room for almost an hour. Typical Space Force snafu. Hurry up and wait. What irritated Johansen the most was that she could have had a second coffee, with plenty of time to enjoy it, if someone had thought to offer them one. But no one did. Finally Admiral Howard and two other flag officers, who Shiloh remembered from the arrival delegation the previous day, entered the room and sat down at the large oval table opposite to him and the XO. Their expressions were grim. All three opened bright red folders, and Howard cleared his throat.

"Thank you for being here on time. Unfortunately when you're the CSO you sometimes have to be late. As my aide told you, we received word by message drone from SFB Bradley that four frigates under Commander Omar, plus the Support Group, were on their way back here. What my aide didn't know, when she spoke with you this morning, was what Omar found when he took those ships back to the system where the battle took place."

He turned to his right and said, "Sergei, we have to find a name for that system. We can't keep calling it the system where the first battle took place."

He turned back to Shiloh and Johansen. "I asked you and Commander Johansen to come here this morning so that we" – he indicated the other two flag officers – "could pick your brains about the next step. What do we do now? That's the question that I'm going to have to go to the Oversight Committee with answers to, and I need as much input as I can find. But before we get to that, you both deserve to know the latest situation. While Cmdr. Omar displayed questionable judgment in returning to the battle system, going against Squadron Leader Torres' orders to retreat, he redeemed himself, in my eyes at least, by his actions once he got there. Upon arrival there was no sign of any Space Force vessel. No distress signals, no energy emissions of any kind, nothing. Commander Omar decided to make a short jump to the opposite side of the system in order to approach the last known location of the 319, 301 and 299 with a vector that could easily be modified into a jump vector back to the staging system and the waiting Support Group. But before actually taking his ships to the site of the ambush on Torres' ships, he deployed a spread of recon drones at high speed to actively scan the area in question. His theory was that if the alien ships had left the vicinity of the ambush, it would be safe to use active scanning. If they were still there, then the active scanning would detect them. That's what happened. The active scanning detected nine ships. Two were apparently adrift and more or less close together, and the other seven were strategically placed around the first two. Preliminary analysis of the scan data suggests that the two drifting ships were the 319 and either the 301 or 299. The other seven are assumed to be alien vessels waiting for another opportunity to ambush more ships. It seems that one of the two ships that stayed behind was destroyed outright. Otherwise, we'd have seen three drifting ships. Once the alien ships were clearly detected, they destroyed the recon drones. Omar then earned himself a commendation by ordering another spread of recon drones to ram the two drifting ships, thereby destroying them. His reasoning was very simple. Even if there were survivors on those ships, and there's no evidence to suggest that there were, there was no way to rescue them without putting even more lives in serious jeopardy. And without rescue, those survivors would either be captured or die eventually from lack of life support and food. By destroying those derelicts, he denied them to the aliens, thereby protecting sensitive information about our location, technology and capabilities. Once the derelicts were confirmed destroyed, Omar ordered his ships to jump back to the staging system where they collected the Support Group and started on their way here. If this preliminary information checks out, then I'm prepared to approve Commander Omar's actions. That pretty much brings you up to date.

"What we'd like to do now is get some ideas from both of you since you two have a unique insight into this alien threat. You are encouraged to speak freely and nothing you say will come back to haunt you. I guarantee it."

As he said that he looked at his two fellow Flag Officers, and they nodded. Howard continued.

"Okay, we've read your reports, of course. I was particularly impressed with the gamut of your recommendations. You've covered everything from short-range weapons, to new ship types, to thoughts on grand strategy. You can both rest assured that our planning staffs will be taking a hard look at all of your recommendations. But what I want to hear from you now is your thoughts on priorities. If you were the Chief of Space Operations, what would you recommend to the Oversight Committee? Commander Shiloh, why don't you start off?"

Shiloh nodded. "Yes, Sir." He paused to collect his thoughts.

"I look at what the initial situation was when 319 encountered the aliens. I see on the one side a single vessel designed for exploration with minimal armor and modest weapons. On the other side I see multiple vessels that seem to be designed for combat. What I can't see is any rationale for the aliens to feel at all threatened by 319's presence. They had numerical superiority. If anyone had a right to feel threatened, it was the 319, and we know that our standing orders specifically require our exploration frigates to attempt peaceful contact regardless of the relative balance of force. And yet the aliens attacked 319, and then used her as bait. That tells me that they didn't just react out of fear. It suggests strongly that they knew exactly what they were doing and had planned for that eventuality in advance. That kind of aggressive attitude is what you would expect from a barbarian horde like the old Mongol invaders. They weren't interested in peaceful exploration, only conquest. If that's the kind of model that they're following, and I think we have to assume that it is, then they'll keep on coming at us no matter what. With that as the scenario in mind, I think we need to do the following right away."

He started counting on the fingers of his left hand.

"First. There should be a crash program to design and deploy drones that pack a bigger punch. I was able to use our existing recon drones because they had built up enough velocity to be destructive, even though they weren't designed with that purpose in mind. Our ships may not have the time to build up velocities like that in future confrontations. We should develop drones that have explosive warheads, kinetic energy warheads, as well as decoy drones and electronic countermeasure drones. They should be simple to make and therefore easy to mass-produce. Smaller drones would mean that our frigates would be able to carry more of them.

"Second. Our ships have to have more armor protection. I realize that Exploration Frigates weren't designed for this kind of combat, but they're all we have right now. We need to modify them quickly so that they have at least a chance of lasting long enough to be able to fight back. We may not even have to add armor to the whole ship. It may be enough in the short run to just add armor to the more critical areas of the hulls, like the Bridge, Engineering, Weapon Turrets, Life Support and Tactical Systems.

"Third. If we're going to go back out there, we should try to achieve numerical superiority ourselves. That means one or more squadrons operating together. It also means developing and practicing multiple ship combat tactics. Up until now we've never had to worry about that and therefore haven't trained for it.

"Fourth. We need to establish an early warning network of passive sensor satellites in key systems so that we have advanced warning of where they are and how many of them there are. That way we can concentrate our strength, such as it is, to the greatest advantage.

"Fifth." He paused for effect. "The whole culture of the Space Force has to be changed. Up until now we've been an interstellar police force concerned with exploration and anti-piracy/anti-smuggling operations. If we're going up against the barbarian hordes, we have to start thinking and acting like an elite fighting force. That means developing the killer instinct, and identifying those officers who have a knack for strategy and tactics."

He took a deep breath.

"I can elaborate further on these ideas if you wish, and I have other thoughts that aren't within the immediate time frame you specified, but that's a quick overview of my thoughts for now."

"Thank you, Commander." Howard turned to look at Johansen.

"Proceed, Commander Johansen."

She leaned forward. "Thank you, Admiral. My thoughts are very much in agreement with Commander Shiloh's comments. In addition, I would like to put forward the following recommendations.

"We don't know enough about the enemy. We don't know what they look like, how they think, where they're from. We don't know what level of technology they have. For all we know, we may be ahead of them in some areas and behind in others. We don't know what star systems they inhabit. We need more intelligence. I see two ways to get it. The first requires that we capture an alien ship. That has to be a primary objective of any military operations. Second, we need to do tactical reconnaissance of star systems that may have an enemy presence. That would entail ships capable of refueling themselves so that they can operate without support for long periods of time. Eventually we should design and build a special purpose long-range reconnaissance type, but in the short run we can use tankers. We should expect them to suffer a high loss rate, so I would suggest that the crews be volunteers. Losing part of our tanker fleet will restrict our ability to operate in the forward areas, so a tanker construction program should be started as soon as possible."

She stopped.

Howard leaned forward. "Is there something else you wish to add, Commander?"

Johansen looked at Shiloh who nodded ever so slightly. This silent communication did not go unnoticed by either Admiral Howard or his two associates.

Johansen continued. "I do have one more idea to put forward, and that idea is this. If we are going to prevail, we'll have to out fight them. In order to out fight them, we'll have to out build them. The only way I can see that we can out build them is if the Space Force develops its own internal industrial and shipyard infrastructure. The best way to do that is to obtain the use of at least one of General Electric Dynamics Universal Fabrication Complexes. We can use one UFC to build more, which can then build the mining robots, processing and fabrication facilities, and the shipyards, as well as the actual equipment for the new ships."

She was about to say more when the Admiral to Howard's right interjected.

"Commander, that's all well and good, but are you not aware that the Space Force has been negotiating with GED for years to buy a UFC? The price they're demanding is far beyond the budget capabilities of the U.E.S.F. There is no way that they would sell us a UFC, when they can use the ones they have to build the ships that the Space Force needs and will pay for."

Johansen nodded. "Yes, Sir. I'm aware of the past efforts to buy a UFC. I was proposing something different. If GED won't sell us one, then we should explore other options, such as leasing one for just long enough to build our own. If GED won't agree to that, well, the Space Force should do whatever it takes to gain access to a UFC, whether GED likes it or not."

"Commander, are you aware that you have just proposed an illegal act, and by doing so you have left yourself open to charges of conspiracy?"

Johansen was about to reply when Howard came to her defense.

"No she hasn't, Sergei. Not only did I guarantee that nothing these people said would be held against them, and I meant that, but with regards to Commander

Johansen's comments, I'm going to interpret them as a hypothetical scenario of what rogue Space Force elements might do if we can't come to some kind of accommodation with GED. Isn't that right, Commander?"

Johansen was just about to reply in the negative when she realized that Admiral Howard was on her side.

"That's right, Admiral."

Howard smiled slightly at her. "Now then, Commander. I would be interested in hearing how, hypothetically of course, a rogue element might go about gaining access to a UFC ... so that we can take precautions against such a possibility."

Johansen was taken aback by this request. "Well, there might be a number of different scenarios, but the one that comes to mind would have some distinct advantages. We know that GED has deployed a UFC on a particularly rich asteroid that's almost on the opposite side of the sun from earth. In another six weeks, I believe, the orbital rotation of the asteroid relative to earth will place the sun squarely in between the two, thereby cutting off direct communication between the UFC unit and GED Central. That won't stop the UFC from continuing its preprogrammed instructions, and if I'm not mistaken, there will be several GED employees onsite to monitor its operations. They live in a support module that can sustain them for months if necessary, although GED has scheduled regular visits by a supply ship roughly every four weeks. I suppose that if a rogue element were able to go to the UFC site, they could essentially commandeer the UFC and ... *persuade* the onsite staff to reprogram the unit. GED may not find out for weeks, or maybe even months. By that time, the newly-built unit could have been moved practically anywhere in this star system, or even to another star system altogether."

"Very interesting. But wouldn't the GED staff onsite eventually report back to their bosses that Space Force personnel had temporarily hijacked the unit?"

Johansen smiled. "Not if the hijackers disguised themselves and didn't wear Space Force uniforms or insignia … Sir."

"No, I suppose not." Howard looked thoughtful. "I think that scenario deserves more analysis ... to make sure something like that doesn't happen. Thank you for your insight, Commander.

"Now that we've heard from both of you on the short term priorities, my colleagues and I would like to go over the reports that both of you submitted and discuss specific items that we'd like greater clarification on. Commander Shiloh, I see on page two of your report you talk about …"

The sessions with the Admirals went on until lunch, at which time the Admirals left the room to eat elsewhere, and food was brought in for Shiloh and Johansen. After that, the Admirals returned and continued questioning the two about their reports for another four hours.

When they were finally satisfied that they had examined every aspect of the reports, Howard closed his folder and leaned back in his chair.

"Okay. That's it. I want to thank both of you for your candor and insights. The Oversight Committee is going to want a briefing in the next 48 hours from me, and at that time I'm going to brief them on what happened, what we know with certainty, and what we think we know with a high degree of probability. They're then going to ask me what we should do next. I'm very likely going to tell them that we are looking into the options that you suggested this morning – most of them that is – to see if they're practical, and how long it would take to implement them, not to mention the cost. I may need to have you nearby as a resource. My staff will let you know when and where that briefing will take place. Commander Shiloh, I'd like you to accompany me to my office for a few more minutes before the two of you return to the hotel."

Several minutes later, Shiloh found himself standing in front of Admiral Howard who was sitting behind his desk. Howard seemed in a good mood. After getting himself more settled in his chair, he spoke.

"I wanted to talk to you privately, Commander First, I want you to know that I've arranged for you to receive a Commendation for your actions during the battle with the alien vessel. It's a good thing you launched those recon drones when you did, Commander. The mission would have ended very differently if you hadn't."

Shiloh felt a shiver go down his spine. Those were the exact same words he 'heard' the Admiral say in his vision. He realized that the Admiral expected him to say something.

"Thank you, Sir."

Howard nodded. "You're welcome. Second is the matter of your next assignment. Once the 344 is repaired, you'll be back aboard as her Commanding Officer. But we're going to give you more responsibility. We're going to make you Squadron Leader."

Shiloh was stunned. "Shouldn't Commander Omar move up to that slot, Sir?"

Howard chuckled. "Yes he should, and he will. You'll be getting another Squadron. SFE144 will need a new SL when her present CO, Commander Delvecio is promoted to Senior Commander and given command of a Task Force that will include a Support Group and at least one Frigate Squadron. SFE144 may very well be assigned to that Task Force, so Delvecio may end up giving orders to his old command again. Any questions?"

"Yes, Sir. Isn't SFE144 the squadron that had one of their ships missing?"

"Yes, it is. 344 will replace the missing 233. Delvecio's ship will get a new skipper, but you'll assume the SL slot. The Command ship that Delvecio will use as his flagship isn't ready to be commissioned just yet, and until it is, he will continue as SFE144's Squadron Leader. When he takes command of the support group, you'll officially take over as Squadron Leader.

"Now I also wanted to discuss the Oversight Committee. I'm pretty certain that the Committee will want a much broader, long term plan submitted to them in due course. Even if they don't ask for it, I know I want to have it. We're going to need a Strategic Planning Group, which will be ad hoc initially but may eventually become a permanent section of the HQ staff. While the 344 is being repaired, which I understand will take at least three weeks if not longer, I want you to participate in the SPG sessions and give the group the benefit of your insights."

"Of course, Sir."

"Good! Well Commander, I won't take any more of your time. Keep yourself available, and my staff will contact you in due course. You're dismissed."

Shiloh saluted and was starting to leave when Howard called to him, "By the way, Commander, I'm curious.

What was it that made you think to deploy those recon drones in that way?"

Shiloh knew he had to answer quickly, but he didn't want to tell the Admiral about his vision. "The thought just seemed to pop into my head, Sir."

"Well, it's a good thing it did."

"Yes, Sir."

When Shiloh arrived back at the underground garage to catch a ride to the hotel, Johansen was waiting for him. On the way back, he told her what the Admiral had told him. She congratulated him on his pending appointment as Squadron Leader. After riding in silence for a few minutes, she turned to Shiloh.

"Do you think we'll be able to beat these aliens?"

"I think we have a chance, but only if our politicians get their heads out of these asses and make the tough decisions in a timely manner. What worries me is that they'll debate, delay and try to make do with half measures. We can't afford that. I'm pretty sure Admiral Howard understands that, too. Let's hope he can convince the Oversight Committee, and that they can convince the rest of the Planetary Assembly."

Johansen was quiet for a few seconds, then said, "What do we do if they can't or won't?"

Shiloh looked at her with a grim expression on his face. "Then we do whatever we have to do."

Johansen nodded her agreement.

Back at the hotel, Shiloh briefed the rest of his officers before they and Johansen left on their shore leave. After saying their goodbyes and agreeing to meet again in two weeks, Shiloh found himself as the only guest of the hotel that night. The next morning, however, the hotel staff informed him that the Support Group and attached frigates under Cmdr. Omar had arrived in orbit around the moon as per standard procedure, and that the hotel had been alerted that the officers of those ships would be checking in later that day. He also received a message that the Oversight Committee would be meeting with Admiral Howard the following day at ten a.m., and that Shiloh was ordered to be at the HQ conference room no later than 0930 hrs. Shiloh didn't see how that left enough time for Howard to meet with Omar and his officers before the meeting with the Oversight Committee. Later, to his surprise, a Space Force limo flying a flag with three stars pulled up to the hotel entrance, and Admiral Howard stepped out. Shiloh went to greet him at the hotel lobby.

"Ah, Commander. How nice of you to greet me. Commander Omar and his people aren't here yet, I take it?"

"No, Sir. Not yet."

Howard looked around. "Well then, they'll be here shortly. There won't be time for me to attend their debriefing sessions tomorrow, since you and I will be in front of the Oversight Committee, so I'm going to set a precedent and have an informal debriefing with Omar and his senior officers here as soon as they arrive. This is what I want you to do, Commander. You wait here in the lobby. I'll tell the hotel staff what kind of arrangements I want for this meeting. When Omar and his people get here, you inform him that the Chief of Operations wants to see him, the other three frigate COs and their XOs, along with the Support Group Leader, immediately. The hotel staff will take care of their belongings. The rest of the group can do as they please for the rest of today. My staff will make sure that everyone knows where they have to be tomorrow, but you'll have to make sure that they know what they have to do tonight. I'm certain they'll all be tired and hungry. Food will be provided during the debriefing. As for their fatigue, well, they'll just have to hang in there a little longer. Any questions, Commander?"

"No, Sir."

"Very well. I'll make sure that you're told what room we'll be using for the debriefing. I'll leave you to it then."

With that, the Admiral turned and walked towards the reception desk, gesturing for the staff's attention. Shiloh didn't have long to wait. A few minutes later several of the ubiquitous Space Force vans pulled up to the hotel entrance. Approximately thirty officers got out, picked up their duffel bags, which even after all these centuries were still the easiest way for military personnel to carry their personal belongings, and wearily climbed the steps to the hotel entrance. Just as they entered, the hotel manager appeared at Shiloh's side and whispered to him.

"Sir. The meeting with the Admiral will take place in the Gagarin Room down the hall on your left."

Shiloh thanked him. He recognized most of the officers who were entering the hotel, and they recognized and greeted him.

Cmdr. Omar walked up to him and said, "Victor. Glad to see you made it. Congratulations on your battle victory. We got the details at our refueling stops. That was a neat trick you pulled off with the drones. You'll be glad to know that the injured you had to leave behind are going to be okay. Gaspar's people did a good job of patching them up."

Omar held out his hand.

Shiloh took it and said, "That's good to hear. I'll thank him personally when I get the chance. I'm also glad to hear that you and the rest of the squadron made it out okay. I heard what happened when you went back there. It's a damn shame about 301 and 299."

Omar nodded before saying, "Yeah. It is. But at least they didn't get any more of us, and we have you to thank for that. I'm just happy to be back. We're all beat as hell. Most of us would normally be in the middle of our sleep shift now. I guess we'll get a quick bite and then sack out …"

His words fell away as he saw Shiloh shake his head in the negative.

"That's not in the works, I'm afraid. Admiral Howard is here to personally debrief you, the other frigate COs and their XOs, plus Gaspar, and he wants to do it right now. Tell those officers to leave their gear here in the lobby. The hotel staff will make sure it gets to your rooms. The rest of your people will be able to check into their rooms now, and are free to do whatever suits them."

Omar was clearly displeased. "Damn it! Some of us have been awake for 24 hours, and we have to debrief NOW?"

"I'm afraid so, Tom. The Admiral has a good reason for doing this now. But at least you'll get to eat during the debrief."

Omar ran his fingers through his hair and looked around. "Okay … well, if the Old Man says jump, then I guess we jump. Where do we go for this debrief?"

Shiloh smiled sympathetically. "I'll show you the way. Go ahead and get your people sorted out and I'll wait here."

Omar nodded, turned and gestured for the group to gather round him. He called out ten names, told them to stay where they were, and then told the rest to walk over to the reception desk and get their room assignments. After they left, he told the remaining group that they were going to meet with the Chief of Operations. The groans were loud enough that Shiloh was worried the Admiral would hear them. Resigned to their fate, they dropped their duffel bags right there in the middle of the lobby, and Shiloh showed them the way to the Gagarin Room. Howard was already waiting for them. He sat patiently while Omar's people found seats and got settled in. Finally they were ready.

"I know that you're tired and hungry. The hotel staff will be bringing in finger food shortly. That will have to do for now. I'm taking the unusual step of informally debriefing you now because I need to get your first hand impressions before I testify in front of the Oversight Committee tomorrow morning. I'll try not to keep you any longer than necessary. Here's how we're going to do this. I'm going to ask Commander Omar to describe the sequence of events of your return to the battle system. If any of you feel that you have something useful to bring forward, and by that I don't mean jokes, good humored insults or other gratuitous comments, then signal me in a non-verbal manner, and I'll make sure that you get the opportunity to express yourself. If this goes on for more than an hour, we'll take a short break.

"Now, unless there are any questions, we'll begin."

There were no questions. As Omar began to relate the sequence of events, Shiloh listened with half an ear and used the rest of his attention to watch the other officers. Gaspar, the Support Group Leader, was listening intently. The other officers seemed to be less interested, probably because of the obvious fatigue that Shiloh could see in their faces. When Omar got to the part where the recon drones started using active scanning to search the target and the aliens destroyed them, one of the XO's signaled that he had something to add. Howard signaled Omar to pause and gave the XO the nod to speak up.

"Well, Sir. I just wanted to make an observation about the destruction of our drones. The aliens didn't just destroy them. They went out of their way to destroy them. It was almost as if they were so angry about being discovered that they lost their temper."

"What made your think that, Commander?"

"Ah, well, I noticed that the alien ships fired on all of the drones, even the ones that weren't close to them, and in some cases they kept on firing at the same drone even when it had stopped its active scanning. It reminded me of a berserk person with a gun, shooting their victim again and again, even after the victim is clearly dead."

Shiloh and Howard exchanged a look as if to say 'hmm, that's interesting'. Shiloh made a mental note to suggest to the strategic Planning Group that someone make an attempt to come up with a forensic profile of the alien race's psychological traits. If they were predisposed to behaving in a certain way, Humans might be able to take advantage of that. The rest of the debriefing went quickly, with nothing coming up that Shiloh didn't know already. When the Admiral was satisfied that he had picked their brains clean, he let them go.

On his way out, Omar came over to Shiloh and said, "Victor, I'd like to hear a blow by blow account of your battle, but I'm just too tired to do it now. How about over breakfast?"

Shiloh smiled and said, "Sure. How's 0730 hrs in the dining room sound?"

Omar sighed. "Too damn early but yeah, I'll be there."

After he left, the Admiral came over to Shiloh and said, "I take it from your expression that you thought the characterization of the alien behavior was significant?"

"Yes, Sir. My barbarian horde scenario is looking more and more likely. If they behave impulsively, we can turn that to our advantage."

"I concur. Well, I'm off to my office. I'll be burning the midnight oil to get ready for the committee meeting. There'll be a staff car waiting to pick you up in front of the hotel by 0815 hrs. Good night Commander."

"Good night, Admiral."

Chapter 4 The Voters Will Never Believe This

The next day started well enough. Shiloh met Cmdr. Omar in the dining room for breakfast at the appointed time. They talked while eating, and Shiloh related to Omar what happened, without getting into the vision-thing. The time went so fast that Shiloh had to wolf down the rest of his breakfast in order to be finished by the time the staff car was scheduled to pick him up. Shiloh was the only one of his crew who had not been allowed to go on leave. But side from a sister and her family, who lived on the other side of the world and to whom he wasn't really all that close, he didn't have family to visit. Both parents had been killed in an aircraft crash when he was still at the Space Force Academy. If he had been allowed to leave, he would likely have gone on a long solitary trip into a wilderness somewhere and camped out for a week or more. But the prospect of spending his time off on Space Force business didn't really bother him. Unlike the normal exploration missions, which at least had the potential for discovering something interesting, the anti-piracy/anti-smuggling patrols were excruciatingly boring. Now that Humanity was in a serious and, to Shiloh's mind, desperate situation, being a Space Force Commander was suddenly a whole lot more interesting.

The staff car dropped him at HQ right on time. An aide showed him to the large room that was set up for committee sessions. Shiloh took a seat near the front. A few minutes later, Admiral Howard showed up with his staff in tow. Howard nodded to Shiloh and proceeded to give his staff some last minutes instructions. With that done, he brought a stack of file folders to the table in front of the raised dais where the committee members would sit. After organizing his materials, Howard turned around and leaned close to Shiloh.

"Glad to see you're here on time, Commander. Let me brief you on how this is going to work. The Committee will show up in 15 to 20 minutes or so. They'll take turns saying a few well-chosen but completely meaningless words. You have to remember that they are elected politicians. Then they'll ask me to give them a verbal report to supplement the written report that I sent them late last night, and which they haven't read yet. After that, they'll ask me questions. The question period can go for as long as they wish. The shortest question period I've ever experienced was half an hour. The longest was a whole day and half of the next. Given the nature of what they're likely to ask me about, I wouldn't be surprised if we're at it all day except for the occasional break. I'll need you to be available during the question period in case I need to check with you about a fact or get your insight on a question that I've been asked. I'm going to ask you to stay in here while I give my report so that you can understand the context in which the resulting questions are being asked. If you absolutely have to leave for some reason OR if you feel that I need to know something that can't wait until a break, ask one of my staff to place a note on the table where I'll see it. That way I won't look silly when I turn around to ask you a question and you're not there. If you and I need to discuss something, keep your voice down so that only I can hear you. Got all that?"

"Yes Sir."

"Any questions, Commander?"

"No Sir."

"Excellent. Now, let me give you a piece of advice. This will be your first and, if you're lucky, only Oversight Committee hearing. I've gone through a few in my time. I'm used to them now. My advice is don't get flustered. Keep your cool, and you'll get through this okay."

"I'll keep that in mind, Admiral."

Howard nodded and turned away.

The committee room gradually filled with people who were either Committee Members' staff or Space Force personnel. The Committee Members themselves began to trickle in at just about the time the Admiral had predicted. The session started half an hour later and proceeded exactly as the Admiral had described. When the self-serving opening statements were finished, the Committee Chair invited Howard to give his opening remarks.

"Thank you, Mr. Chair. Members of the Committee, as you undoubtedly know by now, the Space Force has lost some of its Brothers and Sisters. The crews of Exploration Frigates 319, 301 and 299 have apparently been the victims of an unprovoked attack by multiple armed starships that belong to an unknown alien race. We strongly suspect that the 233, which went missing last month, was also attacked, and it is now presumed destroyed. The report I have filed with the Committee goes into considerable detail about the events that have occurred in the last week. I will now summarize the major events that should be taken note of.

"It began with the routine survey of the target star system by FE 319. As per standard operating procedure, the 319 and the other exploration frigates of squadron SFE089 were each surveying a different star system in proximity to the system where the support group – containing tankers, supply ship and command/support ship – were waiting. When the 319 did not return from her assigned survey target at the expected time, and in light of the disappearance of the 233, the rest of the squadron was sent to investigate. Even though we had not met another alien race up to that point, contingency plans had been created with that possibility in mind. When the squadron, led by Commander Torres, arrived at the system where 319 had vanished, she deployed the squadron according to the approved contingency plans for such a mission.

"One frigate, the 344, was ordered to remain at the edge of the star system at a fixed location to act as a relay for the remaining members of the squadron. Those others proceeded to search for the 319 in a widely dispersed pattern. In order to cover the maximum volume of space in the minimum amount of time, the searching frigates launched reconnaissance drones. After some time had passed, the recon drone launched from Squadron Leader Torres' ship detected a drifting vessel that had the right dimensions to be the missing 319. Now you have to remember at this point that the recon drones were using passive sensors only, as were the frigates. Passive sensors do not emit any electro-magnetic radiation that could be traced back to the sender. What the drone detected was the shifting pattern of reflected sunlight from the 319's slowing rotating hull. Squadron Leader Torres changed course to intercept, and directed the 323 and 299 frigates to rendezvous with the drifting ship as well. The other four frigates were too far away to get there in a reasonable length of time, and at this point, since they weren't sure if the drifting ship was in fact the 319, Commander Torres decided that the other four frigates would continue to search their designated areas. When the drone made a flyby, it became clear that it was indeed the 319, and that she had been the victim of an attack by some kind of energy weapon. Torres then ordered all frigates, except for the 344, to rendezvous with the 319. While the drone was turning to make a second, closer flyby pass, Commander Shiloh, who is present here today and who was in command of the frigate 344 that was performing relay duty at the system's edge, took the precaution of launching three recon drones of his own. They orbited his ship in order to give better sensor coverage of the immediate vicinity. This proved to be prescient because one of those drones detected an unknown and stealthy vessel moving towards the 344 from further out in the system. If the 344 had attempted to jump out of that system in order to bring back the collected data, as per Squadron Leader Torres' instructions, it was highly likely that the unknown vessel would have detected the 344's maneuvers.

"Because the unknown vessel was behaving in a hostile way, and by that I mean moving closer at slow speed without running lights or other normal emissions, Commander Shiloh made the decision, which I fully support and endorse, to open fire pre-emptively. After a short and vicious battle, in which the 344 suffered considerable damage, the alien vessel was disabled and presumed destroyed. This was due mainly to the imaginative use of recon drones as offensive kinetic energy weapons. Shortly after this battle the two frigates that were close to the 319 were attacked by other alien vessels, which apparently had been waiting in ambush near the drifting 319. As we learned later, this second firefight ended badly for our people. None of them was able to escape. There is evidence that their crews were killed either in the battle or later, when Acting Squadron Leader Omar made the difficult decision to destroy the remaining two lifeless hulks that the aliens were trying to use as bait for another ambush. It was the opinion of Squadron Leader Torres, which I share, that had it not been for the pre-emptive attack by Commander Shiloh, which sprang the trap prematurely, all seven frigates would have been ambushed and very likely destroyed. As bad as our losses were – three frigates and their brave crews – we should consider this encounter as a victory in the sense that half the squadron escaped unharmed, and a fifth frigate was able to return with only a handful of dead or injured crew."

The Admiral paused and looked at each of the Committee Members in turn before continuing.

"As important as that is, what is even more important from the larger perspective of Humanity as a whole is that the surviving ships were able to bring back valuable data. Imagine for a moment if the ambush had succeeded as apparently planned. What if all eight frigates had been destroyed? An entire Squadron would have disappeared into the blackness of empty space, and we would have had no idea of what had happened to them. More ships would have been sent to investigate, and they too might have been destroyed. As it is, we have some very valuable data on these aliens. Enough to give us some idea of their technological capabilities, weaknesses, and even the way they think to a limited but important extent. It's this factor that I'll discuss first because I believe that while their technology is important, if we don't understand how they think and react, then we're operating at a severe disadvantage regardless of any technological edge we may possess."

Howard stopped to take a quick sip of water from the glass in front of him.

"I'd like to begin the description of the alien behavioral profile by pointing out what they didn't do. They didn't send out one ship to explore that system the way we did. They didn't send out ships that were designed for exploration. They didn't attempt, so far as we know, to communicate with our ships. What they DID do is the following. They apparently attacked 319 without provocation. I say that because our exploration crews are under standing orders to attempt to make peaceful contact if they should encounter another space-faring race. The aliens also had seven ships in that system, seven ships that we know of. There wasn't time for them to have called in reinforcements. Therefore they had to have been there from the very beginning. Now, as someone who has had military training, I'm here to tell you that you don't send out seven or more ships to explore one star system at a time. It would take far too long to survey any significant volume of space that way. What the deployment of that many ships at one time tells me is that they were engaged in what is referred to in military circles as Reconnaissance in Force. You do that when you know that an enemy is out there somewhere, or if you suspect that an enemy MAY be out there somewhere. If these same aliens were responsible for the fate of the missing 233 last month, then they know that we are out here somewhere, and apparently they consider us the enemy.

"The strategy of setting up an ambush using the 319 as bait strongly suggests preplanning. The ships that they used to attack us seem to be very strongly armored with a single, very powerful energy weapon. That is NOT the kind of design that is optimal for peaceful exploration. It IS the kind of design that would be suitable for offensive operations. Because of the type of ships they deployed and the way they used those ships, I can only come to the conclusion that they weren't out there to make contact. They were out there looking for a fight."

The Admiral paused again to give the Committee Members time to absorb that final statement.

"Now consider that observation for a moment. What kind of race decides to act aggressively against an alien race about which they know almost nothing? That's taking a huge gamble. The race they're attacking could be vastly superior in terms of population, star systems, economic capacity and military might. We tell our people to try to make peaceful contact on the basis that we might be the new kid on the block, and we don't want to piss off an older and potentially more powerful race if we can help it. For those aliens to have acted the way they did from the get go strongly indicates that they have a predisposition towards behaving aggressively. In our own history there have been people who were more inclined to fight than trade. The barbarian hordes that eventually overran Rome are a good example of that. I put it to you that part of the reason Rome fell was that it underestimated the aggressiveness and the determination of the barbarians. We must not make that same mistake. The worst thing we could do now is to shrug this battle off as an isolated incident and continue with business as usual. The SAFE strategy to pursue is to assume the worst-case scenario and act accordingly. In the worst-case scenario the very existence of Humanity is at stake. No less than a crash mobilization of industrial and military resources is required. If, at the end of the day, it turns out that we overreacted, then I will GLADLY offer my resignation, and I'll be able to sleep well at night knowing that my family and all other families are safe. In my opinion, even if we move now with maximum effort, victory will not be a sure thing. However, the longer we delay, and the more we hold back from a full all-out effort, the greater the chances that victory will slip through our fingers.

"Let me explain why I believe this to be true. From the data relating to the combat between the alien ship and Commander Shiloh's ship, we can make some reasonably good guesses as to the combat capabilities of the alien ships. The 344 was hit with a very powerful laser weapon. Experts have looked at the extent of the damage, and their unanimous conclusion is that the alien ship had a laser weapon that produced significantly more energy than both of the lasers on the 344 combined. Sensor data indicates that the alien ship was roughly the same size as the 344. To be able to generate that much more power from a hull of the same size is disturbing. It's safe to say that they know more than we do when it comes to power generation. The combat data also shows that the alien ship was more heavily armored. How much more is hard to say at this point. But what is clear is that right now our ships have inferior weapons and less capable defenses. While we don't know for sure, it's a safe assumption that they have more ships than we do at this point in time. If they had fewer, why would they put a significant percentage of their total fleet in a star system on the off chance of encountering an alien race?

"There are some encouraging indications that you should be aware of as well. At no time did any of our ships detect a sign that the aliens were deploying missiles or drones. That doesn't mean they can't. It may just mean that they don't want to OR perhaps it just means that the type of ships they used in that engagement don't carry them. But if these were their frontline combat vessels, that would tend to suggest that missiles and drones aren't an integral part of their tactical thinking. If that's the case, then we can use that to our advantage IF WE MOVE QUICKLY!"

These last words had been spoken with considerable emphasis, and again the Admiral made eye contact with each committee member before resuming his report.

"If we can develop and deploy combat drones in large numbers, then we may be able to offset their laser weapon advantage with standoff weapons. The other bright spot is what appears to be a much longer recharge time for their laser weapon. If we can get in two or maybe even three shots for each one they fire, and if we can upgrade our lasers, then we have a better chance of beating them in a standup fight. Unfortunately those are the only perceived advantages that we can see at this point.

"The question that I'm sure all of you would like to hear the answer to is this. Given the nature of the threat, what do we do now? A definitive answer will take some time to analyze and cost out. My staff is examining some short-term options that are worth considering right away, and an Ad Hoc Strategic Planning Group is in the process of being put together. They will generate a comprehensive long-term plan. I hope, but can't guarantee, to have something for the Committee to look at in that regard in about a month's time. However in terms of what we can do right now, here are some of the options that are being seriously considered.

"Our Exploration Frigates were not designed for this kind of combat. We can improve their combat capabilities by adding additional hull armor and by upgrading their lasers. That would be just a stopgap measure. In the longer term we'll need larger and more powerful ships, but that will be covered by the report from the Strategic Planning Group. Right now we can improve our chances of winning encounters by changing our operational doctrine. We should not be sending out frigates to a particular star system in anything less than squadron strength. And two or even three squadrons operating together would be even better. I've already ordered the recall of all our Exploration Frigates so that they can be reassigned in light of our new doctrine. The Space Force is going to have to transform itself from a paramilitary organization concerned mainly with catching smugglers and scouting new star systems, to a purely military organization, one that is organized from the outset to deal with external threats. That means we need to start changing the 'corporate culture', so to speak. For example, up until now, the Space Force hasn't had or needed a medal that would recognize exceptional conduct in a ship vs. ship battle. I've changed that. From this point forward, all commanding officers who distinguish themselves in combat will be awarded The Distinguished Combat Medal. It will take the form of a small red star on a jet-black board that can be pinned to the chest or lapel, and it will provide a concrete symbol and reminder of our new orientation.

"Another example of changing the corporate culture will be the testing for, and development of, strategic and tactical skills. Those officers who have an intuitive feel for combat tactics need to be identified in order to be fast tracked to command positions. The Space Force Academy will start teaching classes in tactical combat. Officers will be encouraged to be aggressive in their thinking, and those who aren't able to develop the 'killer instinct', for lack of a better phrase, will be assigned to less critical areas such as logistics and support operations.

"We also need to seriously look at a crash program for the development of drones specifically designed to inflict damage on an armored target. The normal acquisition process, which takes years, is no longer acceptable. Therefore not only will I be submitting a proposal in the immediate future requesting such a crash program, but it will also contain a faster acquisition model that this Committee will have to approve. Speed is now more important than accountability. I cannot emphasize this enough. While I appreciate the fact that this Committee has to make recommendations to the Grand Senate which has the sole authority to approve new spending programs, I also know that this Committee DOES have the authority to authorize the re-allocation of previously approved spending initiatives for emergency uses. I am asking you to approve the use of 200 million Credits that have been set aside for preliminary Pre-Colonization Ground Surveys, for the purposes of initial design, testing and pre-production tooling for the Advanced Combat Drone Program. It will require additional funding later. Because time is of the essence, and we literally cannot afford to waste even a single day, I'm asking this

Committee to approve that reallocation request NOW, this very day.

"There are two other initiatives that can and should be started immediately. We need to have far better intelligence with regard to where the enemy is at any point in time, as well as where they're from. The first requires the establishment of a network of passive sensor satellites in our frontier star systems and in the systems just beyond our frontier. They will take time to design, produce and deploy. However, we can begin to use our tankers in a long-range reconnaissance role, where they will be self-sufficient in refueling capability, giving them a much longer range. In that role, their mission will be to creep into an unexplored star system that may have an alien presence of some kind, and they will then passively scan for any signs of the enemy, including ships, colonies or industrial infrastructure. I cannot overemphasize how hazardous this duty will be. Our tankers will be totally defenseless. If they are discovered, they will likely be destroyed. I'm going to be asking for volunteers, and if a sufficient number of personnel volunteer, we'll only ask each of them to go on one of these long-range recon missions. Multiple missions like this would be tantamount to asking them to commit suicide, and I'm not prepared to do that … at this point.

"There is one final recommendation, the importance of which cannot be overstated. Unfortunately, it is not something that the Space Force can accomplish merely by deciding to do it. Yet its success is absolutely vital to our chances for victory in the months and years ahead. The Space Force needs to build its own internal industrial infrastructure and shipyard capability, and the sooner the better. The kind of force structure that is needed will be impossible to acquire if we must pay private sector companies to build it. Even with this internal capability, the fiscal demands will be onerous.

Without this internal capability, we may as well give up right now and wait for the aliens to arrive. What I'm referring to specifically is the acquisition of, or at least the use of, one of the Universal Fabrication Complexes owned by GED. I'm aware that GED has repeatedly refused to sell a UFC to the Space Force in the past, despite very generous offers. I even understand why they insist on keeping a monopoly on UFCs. The ability to make anything, including more UFCs, using robotic equipment and asteroid-based resources means that GED can manufacture and assemble an Exploration Frigate for a cash outlay of just one or two percent of what it would have cost them using more traditional manufacturing techniques. If they then sell the ship to us, even for a greatly reduced price, they would still make an enormous profit. I have no philosophical objection to GED making money, but I do have a serious objection to their greed threatening the very survival of the Human Race. For the Greater Good, they must be convinced, either by persuasion or by legislation, to give up their monopoly on the UFC technology. I'm not insisting that they be forced to give it to us without some form of compensation. Rather, I'm suggesting that compensation is a question that can be resolved later. We need access to the UFCs NOW! While we won't be able to start building new ships right away because they haven't been designed yet, we can certainly start building more UFCs. The kind of output of ships and equipment that we will very likely need will require hundreds of UFCs. And we can reach that level of capacity through geometric growth if the existing units reproduce themselves, with the new units doing the same over the next few months. The classic example that illustrates this concept is that of starting with one Credit and doubling it every day. Do so, and in less than a month, you'll be a millionaire. To give you some idea of how urgent it is that we start this initiative immediately, let me provide another example. If, as I've been told, it takes approximately one month for a UFC to reproduce itself, and if we wait one month before starting this program, then at any point in the future we will have only half as many UFCs as we would have if we started today. Half as many UFCs will translate into half as many ships. And half as many ships could very well mean the difference between survival and the genocide of Humanity."

The Admiral paused to take another sip of water before adding, "This concludes my opening remarks. I'm now prepared to answer any questions members of the Committee may wish to ask."

The Chairman of the Committee nodded and looked at the other members before responding.

"On behalf of the Committee, I'd like to thank you, Admiral Howard, for that very comprehensive and insightful report. You and your staff have obviously given this unexpected development a lot of thought in the short time that was available to you. Speaking only for myself, I admit that I'm somewhat overwhelmed at this point by what has happened and by what the implications are."

Shiloh saw most of the Committee members nodding their agreement to that. The Chairman continued.

"Given that we haven't had time to read your report as carefully as it warrants, I'm going to ask your indulgence when we ask questions that are already answered in the report. I think you can safely assume that this will be a long session, Admiral. As the Committee's Chairperson, I have the privilege of asking my questions first. My first question is this …"

***

Many, exhausting hours later, when he and the Admiral left the Committee room, Shiloh realized he was sweating.

"What happens now, Sir?"

Howard snorted.

"Now? If by that question, Commander, you mean what am I personally going to do, the answer is I'm going to go back to my office and have a stiff drink, or two. If you mean what happens next in the process here's that answer. The Committee will meet 'In Camera'. That means privately. I think I've convinced them to take this seriously. If they agree with that assessment then they'll report back to the Grand Senate, which will debate the supplementary budget that the Executive Branch will be tabling. Unfortunately that will take several weeks. The government can't just ask for vast amounts of money. They'll need to make a detailed request that will take time to compile. And there's no way around that. That's where you can make a valuable contribution. I'll have my senior planning staff member contact you to start the Strategic Planning Group. The two of you can then figure out who else should be in the group. I will temporarily reassign anyone you need. Don't waste any time with this. We need creative thinking. The end result doesn't have to be a polished report. That's not the group's objective. What I want to get from the SPG is recommendations and ideas, the more ideas, the better. In terms of recommendations, I want to see the whole gamut, ranging from what kinds of R&D we should be conducting, to force structure, deployment, infrastructure, and anything else you can think of. No area is off limits for consideration, but speed is essential. Anything the group comes up with can be revisited and polished later. Cost estimates are a must, but no one expects them to be dead on accurate. Ballpark figures are okay for now. The SPG report will form the skeleton that the Emergency Supplemental Budget request will be built around. Do you understand what I'm asking for, Commander?"

"Yes, Sir, but I do have a question."

"Ask it."

"The group could spend months coming up with ideas. How do we know when to stop brainstorming and give you what we have so far?"

"That's a good question." The Admiral stopped walking and looked thoughtful. "Okay. Here's what we'll do. I'll give you two days to identify and collect the rest of the group, three days to brainstorm ideas, and five more days to crunch the numbers and prepare a report. That means that two hundred and forty hours from now I want a preliminary document in my hand. Remember, substance is more important than format. It doesn't have to be pretty, okay?"

"Yes Sir."

Howard nodded his approval but didn't continue walking immediately. "One more thing, Commander. I'm sure this next point is redundant, but this is too important to risk a misunderstanding. I don't expect the Planning Group to work 24 hours a day, but I also don't expect its members to work from 9 to 5. Do you understand what I'm saying, Commander?"

"Loud and clear Sir."

"Good!"

They started walking again. When they got to the Admiral's offices, Shiloh saw that a Lieutenant

Commander was waiting in the outer office. The Admiral made the introductions.

"Commander Shiloh, this is Lieutenant Commander Amanda Kelly, my senior planner. Kelly, this is the Officer whose reports you've been studying all day. He's going to be temporarily assigned to the SPG until his ship is ready for action again."

Kelly and Shiloh shook hands and exchanged the usual pleasantries. Howard gestured to his inner office and led the way. Once inside, he pointed to two comfortable chairs facing his desk. After everyone was seated, he leaned back and looked at both of them carefully.

"This Strategic Planning Group is an unusual creation. Right now it's very ad hoc and unofficial. Eventually that will change, and it will become a formal department with its own budget and bureaucratic red tape. But for now, because it's unofficial, we have the flexibility to bend the rules a bit. Normally the senior ranked officer would be in charge, and I'm aware that Commander Shiloh is the senior officer. However he will be returning to his ship in several weeks, and I think continuity of leadership of the planning group is more important than following the normal rules of seniority. Therefore I'm going to make Commander Kelly the Team Leader of the Special Planning Group."

Kelly smiled and said, "Thank you Sir."

Howard shook his head. "Don't thank me, Commander. I'm not doing you any favor. The Team Leader is going to get a lot of flak from the legion of armchair critics who think they know more than you do. If I'm doing anyone a favor, it's Commander Shiloh. He gets to fight this war on paper for a few weeks, before going back to doing it for real. Now that I've thrown you into the deep end, Kelly, I'm going to tie one hand behind your back. As

Team Leader you have the ultimate say in how the group operates and what goes into the report. But because Commander Shiloh is the only ship CO who has won a battle so far, his insights deserve to be taken seriously. I'm not saying you have to accept every idea or suggestion that Commander Shiloh makes, but I do expect you to listen to them carefully. I trust that will not be a problem, Commander?"

Kelly shook her head. "No problem at all, Sir."

"Excellent. What do you need to get started?"

Shiloh and Kelly looked at each other, and then she said, "Well Sir, we're going to need physical space to work. The conference room downstairs will do to get started but we're also going to need cubicles and desks, terminals to do research, and eventually we're going to need room to store records that need to be kept in a secured location."

"Yes, I see. Hmm." He pondered that for a few seconds then smiled. "I have the perfect solution. The sub-basement in this building was originally designed to be secure against chemical, biological and radiological attack as a backup facility. It's set up with a conference room, offices, kitchen facilities, storage areas for records, and even temporary sleeping accommodations. Best of all, it isn't being used. Only personnel who are authorized with the necessary biometric data on file can get access, and I'll arrange for your team to get access. That will undoubtedly take a couple of days to arrange, so you'll have to make do with the facilities above. Is there anything else you need to get started?"

Neither Shiloh nor Kelly could think of anything else.

"Good. In that case I'll leave you two to get started while I make some calls."

Shiloh and Kelly saluted, and as they turned to leave, Howard said, "Remember Shiloh, two hundred and forty hours."

Shiloh chuckled and replied, "Yes Sir, I'll remember."

As the two of them walked through the outer office, the Admiral overheard Kelly ask Shiloh, "What's the deal with two hundred and forty hours?"

Chapter 5 You're Not Nearly Devious Enough

After spending the most recent 72 hours in the sub-basement think tank, Shiloh emerged from the Space Force HQ and realized that he had lost track of whether it was day or night. He had been expecting evening dark and instead was blinded by the late morning sunlight. He was dog-tired, but Admiral Howard had his report, and they had completed it within the 240 hour deadline. The Admiral had generously ordered them to take two whole days off, and Shiloh intended to spend the first half sleeping, and the second half eating decent meals. His mind was so preoccupied with the prospect of sleep that he almost walked right by Lt. Cmdr. Johansen who apparently was waiting for him.

"Forgot me already, Skipper?"

Shiloh jumped with surprise. "Angela!"

"So you do remember me. That's nice to know. Jeez, Skipper, you look like hell!"

He laughed. "Tell me about it. I'm not even sure what day it is. My stomach is telling me it's time for supper, but somehow I don't think it's that time of day."

Johansen nodded and smiled. "Lunch actually, and I have a suggestion in that regard. Why don't you join me for a nice, leisurely meal with an alcoholic beverage of your choice, and I'll tell you the good news?"

Now it was Shiloh's turn to smile. "It's a deal. Lead the way, XO."

Twenty-five minutes later they were seated in a quiet and comfortable restaurant, with a beer in Shiloh's hand and a glass of red wine in Johansen's. She broached the subject first.

"I heard that you asked for me to join the planning group."

Shiloh nodded. "Yup. The Admiral said that you were 'unavailable'. He didn't elaborate. Damn strange, too, considering we didn't have any trouble getting anyone else we asked for, even though some of them had to come from a lot further away."

Johansen looked amused. "Yes, well … the Admiral had a little assignment for me. I guess he felt he couldn't risk telling anyone at the time, but I don't see any reason why I can't tell you now. The Admiral wanted my help in convincing GED to allow access to the UFCs."

Shiloh waited for her to continue. When it became obvious that she didn't intend to, he prodded her.

"Well? Did they agree? Come on! Tell me!"

His XO laughed. "Yes they did! All of the UFCs they have now are already busy making more. It won't be long before we have several, then dozens of them."

"That's great! So how did you and the Admiral convince GED's Board to give up their monopoly?"

Johansen looked around before answering. "That's just it. The Board didn't give up anything. We bypassed them altogether. You see, up until now we've dealt with the Board as a whole, and everything was done out in the open. When I suggested to the Admiral that we consider unconventional strategies, he took that to heart. After he appeared before the Oversight Committee, and you joined the SPG, he called me in. We kicked around a few scenarios, starting with the hijack idea I suggested and gradually migrating to other less dramatic and less risky possibilities. What we finally came up with was so damned obvious that we both cursed ourselves for not thinking of it sooner."

She paused for effect.

"We decided to bribe the Chief Executive Officer of GED."

Shiloh was stunned by the simplicity and straightforwardness of the idea, but then he started having doubts.

"Wait a minute. Just because someone takes a bribe doesn't necessarily mean that they stay bribed. What happens if the Board finds out their CEO has sold access to their money machines? They'll just fire him and name a replacement who will countermand the previous orders, stop the production, and transfer of the new UFCs to Space Force control."

He was about to say more but she beat him to it.

"Skipper, you're not nearly devious enough. We're not relying on the CEO's honesty to stay bribed. We are going to make him a series of payments, each one contingent on not only having continued production of the units, but also contingent on the Board not finding out about it. The key is that we secretly recorded the whole transaction and all the conversations. After the deal was done, we let the CEO know that if he double-crossed us, not only would we would tell the Board that he sold out the company's monopoly for a bribe, thereby ruining his career, but we would also see to it that the recordings were leaked to the appropriate investigative authorities, and he would eventually be thrown in jail. And because this is too important to risk something going wrong, we also took the precaution of bribing some of the key technical personnel to make sure that the correct production orders were being carried out, as well as to give us a heads up if the CEO tried anything funny. Naturally we didn't tell him that we had bribed his staff, too. As far as the Board finding out the truth, they'll only know what the CEO tells them. If somehow they eventually do discover the truth and bring charges against him, we have a pardon all ready for him, and he knows that it'll only be implemented if he's been cooperating with us."

It all sounded very plausible to Shiloh, but he still had questions.

"How do we know that the CEO isn't just stringing us along? He may very well want to build more UFCs just like we do, but if he plans on withholding control of the new units when they're finished, then what can the Space Force do about it? We'll be right back to square one again."

Johansen was shaking her head. "Part of the deal with him is that our technical personnel will be present as the new units are built. They'll be fully trained in programming the UFCs. When the new units are finished, they'll be loaded onto Space Force supply ships and redeployed to different and, as far as GED knows, unknown locations where our personnel will have complete control. We can then build anything we want. For a while our UFCs will be building even more UFCs and their supporting equipment. The dispersal strategy means that even if an alien attack on our Home system should destroy the original GED units, they'll only have destroyed a small percentage of our productive capacity."

Shiloh smiled with appreciation. "Very nice. That will make the Strategic Plan much easier to implement."

Johansen leaned forward. "I'm dying to know what the Plan includes. Can you tell me about it?"

"Yeah, sure. I don't see why not. As far as I know, it isn't a classified document. In fact, I wouldn't mind getting a fresh perspective on some of the things we came up with. The Plan isn't cast in stone. We'll be adding to it and revising it as we go along, so your input could be quite useful. I'll tell you what we'll do. Let's order some food, and then I'll tell you the highlights of the Plan."

Which is exactly what they proceeded to do.

After their food and beverage order had been taken, Shiloh leaned forward and said, "Okay, as I recall, there are some 89 specific recommendations in the Plan. The overall strategy calls for limited reconnaissance and raiding operations in the short run, followed by a gradually stepped up tempo with more aggressive missions as the force structure permits. That's where things get interesting. We know from GED records that an Exploration Frigate can be built in eight weeks by a UFC. An FE masses about 20,000 metric tons, so that works out to 2,500 tons per week. The Plan calls for the eventual construction of 800 million tons of warship and support ship capacity."

Johansen whistled in amazement. "My God! Is that even do-able?"

Shiloh chuckled. "It is if you can create hundreds of UFCs through exponential growth. The problem with that huge tonnage figure is that it includes a lot of REALLY BIG ships. I'm talking monsters in excess of a million tons each! Now, even if you have multiple UFCs working together to fabricate parts, these battleships will still take a couple of years to build, at least, and that doesn't include the design phase which will probably take a year all by itself. The Plan recognizes that we can't wait that long to get offensive muscle. We have to acquire something more capable than exploration frigates, and we need them now!"

Johansen nodded. "Okay, so what's the answer?"

"The answer is a series of increasingly larger units as time goes on. Based on our encounter, the group agreed that exploration frigates are too vulnerable in terms of armor to risk in a standup fight. So the Plan calls for the design of an autonomous fighting platform, which you can think of as a super large drone. The AFP will be a generic design that can carry a variety of modular payloads. Everything from a single very powerful laser turret, to multiple decoy or attack drones. Even to a small self-contained refueling unit that the AFP could use to skim gas giants and process small amounts of heavy hydrogen that can be transported back to the Mothership as a way of refueling larger ships without risking them in a gas giant's upper atmosphere. Each AFP would be very heavily armored. They can be carried externally using the same racks that we use to carry smaller drones externally. Empty, they'll mass slightly less than 2,000 tons, so a UFC should be able to build five of them every four weeks, once we get the design perfected. Eventually we'll have large carriers that will carry dozens of them. Until then, they'll have to be carried by supply ships or tankers. They'll be designed to avoid detection both from passive and active scanning, and their small size will make them hard to hit. Since they won't have human crews, they'll be able to withstand acceleration in excess of what our inertial dampeners can handle, and that will make them very maneuverable. And if their primary weapon system is used up or disabled, they'll ram an enemy ship if a window of opportunity presents itself, and the small tactical nuke that each one will carry will detonate on impact – or if the aliens try to dismantle it."

Johansen's face showed an expression of devious delight. "I love it! What else?"

Shiloh chuckled. "Okay. How about a manned vehicle that's about one third the size of an exploration frigate, designed to be carried into battle by a larger ship, with just enough room and life support for four to six crew, for up to 10 days. It will be heavily armored and carry a salvo of fast but short duration missiles, armed with x-ray lasers that will accelerate at high speed and detonate close to the target. The high-energy x-ray laser blast will slice through enemy armor like a hot knife through butter. The gunboats – that's what we're calling them – will be maneuvered in groups. In addition to the combat version, we've also looked at specialized versions like electronic counter measures, and refueling and resupply models. Each gunboat can be produced in about four weeks.

"We also came up with a whole range of ships types. Long range reconnaissance ships, battle cruisers, million ton dreadnoughts, carriers that can carry a combination of gunboats and AFPs, support ships and mine/satellite layers."

"My, oh my. You folks HAVE been busy! Do you have any idea of what they'll go with first?"

Shiloh nodded. "We unanimously recommended that the very first thing that should be put into production is an attack drone. Our drones are basically a standard body with power unit, maneuvering engine, fuel, and a guidance system with room for a modular payload, which up till now has been either a sensor package for reconnaissance/survey work or a data unit for relaying information. There shouldn't be much problem designing a payload that has either a kinetic energy penetrator or a tactical nuke. Now making the attack version harder to detect, and more able to withstand combat damage, will be a bigger challenge and take longer to accomplish, but that can be phases II and III. The x-ray laser version will also take longer to perfect. The main problem we foresee getting combat drones into the field is quantity. The manufacturer wasn't expecting to have to build large numbers of these drones quickly, so it isn't geared up for that. It will take time to change, but I wouldn't be surprised if a few prototypes were ready for field testing by the time the 344 is ready to be taken out again."

The two continued discussing ideas and thoughts for a couple of hours before calling it a night.

It was four days later that Johansen told Shiloh the bad news while they were on their way to HQ for another meeting with Admiral Howard.

"I hear that the call for volunteers for the recon mission has gone out," Shiloh said.

Johansen looked away and nodded. After a few seconds she turned back to Shiloh.

"Yes, I know. I've volunteered."

Shiloh was shocked, and it showed in his voice. "Why did you do that? You know it's practically a suicide mission, don't you?"

Johansen's voice was calm as she replied, "I know that the mission is dangerous, but perhaps not as dangerous as you seem to think it is. First let me explain why. The call made it clear that anyone who volunteers for and survives one of these recon missions will automatically be promoted upon returning to base. That means I'd be promoted to a full Commander, and I'd almost certainly get a ship of my own, which is something I want very badly. How much longer they'll continue to offer that incentive, no one knows, so if I'm going to take advantage of it, it may as well be now.

"Second, as far as the danger is concerned, here's how I see it. The mission profile is to find alien infrastructure, bases or colonies. Maybe even their home world, if we're lucky. We'll be able to scan for energy and electro-magnetic emissions from the edge of each star system we enter. The only time we have to maneuver close to planetary bodies is if we have to move in from the outer system in order to refuel from a gas giant. Some of the internal space that's normally used to carry refueling shuttles will be used to carry recon drones, instead. I hear that they're not exactly known for being comfortable ships, either. "

Shiloh was silent for about twenty seconds and then said, "Okay. I see your point. I guess if I was in your shoes, I might be tempted to do the same thing, but I'm going to be selfish about this and tell you that I wish you hadn't volunteered. Now I'll have to break in a new XO, and it's going to be hard to find someone as good at it as you are."

As he said it, he wondered if he should also tell her of his hope that someday they'd be more than comrades-in-arms, but she replied before he had the chance.

"Thank you. I appreciate that."

They were both silent for a minute or so, and then Shiloh asked, "So when are you due to report to your new ship?"

Johansen replied, "I'm supposed to report aboard the Gnat tomorrow at 0900 hours as her XO. Mission briefing will be later that day, and scheduled departure is for 1800 hrs tomorrow."

"Well, do me a big favor please and come back alive."

Johansen laughed and replied, "Okay. Since you asked, as a favor to you I'll make a special effort to get back."

They both laughed.

Chapter 6 Fly on the Wall

Lt. Cmdr. Johansen called the CO when the ship was half an hour from re-entering normal space at the target system.

"Yakamura here."

"We're half an hour from the target, Skipper."

"Very well. I'll be up the Bridge shortly, XO."

"Understood."

Shortly turned out to be less than two minutes. What Cmdr. Yakamura lacked in physical stature, he more than made up with the intensity of his personality.

As Johansen surrendered the Command Station to her CO, she said, "I have a feeling about this one, Skipper."

Yakamura looked at her in surprise. "Well, XO, that makes two of us!"

Johansen stayed on the Bridge to see what the initial survey results would be. She stood behind Yakamura and off to one side. The remaining time it took to emerge from hyperspace went quickly. After the momentary disorientation of emergence was over, Johansen waited nervously for the initial reports. She looked over to the sensor station and saw several flashing red lights.

Just then the sensor technician turned to look at Yakamura and said in an excited but low voice, "We're picking up lots of EM emissions. They seem to be coming from multiple sources very close to planets, which could mean they have installations on those planets' moons."

Yakamura, acting as if he had expected exactly that news, spoke. "We seem to have hit pay dirt, everyone. Our task now is to be a fly on the wall and get as much information about the alien presence in this system as we can, without taking too many risks. Getting a limited amount of information back to HQ would be better than not being able to get back at all."

He turned to Johansen and said in a lower voice, "XO, I'd like your input into what we do next."

Without waiting for Johansen to reply, Yakamura got up and walked over to stand next to the Astrogator's station. Johansen followed and stood on the opposite side. With both of them leaning over so that they could communicate with the Astrogator without being overheard, Yakamura spoke.

"Okay, Tony. Show me how we're oriented relative to this star system."

The Astrogator acknowledged the request and manipulated his consol controls. A second later, the view screen in front of him changed to show a white disk in the middle, surrounded by several planetary orbits as they would appear if seen from almost edge on. A flashing yellow dot represented Gnat's current position, and a dotted curving line showed what the ship's course would be if allowed to continue on as it was.

Yakamura nodded. "Hm. We're about 30 degrees above the ecliptic, headed down through it. Okay. Now, on another screen, show me our system-by-system path since leaving known friendly territory."

The other screen soon showed a series of straight lines connecting dots with names listed as Zebra 1, Zebra 2, etc., up to their current system, which had been designated as Zebra 9.

Yakamura nodded again and said, "Just as I thought. Our paths through Zebras 1 to 9 has ended up taking the shape of a slight curve as we jumped from each star to the nearest star in the general direction that we wanted to go. So, if we wanted to curve back towards home following a different path, what would be the nearest target system?"

A dashed red line appeared from Zebra 9 through eight more star systems to the slightly green sphere of stars that represented friendly territory. The first star system along that path was a flashing blue dot.

"Do we have enough fuel to jump there? And if so, how much longer could we stay in this system and still be able to jump to that target system?"

That request took longer to fill. While the Astrogator was doing the calculations, Johansen looked at Yakamura.

"I like the idea, Skipper," she said, "but if we don't retrace our path, we run the risk of arriving in a star system that may not have any gas giants to refuel at. On the other hand, we know that Zebra 8 DOES have a couple of gas giants."

"Quite right, XO. And so does THIS system. There's a gas giant on our side of the star. If there are no EM emissions, then I'm very tempted to head there while we continue to observe the activities in the inner system. We can refuel, and that would give us the backup fuel we'd need if this system—" he pointed to the flashing blue dot "—turned out not to have a gas giant."

As it turned out, they did have enough fuel to get to the flashing blue dot system but not enough to spend much time observing enemy activity. The nearest gas giant also turned out to have some EM emissions. While Yakamura and Johansen were discussing whether or not to risk refueling there anyway, the Astrogator took it upon himself to do some calculations and presented his CO with an alternative. Jump back to Zebra 8, refuel, then jump sideways to another star system that was more or less half way between Zebra 8 and the flashing blue dot system. Then, on to the blue dot system in order to proceed back along the new return path from there. Both senior officers agreed that this new route was preferable to any other. And because Zebra 8 was closer to Zebra 9 than the blue dot system, it allowed the ship to spend more time observing enemy activity within the Zebra 9 system.

Yakamura chose not to launch any recon drones. In order to get information that the tanker itself couldn't, the drones would have to get so close to the EM sources that there was a high risk of detection. His orders told him to avoid tipping off the aliens that they were being watched, at all costs. Their fuel situation allowed them to stay for another 36 hours. They'd still have enough fuel to line up with and then jump to Zebra 8 before maneuvering to its gas giant, with a 24 hour supply in reserve. During that 36 hour period, they observed enemy ships approaching and leaving the vicinity of a large rocky planet that wasn't habitable itself and therefore appeared to be a mining outpost of some kind.

Johansen felt like the Gnat was indeed a 'fly on the wall' of this star system. The ships that were leaving were the most interesting. They seemed to head in one of two directions. One direction seemed to be towards another planet with alien activity, but the second direction seemed to head into deep space, and the Gnat's sensors were able to track a few ships actually entering hyperspace. Because these ships were being observed from only one direction, it was impossible for anyone to determine exactly which star system they were headed for, although they could narrow down the field of candidate destinations considerably.

Yakamura and Johansen took turns on the bridge so that they could get some rest. Johansen felt a profound sense of relief when Yakamura finally ordered the ship to line up its heading for a jump to Zebra 8. The jump itself was uneventful, as was the refueling at Zebra 8. However upon arrival at the halfway system, which Yakamura decided would be known as Zebra 10, their plan hit a snag. Zebra 10 was occupied by the aliens. It only had one gas giant, and it appeared that every single one of the dozen visible moons was home to some kind of enemy activity. Johansen was afraid that Yakamura would stubbornly insist on finding a way around this obstacle, but he surprised her by bowing to the inevitable and declaring that they would be jumping back to Zebra 8 and then continuing back the way they had come up the Zebra chain of star systems to friendly territory.

By the time Gnat had returned to friendly territory, Johansen was shocked to realize they had been gone for almost six weeks.

***

Admiral Howard dropped his electronic notepad on his desk, let himself fall into his chair, and immediately reached for the bottle of whisky that he kept hidden in his desk drawer. Admiral Dietrich, Chief of Personnel, and Admiral Kutuzov, Chief of Logistics, grinned in sympathy.

"I'd offer both of you some of this, but I think I'm going to need all of it myself."

Dietrich laughed and said, "Aw, come on now, Sam. That wasn't the worst session with the Oversight Committee you've ever had. Admit it."

Howard took a slug from his drink, slowly nodding, as he said, "No It wasn't THE worst, but it was damn close. I'd still like to know how the Committee learned about the arm-twisting we did to GED's CEO. Any ideas on that?"

Kutuzov looked at Dietrich and said, "I imagine that the Committee has its spies in the Navy. They ARE the Oversight Committee, after all. They're supposed to know what we're doing. Yeah, they reamed you a new one, but at least they didn't reverse the GED strategy. And now that the Committee has implicitly approved it, you no longer have to worry about potential legal consequences. We should thank our lucky stars, and the person who leaked the info, that he or she waited until the Senate had approved the Emergency Funding Bill AND Yakamura returned with the news of the alien outpost. Without that good news, the Committee might not have been so forgiving."

"I think you're right," Howard agreed. "Well Sergei, now that the funding bill's been approved, I imagine you're going to be even busier than before. How's the planning for Operation Dropkick coming along?"

Kutuzov rolled his eyes. "My planners have reached a stalemate. Half want to shift all military industrial activity and shipyard construction to multiple star systems as far as possible from where we suspect the aliens to be, and the other half want to concentrate most of the buildup right here in Sol. As you know, there are Pros and Cons either way. Concentrating most of the activity here simplifies the logistics involved enormously, but then we risk having most of our industrial eggs in one basket. On the other hand, dispersing the buildup minimizes that risk but slows down the pace of the buildup because each industrialized system will have to build its own infrastructure from scratch. And you can't really start building ship and supply factories until you've reached a minimum level of capacity in mining, refining and fabricating raw materials, not to mention the duplication in personnel."

"So what's the answer then?"

Kutuzov looked thoughtful as he replied. "Well, in light of what the Oversight Committee said this afternoon about wanting to see some tangible results from the buildup quickly, I'm thinking that we compromise the two extremes and concentrate the buildup in this system for at least the next six to nine months. Then we'll gradually shift additional capacity to rear area systems as it becomes available."

Howard nodded. "I like it. That would simplify your personnel problems too, wouldn't it, Sepp?"

Dietrich nodded back at him as he replied. "It certainly would. Are we agreed that's the way we'll do it?"

All three men looked at each other and nodded.

"Then I'll get my people started on the personnel side of Dropkick." Dietrich paused before adding, "Now that the SPG's budget has been approved, have you decided who will be running that group on a permanent basis?"

"No," Howard replied, "Kelly's done an outstanding job, but I'm still toying with the idea of giving it to Shiloh. Scuttlebutt has it that so far most of the recommendations from the group originated with Shiloh.

On the other hand, I would hate to lose his tactical skills in the field."

Dietrich jabbed his finger in Howard's general direction and said, "I've been meaning to ask you about Shiloh's actions out there. I've read his combat report, and I can't help thinking there's something he left out. Don't you think it's strange that all of sudden he would deploy sensor drones, for no apparent reason?"

Howard chuckled. "I know what you mean. It's almost as if he had a gut feeling that his ship was under observation. I suppose it's possible that he's too embarrassed to admit that he based his action on what was essentially a hunch. Still, I agree with what the Duke of Wellington said when asked after the Battle of Waterloo whether he'd rather be lucky or good. He said 'I'd rather be lucky'. If Shiloh's victory was just plain dumb luck, then I'll take it for what it is."

Kutuzov leaned forward. "Well, whatever you decide to do with Shiloh, you're going to have to make up your mind soon. If Shiloh's going to steer the Strategic Planning Group, Dietrich will have to find another Commander to take the 144th."

Howard nodded and considered his options. He had the strange feeling that this decision was going to turn out to be very important in the long run, and yet Shiloh was only a Commander, one of just over two hundred currently qualified for ship command. How could the outcome of this war depend on this one man? With Dietrich and Kutuzov starting to become impatient, Howard made up his mind and spoke.

"Okay. I've decided. Regardless of whether Shiloh's a tactical genius or not, he's an experienced ship jockey, and when we start getting new ships out of our construction program we're going to need all the experienced officers we can lay our hands on. So Shiloh will keep his SL slot for the 144th, and Kelly will be promoted and confirmed as Head of Strategic Planning."

The three admirals moved on to discuss other issues, and eventually the meeting broke up with Dietrich and Kutuzov going back to their offices. Howard wondered if he had made the right decision. He also wondered if he would ever know. Sometimes he couldn't help thinking, *being an Admiral sucks.*

***

Shiloh entered the main auditorium at Space Force HQ and spent a few seconds taking in the view of hundreds of SF personnel milling about and chatting prior to Admiral Howard's briefing. It seemed as though every officer, and quite a few of the NCOs and enlisted personnel presently on Earth, were here. Shiloh understood why, perfectly. Howard was about to present a proposal for the first offensive action against the aliens, and EVERYONE wanted to hear about it firsthand. With time running out and empty seats disappearing quickly, Shiloh decided to take a seat in a row that was near the back of the room. It happened to be quite close to one of the large view screens strategically placed around the auditorium, so that those in the middle and back could see any presentation just as well as those in the front. It wasn't long before the rest of the empty seats were filled, and the doors at the back were closed. When the overhead lights dimmed, the background chatter died away quickly. Shiloh saw Admiral Howard step out onto the stage and walk over to a podium. Behind, and to one side, a very large view screen dropped down and came to life. It showed a star chart, with Space Force Base Bradley in the lower left corner as a green dot, and a pulsing red dot in the upper right corner, with white dots in between. Just as the background chatter started up again, Howard started speaking.

"This briefing will now commence. If you're wondering why the CSO is giving this briefing, you're not alone. I'm wondering the same thing!"

That generated a wave of laughter.

"The answer to that question is that a briefing like this has never been necessary before. But now that the Space Force is transitioning to an elite military unit that can and will conduct offensive operations, there will have to be some changes here at HQ. That's why this is very likely to be the one and only time you'll see the Chief of Space Operations give a briefing like this. In future, I would expect that my soon to be announced Deputy CSO will be doing the honors. Be that as it may, this time it's my turn, so let's begin."

He paused to collect his thoughts.

"As I'm sure all of you have heard by now, our first attempt on long range reconnaissance was very successful. Cmdr. Yakamura and his crew of volunteers were able to sneak into a star system, indicated by the flashing red dot on the screen, which clearly has an alien presence that looks as though it's primarily mining-related."

The display now showed a blue line leading from SFB Bradley to the alien system.

"Analysis of Gnat's sensor data has revealed that this target system, Zebra 9, has half a dozen different locations where industrial activity of some sort is going on. Now that we have a fixed target, the Space Force has requested and been granted permission to engage in a raid on Zebra 9. Therefore this briefing will describe how we intend to conduct that operation, which will be called Operation Dropkick.

"The raid will consist of three phases. The first phase will be to make sure that we retain both strategic and tactical surprise. In order to do this, each of the 13 star systems that lie between our Bradley Base and Zebra 9 will have all gas giants monitored by orbiting recon drones. They will report any alien activity to the message drones that will be deployed at specific locations at the edge of these star systems. As the raiding force enters each intervening star system, it will make contact with the message drone in that system and verify that it's safe to refuel at the gas giant. If enemy activity has been detected near a refueling point, the raiding force commander will have several options. He or she can call off the raid altogether, use their remaining fuel to leapfrog past that system to the next star system in the line of advance, or they might decide to wait a while to see if the alien presence is only temporary. I would like to point out here how lucky the crew of the tanker Gnat was to have been able to refuel undetected in the star systems closest to Zebra 9. Given what happened to our ships in these other two systems—" the display showed two new yellow dots, both off to one side of the blue line "—one would have expected there to be picket ships in the systems surrounding their mining operations to guard against exactly what we were able to do.

"Once all of the refueling points along the way are under our observation, Phase Two will commence and the raiding force will leave SFB Bradley and proceed to the target. The raiding force will be designated Task Force 79 and will consist of a Command/Support squadron made up of a command ship and twelve tankers, plus six frigate squadrons."

He paused as the audience reacted with surprised chatter. He let it go on for a few seconds before he resumed speaking.

"Let's settle down, people." When it was quiet again, he continued. "Committing one third of all active squadrons may sound like overkill, however we do NOT want to underestimate the enemy. We've allocated one frigate squadron for each of the six mining locations in Zebra 9. When TF 79 enters the outer edge of Zebra 9, it will do so at a point that is equidistant from all six target locations, or as close to that as possible. Three of the target locations are moons orbiting two gas giants. The commander of TF79 will observe the level of enemy activity at both gas giants and, based on that information, will pick one as a refueling point. Phase Three will then begin with a high-speed pass by each frigate squadron past its designated target. Depending on the effectiveness of the damage inflicted and the strength of their defenses, the task force commander will have the flexibility to order additional attacks. In any case, when the chosen gas giant has been cleared of enemy defenses, the 12 tankers will move in to refuel, escorted by a frigate squadron, and then head back to a predetermined rendezvous point, where all ships will be refueled enough that they can make a long jump to the farthest refueling system possible. The idea here is that the task force will make the minimum number of hyperjumps back to Bradley in order to get out of the enemy zone as quickly as possible. When the task force reaches Bradley, any casualties will be transferred to the base, and the task force will then return to Sol. In the meantime, Task Force 80, consisting of four frigate squadrons, will be assigned the mission of protecting our Bradley base against any enemy retaliatory strikes that may occur subsequent to our raid. Four frigate squadrons will remain at Bradley from now on, with each tour of duty lasting four weeks. While TF79 will do everything it can to avoid revealing the location or direction of SFB Bradley, we shouldn't assume that the enemy won't be able to figure out where to go for a counter-strike. Since Bradley will be a forward base for some time to come, we'll start taking a series of defensive measures to protect it.

"Task Force 79 will be commanded by Senior Commander Yakamura, whose familiarity with Zebra 9 will stand him in good stead. The six frigate squadrons will be the 51st, the 77th, the 98th, the 102nd, the 144th and the 153rd."

He paused again, then said, "That concludes the overview of Operation Dropkick. I will NOT be taking any questions. However, if any of you have comments or suggestions that you feel would help make this operation a success, you're welcome to submit them in writing to my Office. Before I end this briefing, I have a few other items to communicate to all of you."

"Since meetings like this won't happen very often, now would be a good time to bring you up to date on what will be happening here on the Home Front over the next weeks and months.

"First, two new types of attack drones have been successfully tested and will be put into volume production very soon. One type has a depleted uranium kinetic energy penetrator warhead, while the other has a sub-kiloton tactical fission warhead. Unfortunately, neither one will be available for Dropkick, but we expect to be able to equip some squadrons with a few of these beauties before too long.

"Second, an in-house ship design bureau has now been established. It has already started working on detailed designs of a long-range reconnaissance ship, as well as a combat frigate that will have 150% more tonnage than an exploration frigate, with hull armor, more powerful lasers and enhanced ECM/Stealth capabilities. When we are far enough along the design process that we feel we can begin actual fabrication of parts, we will NOT be going with the old process of building one prototype ship first, to be extensively evaluated before any more are built. We can't afford the time for that anymore. Multiple combat frigates and, to a lesser extent, long-range recon frigates will be built at the same time. While that is going on, a SEPARATE design team will be working on an Autonomous Fighting Platform which can be thought of as a very large drone, with high endurance and capable of carrying its own standoff weapon systems. Once we have that design perfected, actual construction will be relatively quick. You can expect to see big changes in our force structure before the end of this year.

"That brings this briefing to an end. Let's all wish the men and women of TF 79 good luck and good hunting."

With that, Howard turned and left the stage. The lights came back up, and everyone started to leave while they chatted with one another. Shiloh stayed seated. He didn't mind being one of the last to leave while he pondered the raid profile. He was both excited and apprehensive about his squadron being part of the raiding force.

***

When Shiloh stepped back onto his repaired ship, it felt like coming home. Even though all Exploration Frigates were nearly identical in basic design, somehow this particular ship gave him a sense of familiarity that would have been missing from any other ship. As he stepped through the airlock connecting the asteroid repair facility to the ship, he saw his new XO standing there to greet him. With Johansen back from her recon mission and now waiting for a command of her own, Admiral Dietrich had paid Shiloh a singular honor by letting him pick his new Executive Officer. After going through the dossiers of several dozen potential candidates, Shiloh had picked Lt. Cmdr. Svetlana Chenko. The main reason he picked her was the persistent reports by her superiors to the effect that Chenko brought an unusually serious attitude to her duties, and Shiloh thought that would be exactly what the Space Force in general, and his ship in particular, now needed.

"Glad to see you were able to report to the ship so quickly, Commander."

Chenko saluted and said, "Thank you, Commander. I understand that you specifically requested me as Executive Officer."

Shiloh returned the salute and responded with, "Yes I did. I'm certain that we'll work well together."

With the saluting out of the way, Shiloh started walking towards the Bridge and said, "Has the ship's new second Officer arrived yet?"

Chenko, who had fallen in step with her CO, said, "Lieutenant Commander Farnsworth arrived on the previous transport. I've asked him to get up to speed on the current status of the ship's repairs. I understand that it's taken longer to finish them then was originally estimated."

Shiloh grimaced. "Yes, the estimate of three weeks was overly optimistic, but I understand that most of the delay is the result of last minute modifications that were ordered by our Chief of Operations. I've been told that at least one of her lasers is being upgraded to a more powerful model and that some of the ship's hull will have armor added to it."

He paused and then asked, "What percentage of the crew is aboard right now?"

Chenko didn't hesitate in responding. "We currently have 34 out of 77 onboard. Do you have some idea of when the ship will be expected to be ready for duty, Commander?"

Shiloh realized that Chenko was not likely to call him Skipper the way that Johansen did.

"Admiral Howard is anxious to get Task Force 79 up and running. Senior Commander Delvecio will be taking command of the Marathon soon and she should be ready to leave dock in less than a week. That means that I'll be stepping in as SFE144's Squadron Leader, and a squadron leader should be with his squadron, not sitting in a repair dock. I'm anxious to get the Old Girl fixed up and ready to dance as soon as possible."

Chenko did not smile at the reference to the 344 as the 'old girl'.

"I see your point, Sir."

By this time, they were entering the Bridge. It looked pretty much the same as before and was unoccupied since the ship was still berthed in the repair dock. Shiloh walked over to his command station and manipulated several controls. The large Tactical display on the wall came to life and showed the overall deployment of Space Force vessels in the Solar System. There was a dense cluster of green dots in orbit around Earth with a scattering of green dots elsewhere in the system, including the asteroid shipyards where the 344 was located, as well as in transit between Earth and other locations. Shiloh made the display zoom in to the cluster around Earth. The screen filled with green triangles showing ship identification. Never before had he seen so many exploration frigates in Earth orbit at one time. Admiral Howard had called back virtually every frigate the Space Force had. Exploration had ground to a halt. Shiloh wondered how many years it would be before exploration efforts started up again.

With Chenko helping him, Shiloh was able to convince the shipyard to finish their repairs on the 344 before the new command ship Marathon was ready. So it was that when Sen. Cmdr. Delvecio officially gave up the post of Squadron Leader of SFE144, Shiloh's ship was already back in Earth orbit and in formation with the rest of the squadron. Twenty-four hours after that, Task Force 79, under Sen. Cmdr. Yakamura, left Earth orbit.

Chapter 7 The Best Laid Plans of Mice and Men

It took 16 days for them to get to SFB Bradley, and then there was another two weeks of careful jumping along the Zebra route. The previously deployed recon drones around each star system's gas giants were checked for any signs of alien activity. None were found. When the task force arrived at Zebra 7 and confirmed that no enemy activity had been detected, Yakamura called an electronic conference with his squadron leaders.

"Well, we've verified that no enemy activity has been detected near this system's gas giant in the five weeks since the recon drone was deployed. Quite frankly, I'm surprised by this lack of enemy activity so close to their mining system. But, I'll take whatever luck I can get. However, that's not the reason I called this conference. Whoever calculated our projected fuel consumption was overly optimistic. I've just checked the task force's total remaining fuel supply and compared it to the estimated consumption that we expect to realize in jumping to Zebra 9, making our planned attacks, and then jumping back here. I'm concerned about the numbers. The plan calls for us to arrive back here with a minimum reserve of not less than 10%. If we continue with the Plan as it stands now, our reserve will be only 6.5%, and that's for the entire task force. Individual ships' reserves could be much lower. I'm not prepared to risk that. So here is what we're going to do. Shiloh and Dejanus, you two will take your squadrons and escort all 12 tankers to this system's gas giant, where they will skim heavy hydrogen until our estimated reserves are back up to 15%. You'll then escort them back here, and when the task force is together again, we'll proceed with the rest of the mission. Are there any questions or concerns?"

Cmdr. Dejanus spoke up. "Yes there is. Am I correct in thinking that as the senior Squadron Leader, I'll have tactical command authority during this refueling mission?"

Yakamura nodded and replied. "You are correct, Commander Rolen, you'll still have operational authority for the actual refueling of your tanker squadron, but in the event of contact with the enemy, you'll follow Dejanus's orders. Clear?"

"Clear, Sir."

"Commander Shiloh, that goes for you too."

"Understood, Sir."

"Good. Now, if there are no other questions ..." – there were none – "then let's proceed."

When the communication channel with the command ship terminated, Shiloh switched over to the open com channel with the rest of his squadron and gave them the news. By the time he had finished that, all of the ships involved in the refueling operation had received a data burst from Yakamura with detailed instructions.

Once underway, Dejanus issued his own orders regarding formation. SFE144 would lead the way, with the tanker squadron in the middle and SFE077 in the rear. Apparently Cmdr. Dejanus did not see the need to lead from the front. Shiloh didn't think much of that decision, and he was certain that most of the other ship commanders wouldn't either. With the transit to the gas giant expected to take almost 10 hours, Shiloh was glad that his command shift was nearly over. He wanted to be well rested and on the Bridge when they neared their destination.

As it turned out, the entire operation was completely uneventful and, in fact, quite boring. When all three squadrons joined the rest of the task force just over 32 hours later, Yakamura congratulated everyone on a smooth operation and ordered the task force to head on course for the jump to Zebra 9. Jumping past Zebra 8 directly to Zebra 9 took almost 50 hours. The tension aboard the 344 was palpable, and Shiloh was certain that it was the same aboard the other ships. The only person who seemed to be immune to the tension was Lt. Cmdr. Chenko. She remained as totally calm and serious as before. Shiloh found out that Chenko was an enthusiastic chess player. Wanting to get to know his new XO better, he borrowed a chess set from one of the crew and offered Chenko a game in the officer's wardroom during their overlapping off duty shift. It wasn't long before he realized that he was out of his depth. When Chenko moved her Queen all the way down to Shiloh's end of the board in order to pressure his King, Shiloh experienced another vision. In it, he saw Task Force Leader Yakamura on a view screen saying, 'I'm approving Commander Shiloh's request that all frigate squadrons be refueled before they split up to start the attack.'

The vision must have made his expression change because Chenko asked, "Are you alright, Sir?"

Shiloh quickly regained his composure and replied in the affirmative. Four moves later Chenko declared checkmate, and Shiloh tipped over his King.

As he was putting the pieces and board away, he said, "Before we emerge into Zebra 9, XO, I'd like to see a calculation of the squadron's fuel reserves and the estimated consumption for carrying out the mission and jumping back to Zebra 7."

Chenko acknowledged the order, and Shiloh left the wardroom.

When TF79 finally arrived at Zebra 9, their sensors revealed a big surprise. The entire system was EM dark. No artificial emissions were detected at all. Yakamura immediately called another conference session with his squadron leaders. As Shiloh listened to him explain how the recon mission had definitely detected six strong point sources of EM emissions along with other signs of industrial activity, he reviewed once again Chenko's report on SFE144's fuel situation. Due to the detour of escorting the tanker squadron to and from the gas giant, SFE144's remaining fuel was now below the minimum required for conducting the raid itself and the return jump. Once he had that conclusion clearly in his mind, he returned his full attention to the conference discussion. SFE153's Cmdr. LaRoche was speaking.

"—appears that they knew we were coming and shut down all energy sources to make it harder for us to pinpoint them. That suggests we should reconsider this mission if the element of surprise is gone."

SFE051's Cmdr. Cabrera started to respond but Yakamura cut him off.

"This mission will proceed regardless of whether we still have the element of surprise or not. I will not abandon this mission merely because they might be expecting us. What kind of signal would that send them? Any other comments?"

Shiloh spoke up. "Yes, Sir. I have a concern regarding my squadron's fuel situation. Our tanker escort mission depleted our reserves to the point where we won't have enough fuel to jump back to Zebra 7 if we're unable to refuel after the attack. I'd like to request that all of the frigate squadrons be refueled now, prior to the start of the attack. That way there'll be no risk that any ship will end up being stuck in this system and unable to jump back to Zebra 7. I realize that this request will delay the start of the attack, however it seems to me that we're more likely to have time to refuel when the enemy doesn't know we're here, than after the attack when whatever enemy ships are in this system are alerted to our presence."

Yakamura turned to the other screen and said, "What do the rest of you think of this suggestion?"

Only one squadron leader wanted to attack first and refuel later, and his argument was only half-hearted. All the others agreed with Shiloh. Yakamura nodded.

"Very well, in light of the support for this request, and because I feel the risk imposed by the delay is minimal, I'm approving Commander Shiloh's request that all frigate squadrons be refueled before they split up to start the attack. My XO will coordinate the refueling. That's all for now."

After the conference ended, Shiloh passed the refueling order to his squadron and ordered his Helm Officer to follow the instructions of the tanker assigned to the 344. While that was going on, he called Chenko to the Bridge. When she arrived next to his Command Station, he turned toward her.

"You heard the news about the emissions blackout?"

Chenko nodded.

"Comments?"

She thought carefully and then replied. "I agree that they are probably expecting us, and that begs the question of how did they know we were coming."

Shiloh nodded. "Yes, and the only answer I can think of that makes any kind of sense is that they detected our recon ship and figured out that we would follow up with a massed attack. But how did they detect the Gnat? She never approached the inner system, nor did she detect any enemy vessel. She was far enough out from this system's star that any reflected light would have been extremely difficult to detect, unless an enemy ship happened to be relatively close. And the odds of that happening are literally … astronomical. I can't help feeling that we've overlooked something. By the way, I've convinced Yakamura to let all frigate squadrons refuel now. I've passed the word to the squadron, and Lt. Verlander is looking after our refueling."

He paused, still wondering what implications the latest vision had in store for them, and then continued. "When the 144th is ready to start its attack run, I'm going to stay on the Bridge but only in my capacity as Squadron Leader. You will take the Con for this ship. I'll use this Command Station and you will con the ship from the Helm Station. Any questions?"

Chenko thought for a moment, then said, "No, Sir. That's clear enough and I can see why you want to do it that way. Having responsibility for both the ship and the squadron in a combat situation might be overwhelming for one person to handle."

"Excellent. You can wait until I send the Squadron to Battle Stations before you take over Verlander's station."

Chenko acknowledged that and left the Bridge.

When Shiloh returned his attention to the refueling, he saw that 2 of the 12 tankers were refueling each frigate squadron. As the fuel shuttle approached the 344, Shiloh felt himself getting impatient. His ship had refueled this way dozens of times before, but this time the process seemed to be going slower than usual, although a glance at the chronometer told him it wasn't. It was his own sense of time that was off, and he wondered if he was experiencing a rush of adrenaline. It would account for his distorted sense of time, but as to why he would be feeling a rush of adrenaline now when their scheduled attack was still a couple of hours away, he had no idea.

In point of fact, 20 minutes later that all eight frigates in SFE144 were finished their refueling. Shiloh watched with satisfaction as the last fuel shuttle disengaged and returned to its tanker. He immediately activated the com channel to the command ship, and Yakamura's face appeared on the view screen.

"All finished refueling, Commander?" asked Yakamura.

"Yes, Sir. Request permission for the 144th to leave the Task Force and proceed to the target."

Yakamura's face showed the barest hint of a smile as he said, "Permission granted. Good hunting, Shiloh."

"Thank you, Sir. See you on the other side."

"Absolutely! Yakamura out."

The screen went dark. Shiloh turned to his squadron com channel and said, "Squadron Leader to squadron. Prepare to execute course change."

He then waited for all his ships to electronically acknowledge their readiness for the computed course change. As soon as all eight ship's Helm Officers had signaled ready, Shiloh touched the flashing amber EXECUTE symbol on his Tactical Command Screen. Maneuvering computers pre-programmed with the desired course took control of each ship and made the exact same turn. At these speeds, leaving the course changes for a formation of ships to manual control was asking for collisions. Shiloh watched the squadron's actual course come around very slowly to the desired course. With the residual speed left over from the hyper-jump, making a micro-jump to the vicinity of the target would take only a few seconds. To retain the element of surprise for all of the targets, all six frigate squadrons would micro-jump at the same time, which meant that none of them could jump until all six were on the proper heading for their target. Shiloh checked a smaller screen, which showed the status of all the Task Force's squadrons, and noticed that squadrons 098 and 102 were still listed as undergoing refueling. He also noticed that the Command Ship, all of the tankers, and the 16 frigates that were not finished refueling, had already changed course for the heading that the Command Ship and the tankers would use to micro-jump to the other side of the star system, where the rendezvous point was located. Shiloh was just about to make a comment that Senior Commander Yakamura was in a hurry to get to the rendezvous point, when the Com Tech suddenly sat up and yelled out.

"Firefly's shuttle just reported that Firefly has suffered some kind of hull rupture!"

Shiloh looked over at him to see if more information was coming. The Com Tech started to say something and then stopped abruptly, but only for a second or two.

"No communication from— Dragonfly reports she's taking laser fire!"

Shiloh was about to ask 'from where' when the Com Tech continued.

"Sprite's shuttle stopped transmitting in mid-sentence!"

Shiloh looked back at the squadron status board. The yellow symbol indicating refueling operations beside the tanker squadron suddenly changed to flashing red, meaning they were under enemy fire. The symbol beside the Command Ship also changed to a flashing red. Shiloh switched on the main com channel that the Command Ship usually used.

"—ships, all ships, we're under enemy fire! Ships from the 98th and 102nd are ordered to go active on all scanners and return fire at will! Cabrera, Dejanus, Shiloh and Laroche, you're ordered t—"

The voice was cut off so abruptly that Shiloh was startled. He quickly checked to make sure that the interruption wasn't a technical snafu on his end. It wasn't. Yakamura's ship had stopped transmitting. Shiloh touched the electronic screen pad that sent his ship to Battle Stations.

"Com, signal the squadron to go to Battle Stations with Condition—"

He was about to say, 'One', which would have resulted in all his ships actively scanning and immediately firing on any unidentified contacts, but then he realized that Condition One might not be the best thing to do. As far as he knew, his ships were not being fired upon, at least not yet. And that could be for a number of reasons, such as them being out of range, but it could also be because they hadn't been detected yet. If they suddenly went to active scanning, not only would they detect enemy ships, but they would also be detected. He made a snap decision to give himself more options by saying, 'Four'.

Condition Four put all ships at Battle Stations, but with passive sensors only, and holding their fire until ordered otherwise. Without him ordering it, the large display screen on the wall switched from long-range astrogation mode to short range tactical mode. The tactical situation was not good. SFE144 was heading away from the main body of the Task Force, as were Jessica Cabrera's 051, Raphael Dejanus' 077, and Hiram LaRoche's 153. Mbutu's 098 and Bettencourt's 102 squadrons were still close enough to the tanker squadron that they could be considered part of the main body of ships. Shiloh could tell when ships from those two squadrons started actively scanning. A cluster of red triangles appeared at the Task Force's 8 o'clock position at a surprisingly close range! Shiloh counted the red triangles. Twenty-eight! The hair on the back of his neck stood up. How did 28 enemy ships get this close, this quickly? Something wasn't right. He tried to find out where the Command Ship was in the cluster of green hexagons that represented friendly ships. The Command Ship's hexagon should have been a brighter green. Shiloh couldn't find it, and suddenly he realized that the reason he couldn't find it was because it wasn't there! He also realized that some of his squadron's COs were trying to talk to him.

"144 squadron, standby! I'm going to try to re-establish communications with the Task Force Leader!"

Turning to the Com Tech, he said, "See if you can raise the Valley Forge again!"

While he was waiting for the results of that effort, Chenko rushed onto the Bridge. Shiloh saw her, nodded, and pointed to the Helm Station.

"XO, take the Con," he told her. "Lt. Verlander, the XO will be conning the ship from your station! Remain on the

Bridge in case I need you! I'll retain squadron command!"

Turning back to the Com Tech, he said. "Any word from Task Force Leader?"

The answer surprised him.

"Sir! I have Yellowjacket's CO on the line."

Shiloh nodded to him and heard the com channel switch over to a static filled line.

"Shiloh! Valley Forge has been shot to pieces! We were close enough to see it visually on our screens! Who's in command of the Task Force now?"

Shiloh thought fast. "It's Mbutu! Does he know about Yakamura?"

"Don't know! Hanson! Contact Mbutu's frigate. Notify him that Yakamura's gone and he's in command now! Victor, you still there?"

Shiloh nodded even though Frank Rolen couldn't see him. "Yes, Frank. I'm still here. My squadron is still shaking down to Battle Stations! What's your squadron's status?"

"Not good. Dragonfly's lost all power! Firefly's not maneuvering anymore either, and we can't raise her! My ship's suffered a glancing hit! We're losing fuel and atmosphere but we're still underway! I want to jump my ships outta here, but I also don't want to jump the gun if Yaka– Mbutu has other plans! God, Victor, where did these bastards come from?"

"I don't know, Frank, but you can't afford to wait for Mbutu to give you permission to jump. If your tankers are taken out, NONE of us will get back home! My advice is jump your ships away from here right now on your current heading, then dogleg it to the rendezvous point!"

"SHIT, VICTOR! Some of my ships still haven't recovered their shuttles yet! We can't leave them behind!"

Shiloh thought fast and replied. "We may have to, Frank! You may be able to pick those shuttles up later if the enemy leaves, and we come back here. If the tankers are destroyed, those shuttle crews are dead anyway!"

"You're right, Victor. DAMN! Sprite's just blown up! Okay! Hanson! Message to all tankers! Micro-jump immediately and proceed independently to the rendezvous point! Tell those shuttle crews we'll try to come back and pick them up later! Victor, we're outta here! See you at the rendezvous point!"

The channel cut off and Shiloh watched the green hexagon that was the tanker Yellowjacket fade out. Other tankers' symbols also faded out, but two hexagons, Hummingbird's and Pixie's, broke into pieces indicating that the ships had been blown apart by internal explosions presumably caused by enemy fire. Shiloh checked his squadron's status board and saw that all ships were at Battle Stations. He then looked back at the Tactical display. Switching back to the squadron Com channel he heard an angry voice.

"—when can we open fire, dammit?"

Shiloh replied before anyone else did.

"This is Shiloh. Here's the situation. TF Flagship has been destroyed. We have to assume that Mbutu is TF Leader now. Those tankers that were still able to jump away have done so and are headed for the rendezvous point. I'm going to try to contact Mbutu. Standby."

Shiloh cut short his message to the squadron when he noticed the Com Tech had switched Shiloh's audio speakers to another channel with Task Force Leader Mbutu on it.

"This is Mbutu. I've taken command of the Task Force. Most of the tanker squadron has jumped away. My squadron and 102 are now taking laser fire from enemy ships! All squadrons are ordered to close with the enemy force and open fire! Squadron Leaders acknowledge these orders!"

As per standard operating procedure, squadrons replied in ascending order of squadron number.

When it was the 144th's turn, Shiloh said, "144th acknowledges!" As soon as that was out of the way, Shiloh switched back to the squadron channel and said, "We've been ordered to close with the enemy force and open fire. Course changes will be downloaded shortly. Maneuvering will be by autopilot. We'll use one recon drone from each ship to triangulate the exact position of enemy ships. Until that data is available, take your best shots, using passive sensors only. I repeat, passive sensors only. No sense letting the enemy pinpoint our location from our active sensors. Keep this channel open."

Shiloh muted his microphone and looked over at Chenko. "XO! Plot a course change for the squadron that will put us on a heading we can use for a dogleg micro-jump closer to the rendezvous point if we should need to do that! You may also fire at will!"

"Acknowledged. Weapons Officer, you may open fire. Goran! Launch a recon drone and send it towards the enemy force at maximum speed. Begin active scanning as soon as possible. Course change is coming up! Course change is set and all ships have acknowledged receipt. Squadron is ready to change heading at your discretion, Sir!"

"Very good, XO. Here we go!"

Shiloh touched the electronic screen's flashing red button that activated the autopilots on all eight ships to maneuver in sync. He looked at the Tactical display and heard Chenko say, "Squadron is coming around to the new heading!"

It was too soon to be able to confirm that from the larger scale of the Tactical display. Shiloh used his Command Station controls to rotate the Tactical display to get a better idea of the relative positions and vectors of all the various clusters of ships. The Task Force had emerged from hyperspace more or less above the orbit of the farthest planet with a heading that would take it even further from the system's star. As each frigate squadron finished refueling, it pulled away from the Task Force and headed towards the planet where the enemy installations were expected to be. So from the Task Force's point of view, the four fueled squadrons had angled 'down' and were now below the remaining two frigates.

The enemy force, meanwhile, was approaching the two frigate squadrons from below and off to one side, although the 98th's and 102nd's vectors were sufficiently fast that the enemy's relative position to them was rapidly shifting to their rear. What this meant was that all four refueled squadrons had to 'pull up sharply' in order to narrow the range to the enemy ships. It was clear from listening to the Weapons Officer's report of miss after miss, that at this range and with passive sensors only, Shiloh's squadron was just too far away. Once the squadron deployed its recon drones and was able to triangulate their active scan data, they would be able to improve laser fire accuracy somewhat.

The only way to tell from the Tactical display if a ship was hit by laser fire was if the ship's display symbol slowed down, moved erratically, or broke up altogether. While a few of the enemy ships were clearly damaged, the frigates of the two squadrons closest to the enemy force were taking crippling hits at a faster rate and falling behind the others as the damaged ships stopped accelerating. Shiloh winced as one of Mbutu's ships broke up and disappeared. A few seconds later another frigate did the same thing. The enemy force appeared to concentrate their fire on one target at a time. It was clear that while the Task Force outnumbered the enemy in total number of ships, the frigates that were close enough to be hit were outnumbered almost two to one. When another of Mbutu's frigates stopped maneuvering and fell behind, Shiloh called out to Chenko.

"XO! Check to see who's next in line for command of the Task Force if Mbutu is taken out!"

Chenko checked and said, "Bettencourt is the next most senior, then Dejanus, Rolen, Cabrera, LaRoche and then yourself, Sir!"

"Thank you, XO."

Shiloh manipulated his com channel controls. The channel to Mbutu was open but silent. "Shiloh to squadron. I'm monitoring communications with the Task Force Leader, but he's not transmitting at the moment. I'm going to keep this channel open until further notice. We should start to get triangulated targeting data from our recon drones any second now. When we do, my Weapons Officer will designate a target, and I want the entire squadron to fire on that target and keep firing on it until a new target is designated."

While he was talking, he noticed that Chenko quickly rushed over to the Weapons Station and huddled with Sen. Lt. Sykes.

Shiloh called to him. "Sykes!"

The Officer looked up, as did Chenko.

"Sir?"

"Your targeting priorities should be the ship closest to our frigates. As soon as the target loses the ability to keep up with their formation, I want you to switch to another target. If we damage their ability to maneuver, then our ships will eventually pull out of their effective weapons range! Right now that's all I'm going for."

"Understood, Sir!"

Sykes and Chenko resumed their low-voiced consultation. One of Shiloh's ship commanders responded.

"Even if we cripple some of their ships, those cripples might still be able to fire! We should keep firing on the same target until it's completely destroyed!"

Shiloh bit back a curse just in time and said, "Negative! We could end up wasting shots on a lifeless hulk that refuses to blow up! We need to even the odds against the 98th and 102nd as fast as possible, and that means knocking as many enemy ships out of the fight as we can. When we whittle them down enough, I think they'll break off the attack altogether, and then we can pick off the stragglers at our leisure!"

A shout from Sykes told Shiloh that they now had more precise targeting data from their recon drones. Shiloh noticed from the Tactical display that the other three squadrons had also followed his lead and launched their own recon drones. Enemy ships started falling behind at a noticeably faster rate now, although by this time Mbutu's squadron was down to only four ships still able to accelerate away, and Bettencourt's squadron was down to just three. Chenko had finished coaching Sykes and was back at the Helm. Shiloh did a quick recount of the remaining enemy ships still able to keep up with the frigates. That total was now down to 18. The range from squadron 144 to the enemy was starting to drop much faster as the squadron's heading was steep enough that it would eventually pass behind the enemy formation, unless those ships made their own radical course change, which is exactly what they proceeded to do.

"They've broken off!" yelled Chenko.

Shiloh had enough presence of mind to realize that this was the first time he had seen Chenko get excited about anything. He checked the display and saw that Chenko was correct. The projected course of the enemy's main body of ships was now swinging away from all six frigate squadrons. Shiloh was about to speak when he heard Cmdr. Mbutu's voice.

"All squadrons, the enemy is attempting to break away! Victor, Jessica, and Hiram, I want your squadrons to pursue the enemy main body. Raph, rejoin the Task Force while we collect our stragglers, and take out any enemy cripples that are in range!"

Shiloh responded with, "Squadron 144 will pursue enemy main body as per Task Force Leader's order, along with the 51st and the 153rd. Shiloh to squadron. Let's keep our recon drones on their tails! You'll be receiving a new course change for your autopilots momentarily. XO, you know what has to be done?"

"Yes, Sir! I'll have that new course computed in a few seconds!"

But before Shiloh could implement Chenko's new course change, all of the enemy ships, except for two stragglers, micro-jumped away. Shiloh was taken aback by the change in alien strategy but when he thought about it, it suddenly made sense. As soon as the enemy fleet had started suffering more damage than they were dishing out, their Commander had made the correct decision to cut their losses and disengage via a micro-jump. With the other four squadrons rapidly making their superior numbers felt, the odds had shifted in favor of their enemy, and they knew it. Shiloh wondered if Mbutu would still order the planned attack on the enemy installations. He was thinking over the pros and cons when Mbutu come back on the com channel.

"Mbutu to all ships. It appears that we have our second tactical victory as the enemy has left the field of battle! In light of the reduced strength of the 98th and 102nd squadrons, plus the fact that the number of apparently undamaged enemy ships is equal to two full strength squadrons, I've decided that we will not split up into individual squadrons as per the planned attack. We'll keep the Task Force together, recover any survivors from our crippled ships and then reunite with the tanker squadron at the rendezvous point."

As Mbutu kept on talking, Shiloh noticed that Chenko had an alarmed look on her face. He motioned for her to come over to his Command Station. When she got there, he switched his com channel pickup to mute before speaking to her.

"What's bothering you, XO?"

She hesitated for only a second and then said, "I can't help wondering how they knew we were here so quickly!"

"Well, it must have been a lucky fluke that they happened to be in the vicinity of our emergence from hyperspace. Right?"

"And what if it wasn't a lucky fluke? What if they DETECTED our emergence from hyperspace?"

"Then that's a problem alright, but I don't see—"

Chenko interrupted. "If they detected our emergence, then they can probably detect the tanker squadron's emergence from their micro-jump too!"

Shiloh was stunned by Chenko's conclusion. He quickly decided that it wasn't a risk worth taking. Turning the audio pickup back on, he heard Cmdr. Cabrera ask who would run down the two enemy stragglers. Before Mbutu could respond, Shiloh jumped in.

"Commander Mbutu, my XO has just raised a disturbing possibility that I think needs to be brought to your attention immediately."

"Go ahead, Victor."

"The fact that a concentrated force of enemy vessels was able to arrive at our location so quickly after emerging from hyperspace, raises the possibility that they can detect when and where ships emerge from hyperspace, and if that's true, then our tanker squadron is in deadly danger as well! I urgently recommend that at least two squadrons be ordered to proceed to the rendezvous point as fast as possible!"

Mbutu was silent for what seemed like a long time. None of the other squadron leaders spoke. Finally Mbutu spoke.

"I hope you're wrong, Victor but prudence demands that we err on the side of caution. So you and Hiram take your squadrons to the rendezvous point asap and link up with the tanker squadron. Send a message drone back here when you arrive. Until the rest of the Task Force arrives there, Commander Rolen will be in charge. Is that clear?"

Both LaRoche and Shiloh said that Mbutu's orders were clear.

Chapter 8 The Other Shoe Drops

Even though Chenko, with Lt. Verlander's help, calculated the required course change and micro-jump in record time, getting to the point of being able to make the micro-jump seemed to take much longer than usual. Shiloh knew that his sense of time was off, likely because of the adrenaline rush of the combat and anxiety over whether the tanker squadron might be under attack. The actual micro-jump took only seconds. Shiloh's squadron arrived first and began to actively scan the area. It wasn't long before they picked up the tanker squadron's homing beacon operating as per standard orders. The rendezvous point was sufficiently far from any of the suspected locations of alien infrastructure that it would take hours for the homing signal to reach any of them. The tanker squadron was almost half a light second away. Once both squadrons achieved contact with each other, arrangements were made to join up. When SFE153 arrived and made contact, it too adjusted its heading to link up. Shiloh briefed Frank Rolen about the outcome of the battle. Rolen sounded relieved to hear that the crews of the tankers and shuttles left behind would be picked up, but then Shiloh explained the fear that the aliens were able to track ships emerging from hyperspace.

"Oh God, Victor, that's all we need! This mission is rapidly turning into a clusterfuck! I'm worried about what we should do if that enemy force turns up here before the rest of the Task Force arrives."

"Well Frank, first of all it won't be like last time because both LaRoche's squadron and mine are actively scanning the area, which means that the enemy force won't be able to sneak up on us undetected. Second, to avoid being caught at close range if they should happen to jump that accurately, I recommend we make a radical course change and leave behind a message drone as a communications relay. Third, in the unlikely event that your tankers are taking laser fire, we should have a backup plan for your squadron to jump to Zebra 7 for a new rendezvous there. We'd have to check everyone's fuel situation to make sure, but I think everyone should have enough fuel to get to Zebra 7. How's that sound?"

There was silence for a few seconds, then Rolen said, "Yes, that sounds good, Victor, especially in light of the fact that my squadron is down to just five tankers. Can you believe it? FIVE! Yellowjacket is damaged and unable to skim gas giants but still has enough fuel to get to Zebra 7. And if we take the time to seal off the damaged sections, she can carry fuel that the other tankers can skim and transfer over. As far as everyone else being able to get to Zebra 7 is concerned, unless they sustained damage to their fuel storage, they should be okay, too. What's your opinion, Hiram?"

"I would actually go further than Victor and recommend that you take your tankers to Zebra 7 right NOW and take both frigate squadrons with you to ride shotgun. Refuel at Zebra 7 and wait for the Task Force to catch up. When Mbutu and the Task Force gets here, a message drone will update them, and they'll know where to find us."

Before Rolen could respond, Shiloh spoke.

"I would advise against that, Frank. If we're right about the aliens being able to detect ships emerging from hyperspace, then the enemy force might be waiting here in ambush when the rest of the Task Force, with its under-strength squadrons, arrives. We should try to unite the Task Force if at all possible because there's safety in numbers. Besides, with a little luck, Mbutu and his ships will arrive first, and then we might be able to ambush the enemy force for a change."

Rolen started to reply when the sensor alarm on board both Shiloh's and LaRoche's ships started wailing. As Shiloh looked up at the Tactical display, he saw a cluster of red triangles emerging from hyperspace behind the tanker and the two frigate squadrons. Turning back to the view screen with Rolen on it, Shiloh spoke quickly.

"Frank, they're here! No time to debate things! You've got to get your tankers to safety! Let's rendezvous at the gas giant in Zebra 7!"

"Yes. Okay, Victor! We'll see you there! Good luck!"

Shiloh heard the com channel cut off and shifted his focus back to the squadron channel. The squadron was still at Battle Stations so he said, "Shiloh to squadron! The enemy is back for more punishment. Concentrate your targeting as before and open fire!"

Shifting to the channel with LaRoche, he said, "Hiram, we've got to keep them busy while the tankers jump away!"

"Okay, Victor! The 153rd will back you up!"

Shiloh remembered that Mbutu had ordered Rolen to do something he might not be able to.

"Shiloh to squadron. Each frigate will launch a message drone to jump back to the Task Force with a tactical update asap!"

With eight message drones launched, even if the enemy detected them and fired on them, there was still a good chance that at least one would get through. Even if the others were destroyed, at least they would divert some of the enemy fire. Shiloh hoped that LaRoche would order his squadron to launch their own spread of message drones as soon as they detected those from the 144th. Turning his attention back to the Tactical display, Shiloh saw that the enemy vector was almost at right angles to the frigates, but he could already tell that the enemy ships were clawing their way around in an effort to keep the range from opening further. Shiloh made the display zoom in. He saw the 144th launch message drones, and a few seconds later the 153rd followed suit. Almost at the same time, enemy ships started taking hits and falling out of formation. Shiloh checked to see if the tankers had jumped and couldn't find any still there. He spoke out loud, to no one in particular.

"Did all the tankers jump away?"

It was Chenko who answered.

"Yellowjacket was destroyed almost immediately. The others managed to jump away."

"Damn!" Shiloh pounded the armrest of his Command Station chair. He was about to say more but Chenko spoke first.

"307's lost maneuvering ability!"

307 was one of his ships. Shiloh quickly switched com channels and 307's CO appeared.

"What's your situation, Tom?"

"We're in bad shape, Sir. Main power's go—"

The picture and sound cut off abruptly. Shiloh looked up just in time to see the breakup of the green hexagon symbol that was Frigate 307. Before he could react, one of LaRoche's ships also broke apart. LaRoche was still on the open channel, and just as Shiloh turned to the screen to say something, every light and electronic device on the Bridge went dark. Shiloh felt the artificial gravity fail, as well as his Command Station chair's automatic restraints locking in. In half a second, the emergency lights came on, but nothing else.

Not hesitating for a second he said, "XO! I'm taking back the Con. Get down to Engineering and find out what happened. If they still have power down there, you'll have to pilot the ship from Engineering. We've got to maneuver in order to avoid being a sitting duck!"

As Chenko braced herself to push off for a leap in zero G at the access tube, Shiloh turned to the Com Tech and said, "Do we have any ship to ship communications at all?"

The Com Tech shook his head. Shiloh hit his chair armrest again. His ship was blind, deaf and crippled. It was liable to be cut to pieces with concentrated laser fire any second, and there was absolutely nothing he could do about it! Seconds seemed to last minutes. He knew that Chenko would be trying to get to Engineering as fast as possible, but with no gravity, moving down the length of the hull would take time. As the seconds and then minutes passed with no lethal blow, Shiloh began to hope that they would survive this nasty turn of events.

Finally, after almost five excruciating minutes, the power came back on just as suddenly as it had cut off. To avoid serious injury, the artificial gravity came back on very slowly. As the Com Tech tried to re-establish communication channels, Shiloh watched the Tactical display sort out the incoming data from sensors. When the display settled down, Shiloh saw that that there were NO red triangles at all! Instead there were a lot more green hexagons. It looked as though the rest of the Task Force had arrived. One of Shiloh's com screens light up to reveal Task Force Leader Mbutu.

"Ah! Glad to see that you're back, Victor!"

Shiloh nodded. "Yes, Sir. We seem to be operational again. What happened, Sir?"

"Well, the enemy force jumped away, almost literally, as soon as we showed up! I understand from Hiram that four of our tankers managed to get away, and that we will meet up with them again in Zebra 7."

"I hope so, Sir. The tankers weren't lined up for a jump directly to Zebra 7, so they would have had to micro-jump somewhere else in this system first, then change heading for the jump to Zebra 7. I just hope that the alien force didn't ambush them before they were able to jump outsystem."

Mbutu looked thoughtful. "Yes. Let's hope so. Given that they arrived here so quickly, there doesn't seem to be any doubt now that they're able to detect ships emerging from hyperspace. Thank God you recommended sending two squadrons here asap! If we hadn't done that, all of the tankers would likely have been destroyed, and then the entire Task Force would have been lost from eventual fuel exhaustion."

He paused before adding, "While my squadrons are maneuvering to link up with yours, the 144th and 153rd can finish transferring survivors from your damaged ships. As soon as all that's done, we'll head straight for Zebra 7. Commander Tanaka will be temporarily assuming the post of squadron leader for the 153rd. Any questions?"

"No, Sir."

"Fine. Mbutu clear."

As Shiloh was about to attempt to reconnect with the rest of his squadron, Chenko returned to the Bridge and walked quickly over to him.

"What happened to us, XO?"

"We took a partial hit that penetrated just deep enough to sever a main power linkage from the power plant to the rest of the ship. I checked our repair log from the shipyard, and that particular section of the hull wasn't armored. The actual amount of energy used to cut the linkage was relatively small compared to the impact of the damage. It seems to be a design flaw that might explain other ships being crippled in battle. We were lucky that we didn't suffer any more hits after that. Offhand I'd say we probably took a hit that was aimed at someone else and missed."

"Good work, XO! I've just spoken with TFL Mbutu and we're in the process of reforming the Task Force. After that we'll head for Zebra 7, hopefully find the remaining tankers, and then head home. Until we're in hyperspace, I want you to con this ship from the Helm as before while I con the squadron."

"Yes, Sir."

Chenko moved to the Helm Station where Verlander was already getting up to move aside. Shiloh held a hasty view screen conference with his remaining six frigates, none of which had suffered any serious damage. All six COs seemed to be relieved to hear that the Task Force was heading home. With a roughly 55 hour hyperjump ahead of them, there was not the sense of urgency that they had experienced with the micro-jump. By accelerating to a higher speed, the Task Force was likely to arrive at Zebra 7 star system before the tankers did, however at that distance it was very unlikely they would emerge anywhere near each other. With only one gas giant, the rendezvous point was obvious. If the tankers got there first, they would refuel and wait for the Task Force to show up, using passive sensors only. When the Task Force arrived, it would scan the vicinity of the gas giant with active sensors. If it detected four ships, it would attempt to make contact from a safe distance. The Task Force regrouped, changed heading and entered hyperspace, all without further enemy contact. Once in the safety of hyperspace, Shiloh cancelled Battle Stations and the ship returned to its normal routine.

During the hyperjump, Shiloh briefed each off-duty section of the crew about the details of the two encounters so that everyone knew what happened. Most of the crew were upset that Mbutu had chosen to abort the mission, but Shiloh explained to them that with only four tankers left to get the rest of the surviving frigates home, it would be reckless to remain in Zebra 9. The enemy clearly recognized what the tankers were, and were gunning for them. He also started working on his After-Action reports. Once again he omitted the vision he experienced that had prevented an even worse outcome. If all six frigate squadrons had not taken the time to refuel upon arrival at Zebra 9, it was highly likely that the command ship and tanker squadron would have been ambushed and destroyed before any frigate squadron could come to its rescue. Even if the tankers had micro-jumped away, the alien ships would have detected their emergence location and micro-jumped after them. Without the tankers, the rest of the Task Force would have been destroyed either fighting the superior enemy force one squadron at a time, or they would have jumped to another star system only to eventually run out of fuel altogether, their crews eventually dying from lack of oxygen. In Shiloh's mind the whole operation was a tactical defeat, yet a strategic victory in the sense that the enemy force had tried and ultimately failed to use its hyperspace emergence technology to completely ambush the expected attacking force. If no ship survived to return to base with that crucial information, the aliens would continue to have that advantage and perhaps ambush more squadrons. So, for the loss of 13 frigates, 8 tankers and 1 command ship, but thankfully not all of those crews, Space Force had acquired some very valuable intel, and 35 frigates and four tankers –hopefully – would make it back to live and fight another day. It was a painful price to have to pay, but Shiloh felt it would ultimately be worth it.

The arrival at Zebra 7 was, as expected, uneventful. Having emerged in the outer edges of the system, the Task Force had to proceed under normal space drive to the gas giant. The recon drone left in orbit around the gas giant to monitor enemy activity had downloaded sensor data that showed no discernible activity, enemy or friendly, during the time since the last visit here. That didn't concern Shiloh very much. Mbutu had ordered the Task Force to accelerate prior to jumping, which meant that they could easily have arrived first, having passed the tankers somewhere in hyperspace. Once in orbit around the gas giant, the Task Force spent a nervous 14 hours until a signal from the tankers confirmed their arrival insystem. As soon as the tankers entered orbit, they began the task of refueling the Task Force. Since that task would take almost 33 hours to complete, any frigate not being refueled at any given point in time was in a higher orbit, actively scanning for enemy ships.

On a hunch, Shiloh ordered his squadron to also scan the surfaces of the 13 moons orbiting the gas giant. After multiple passes, one of those moons finally revealed its secret. An alien device that was too small to be anything other than a passive detection device was spotted from its very tiny radar reflection. Given that no ship had been detected deploying the device after the recon drone was deployed in orbit, it was clear that the ground unit had been placed there before the raid was even contemplated. Perhaps even before Yakamura's reconnaissance mission! If that were the case, then the aliens would have a rough idea from which part of the sky Space Force ships were coming. When Shiloh had notified Mbutu about the alien device and his concerns about leading the enemy back towards Human Space, Mbutu concurred and said that when the Task Force was ready to leave, it would take a detour in the wrong direction before resuming its journey back home. The two of them debated whether to leave the device alone and pretend they hadn't noticed it, or destroy it now. Shiloh was in favor of leaving it intact in order to preserve the options of some kind of strategic deception operation in the future. Mbutu disagreed, and in his capacity as Task Force Leader, he ordered Shiloh's squadron to destroy the device immediately. Shiloh decided that the 344 would do the task. One well-aimed laser shot turned the device into a slag pile of melted metal.

At last the entire Task Force was refueled, and the tankers were topped up as well. Mbutu ordered the Task Force to retrace its inward path in order to confuse the enemy, just in case there was another detection device watching them. When the Task Force was almost a light hour from the gas giant, TF79 turned back towards their real destination, which was Zebra 3, bypassing 4, 5 and 6 altogether. The recon drones left to monitor Zebra 3's two gas giants didn't reveal any sign of enemy activity, and the ships of the squadron took a very close look at the moons of both of them without finding any alien devices. With that refueling going off without a hitch, and the task force back in hyperspace on its way to one more refueling stop before arriving back at SFB Bradley, Shiloh and the rest of his crew began to relax. The arrival back at Bradley was anticlimactic. Since all Space Force bases were close enough to each other to be reached with one full load of fuel, TF79's frigate squadrons were no longer dependent on their tankers, which were detached as per orders that were waiting for them. TF79 arrived back in Earth orbit almost two months after heading out on the attack mission. No sooner had the task force settled down into its parking orbit than orders arrived from the Chief of Operations for all COs and XOs to report to HQ asap. Shiloh had a feeling Admiral Howard would not be happy.

Chapter 9 Payback's a Bitch

It was night and raining when the shuttle, carrying Shiloh, Chenko and the other COs and XOs from his squadron, landed at the spaceport outside Geneva. Space Force vans were waiting to take them to Headquarters. Some of the other squadrons had already landed their officers. When they arrived at HQ, they were shown into the same large auditorium where Howard had briefed everyone on the first encounter. Since not everyone was there yet, those officers who had arrived were allowed to walk around and chat with others. Mbutu's squadron, what was left of it, had already landed its officers, but Mbutu himself was not in sight. Shiloh overheard one of his officers say that Mbutu was in a private debriefing with Admiral Howard himself. After a while, more officers showed up, and soon after that one of Admiral Howard's staff came and asked everyone to take a seat. Shiloh and Chenko sat at the end of the second row. Just as everyone was getting settled down, the staff officer shouted out.

"Attention on deck!"

Everyone jumped to attention and stopped talking. Admiral Howard entered the auditorium followed by Cmdr. Mbutu, who took the nearest vacant seat. Howard strolled leisurely to the center of the stage, folded his arms across his chest, and began.

"Well, here we are. Space Force has lost … one command ship, eight tankers, 13 frigates ... and 987 officers and crew. I've just spent the last hour with Acting Task Force Leader Mbutu going over his summary of what happened, and I've skimmed the After-Action reports of the various squadron leaders who transmitted their reports while en route to Near Earth Orbit. I have a pretty good idea of how Operation Dropkick went down."

He paused to look around at his audience. The room was dead silent. Howard started to pace slowly across the front of the stage, from side to side and back again, speaking as he went.

"In the days and weeks to come, those who weren't there will look at the results, including the fact that none of the alien infrastructure facilities in Zebra 9 were damaged or destroyed, and they'll conclude that Operation Dropkick was a disaster, a major defeat for the Space Force. That is not my view of the operation, and it shouldn't be yours. Granted, you did not inflict any damage on the alien mining operations, but their destruction was never expected to be more than an inconvenience to the aliens. The raid was primarily intended to give the participating squadrons some combat experience, along with experience in working with a larger formation, as well as obtaining additional insight and intel on alien capabilities, tactics and operating procedures. From THAT perspective, the mission was at least partially successful. Let's also not forget that the enemy took some losses too! Only five enemy ships were confirmed as destroyed outright, but another seven suffered obvious damage, and we can reasonably expect them to be out of action for a while. Given that they clearly have the ability to detect ships emerging from hyperspace, and were therefore able to catch TF79 by surprise, I'm actually impressed that our losses weren't higher. Now that we know about their detection capabilities AND the fact that they've planted automated detection stations beyond their actual sphere of operation, we can adjust our plans accordingly. I consider getting that intel back to us here to be a major accomplishment. So while it's perfectly acceptable to mourn our lost comrades-in-arms, you should also feel that their sacrifice was NOT in vain!

"So what do we do now? Well, frankly not very much. The loss of those tankers is going to effectively curtail any possibility of conducting offensive operations in strength, much beyond the support range of our forward bases. In the near term, that means that Space Force will have to remain on the defensive while we rebuild our tanker capability. So, no more raids for at least six months. That does not mean, however, that we'll be sitting on our hands. Once my staff works out the details, we will deploy our frigates in a way that hopefully will allow us to detect any enemy incursion into star systems that would put them within striking distance of those forward bases closest to them. While that is going on, our shipyard capacity will continue to expand, and we'll start to see new ship designs becoming operational. Here's what you can look forward to."

He motioned to his aid, who manipulated a device, and the large view screen behind Howard came to life. It showed two ships. Howard continued.

"I'm sure you recognize the design at the bottom as the exploration frigate that all of you have come to know and love."

Howard's playful sarcasm generated a ripple of chuckles from the audience.

"The FE class of frigates are 245 meters long, 44 meters wide, mass approximately 22,000 metric tons, carry up to six drones externally and are armed with two laser turrets, one on top and the other below. The other ship will be the new FA class of armored combat frigates. Don't be misled by its shorter length. It's actually a much larger ship massing almost 50,000 tons. It doesn't seem larger because you're looking at it from the side. Here is a better view from above."

The image changed and Shiloh heard whistles of appreciation.

"As you can see, the combat frigate is much wider and looks like an arrowhead that has had its point chopped off. However, unlike the FE class, the combat frigate will be highly streamlined and will have the capability to skim gas giants to refuel itself without the need to refuel from tankers. It will be armed with three double laser turrets! That's six laser cannon! All three turrets can be retracted during gas giant skimming. It will also be able to carry up to 20 drones internally."

The picture changed again to show a much smaller vehicle beside the two frigates.

"This is the new AFP. The first AFP prototype is nearing completion and is scheduled to begin its test phase within the next two weeks. It will be a modular design that can be configured several ways, including a standoff strike version that will carry four VERY fast attack drones … like this."

The picture changed again to show the wedge-shaped vehicle with a detachable middle section, which contained four cone-shaped objects.

"Now when I say that these attack drones are fast, I mean REALLY fast. The FE class frigate can accelerate at a maximum of one point three kilometers per second squared which is equivalent to about 133 gravities. Our standard drones can just about double that rate of acceleration, as will the new combat frigate. The AFPs will be able to triple that rate to about 400 gravities. These new attack drones will be designed to accelerate at almost 800 gravities and the techies are sure they can eventually double that again! But the problem is that these attack drones won't be able to maintain that acceleration for very long, which is why the AFPs will be carrying them instead of the frigates themselves. The AFPs will have to carry them in close enough that the velocity of the AFP, combined with the acceleration of the attack drone, can reach the target before the attack drone runs out of power and can't conduct terminal maneuvers to guarantee a hit. The effective range of these attack drones will depend on how fast the AFPs are going when the drones are launched. I should point out here that standoff strike AFPs carried by combat frigates will only be able to attack once. This is because externally mounted AFPs can't be reloaded until the frigate reaches a base where the AFPs can transfer, too. The long range answer to that problem will be the AFP Carrier, and as soon as we get the bugs worked out of the AFP prototypes and accumulate some operational experience with them, we'll start designing the carriers for them. We estimate it will take at least a year just to build a carrier, so don't hold your breath waiting for them."

That brought forth more laughter. Howard nodded to his aide and the view screen went dark.

"That's just a peek at what's coming down the pike. I'm showing you this so that you're aware we ARE making progress. Unfortunately it also means that the lowly exploration frigate will have to carry the burden of our defense for a while longer. So, here's what's going to happen now. The 102nd and 98th will each contribute two frigates towards filling the gaps in the 51st, 144th and 153rd. Those three squadrons, along with the 77th, will be redeployed after their crews stand down for a one week rest period. What ultimately will become of the 102nd and 98th has not been decided yet. We may disband those squadrons altogether, or rebuild them with new ships coming off the shipyards, but that's yet to be determined. Now, before I dismiss you so that you can get your crews on the ground, it's important that we have all After-Action reports before you go on R&R. If you haven't already filed your AA report, you had better do so within the next 24 hours."

Shiloh heard a few groans and wondered if Admiral Howard heard them too. If he did, he gave no sign of it.

"Okay, that's it! You're dismissed!"

Shiloh turned to Chenko and said, "XO, I'll leave it to you to arrange the details for our crew to be brought down. When you decide where you're going to spend your R&R, make sure I know how to reach you if I need to. I have a feeling that Admiral Howard isn't finished with me just yet."

Chenko nodded and said, "Yes, Sir."

Shiloh looked back at the Admiral and saw that he was whispering something to his aide, who nodded and looked around the room at the departing officers, saw Shiloh, and quickly walked over to him.

"Commander Shiloh, the Admiral would like a word with you in his office."

"Certainly, Lieutenant."

Before following the aide, Shiloh looked at Chenko and said, "See what I mean?"

By this time, Howard had already left the auditorium. Even though he knew the way, Shiloh let the aide lead him to the Admiral's office.

When they arrived, Howard waved him in and said, "Have a seat, Commander."

Shiloh sat down in the indicated chair, with Howard facing him from the other side of the desk.

"I wanted to speak with you in private because Commander Mbutu's After-Action report has raised some questions about your conduct, and I wanted to hear your side."

Shiloh's surprise was clearly evident to Howard.

"I see that you didn't know about Mbutu's criticisms. Well let me enlighten you. In your report, you say that you advised Commander Rolen to jump his tankers away, without waiting to get orders from Mbutu, the Acting TF Leader. Mbutu claims that you acted as the defacto Task Force Leader knowing full well that he, Mbutu, was senior to you, and that he was in command of the Task Force. Furthermore, you encouraged Rolen to ignore the proper chain of command. I assume that you'd like to respond to that?"

"Absolutely, Sir. Rolen's tankers were clearly being targeted by the alien force, and with that concentration of fire, his tankers wouldn't have lasted very long. He himself told me that his instinct was to order his squadron to jump away immediately, but he was hesitating to do so because of lack of orders from Commander Mbutu. My advice to Rolen was from the point of view of one Squadron Leader to another, to protect not only his command, but also the whole Task Force as best he could under the circumstances. At no time did I say or imply that Rolen should ignore orders from Mbutu, Sir."

"I see."

Howard said nothing while he trimmed and lit a cigar. After taking a puff, he said, "I presume that the audio recordings made at the time will verify your explanation?"

"Yes, Sir."

"Well, that being the case, I'm inclined to accept you weren't trying to usurp Mbutu's authority. Although I have to say, Commander Shiloh, that you came pretty close to crossing that line. Now that I've heard your side of the story, I'll have another chat with Mbutu. I think I'll be able to convince him to let this issue go, but if he insists on pursuing it, that's his right, and there will have to be a formal Board of Inquiry at which point your audio recordings will be presented as evidence. It's unfortunate this issue has raised its ugly head because that it tarnishes the credit you earned by convincing Yakamura to refuel the Task Force before commencing the attack. It's clear to me that if you hadn't done that, the command ship and tanker squadron would have been caught without any support from the frigate squadrons. They would have been too far away by then, and it's highly likely that all the tankers would have been destroyed, thereby stranding the rest of the Task Force without the ability to return to friendly territory."

He took another puff of the cigar and continued, "By the way, congratulate Commander Chenko for me for having that flash of insight into the aliens' ability to detect ships leaving Jumpspace. The two of you make a good team. You both seem to have some kind of sixth sense when it comes to critical combat situations, and that's something that should be recognized and encouraged."

Shiloh was very tempted to admit to his own visions but decided not to. Having an inspired thought was one thing, having a full-blown vision was quite another.

"Very well, Commander. Unless there's something you wish to ask or discuss with me, you're free to go."

"No, Sir. I have nothing more to add."

Shiloh got up, came to attention, saluted – which Howard returned – and left the office. After assuring himself that arrangements for his crew's R&R leave were under way, and having received a short message from Chenko letting him know where to reach her during her leave, Shiloh accepted an invitation to join several other officers from his squadron at a resort on the Mediterranean Sea in Egypt. The leave went far too quickly, and 170 hours later Shiloh and his squadron were on their way back to Bradley Base for system patrol and quick reaction duties in case enemy forces showed up in, or within striking distance of, the star system containing SFB Bradley.

Chapter 10 Give As Good As We Get

The next four months were boringly uneventful. Single frigates were on picket duty in the star systems forming a buffer zone in front of the system containing the Bradley Base, each in contact with a dozen or more recon drones strategically deployed throughout those systems. Shiloh and the other squadron leaders and frigate COs were confident that the enemy could not sneak up on Bradley Base without being detected. So it was, with only three more days to go before SFE144 was due to be rotated back to Sol for a longer stand down, that the period of boredom ended.

Shiloh was asleep in his cabin when the call from the Bridge came.

"Shiloh here."

"Chenko here, Sir. A message drone has just arrived and is signaling that picket ship 257 in Tango Delta 11 has detected a minimum of three unknown ships moving towards one of that system's gas giants."

Shiloh sat up quickly and said, "Any word from Base Command yet?"

"No, Sir, but I expect we'll hear something any minute now."

"I agree, XO. Put the ship and the squadron on alert. I'll be on the Bridge shortly. Shiloh out."

He quickly put on a clean uniform and then ran out of the cabin and down the short corridor to the Bridge. When he got there, he heard the voice of the Base Commander over the loudspeakers.

"—signs of enemy activity in Tango Delta 11. Therefore I'm activating Plan Alpha III. The 55th will immediately jump to Tango Delta 9, the 77th to Tango Delta 8 and the 144th to Tango Delta 6. Truman out."

As Chenko got up from the Command Station, Shiloh waved her back down and said, "I'm not taking the Con just yet, XO. Let's acknowledge our orders to the Base Commander and get the Squadron onto the right heading for TD 6."

"Yes, Sir. Specialist Fletcher, acknowledge the144th orders. Lt. Millar, plot a course change to Tango Delta 6."

Shiloh walked over to the Communications Station, waited until the Com Tech had sent the acknowledgement, and then said, "Open an audio channel to the Squadron."

"Channel open, Sir."

"This is Shiloh. Plan Alpha III has just been put into effect. The 144th has been ordered to Tango Delta 6 asap. You'll be receiving the necessary course change data shortly. Because of the short distance to TD6 and back, we won't have to worry about fuel consumption, and therefore we'll be making a high-speed jump. If the enemy chose that star system as their next destination, it's imperative that the 144th get there before they do. Once we arrive at TD 6, I'll contact our picket ship already stationed there, and then I'll determine how we'll proceed based on the situation at that time. Shiloh out."

He turned back to look at Chenko who said, "Course and speed for Tango Delta 6 has been plotted and uploaded, and all ships report ready to execute, Sir."

"Very well, XO. Helm, execute the course change!"

"Executing course change now, Sir."

As all eight frigates began to both accelerate and change their headings via autopilot, Shiloh looked at the Tactical display and saw that the other two squadrons were also coming around to the new headings for their own high speed jumps. Two more frigate squadrons remained as they were. They would continue to defend this star system in case the enemy jumped past Tango Delta 6, 8 and 9 altogether. That was highly unlikely, but nevertheless had to be guarded against because the base itself had minimal defenses.

The optimum combination of normal acceleration and Jumpspace speed enabled the 144th to arrive at the outer edges of the Tango Delta 6 system in just over 12 hours. Even as the squadron decelerated, Shiloh sent a tight beam transmission to the point in the system where the frigate on picket duty was supposed to be. With the distance between them measured in light hours, it was almost seven hours later when Shiloh received a reply from the picket ship. No sign of enemy activity so far. Shiloh happened to be on the Bridge when the 339's message arrived. When Chenko arrived to take her regular duty shift, Shiloh shared the message with her and asked for her comments.

"Well, Sir. I don't think we can jump to any conclusions just yet, even though TD 11 is just over four light years away, and it wouldn't take those ships long to get here. They may still be in TD 11, or they might have turned around and gone back home OR they could easily have jumped to TD 8 or 9 instead. How long we wait here is a good question."

Shiloh nodded. "I agree with your assessment. The question I'm now trying to grapple with is how close we take the squadron to the picket ship. I don't want to give away her position if those alien ships do show up, but then again, waiting for hours for a transmission to reach us eliminates a lot of tactical options. What do you suggest?"

Chenko pondered that for a few seconds while Shiloh waited. Finally she said, "My recommendation would be that the Squadron not be any further away than five light minutes. It's unlikely that the tactical situation would change drastically in that period of time, but further than that could be problematic."

"Yes, I agree. When you take the con for your duty shift, that's what I want you to arrange. Let's put the squadron within five light minutes of the picket ship, on a heading that's in the general direction of the nearest gas giant, at a speed of ... 1500 kps. At some point, I'll want the squadron to loop back around, but we don't have to worry about that now. Let's keep our link to the picket ship active at all times so that they know our position and vector. Also keep a message drone ready to deploy in case something develops that Base Commander Korolev needs to know about."

"Yes, Sir. Even though I'm early for my duty shift, I can relieve you now if you wish."

"Thank you, XO. I'll take you up on your kind offer." In a louder voice Shiloh said, "The XO has the Con!"

As Chenko took his place at the Command Station, Shiloh took one last look around and then left the Bridge for a bite to eat in the Wardroom, followed by a short power nap in his cabin.

When no sign of the enemy ships appeared during the first 12 hours, Shiloh felt more relaxed. He ordered the crew, which had been on alert status, to stand down to normal routine. When another 24 hours went by without news, the all too familiar sense of boredom that he and the crew had suffered through while on defensive patrol at Bradley base, seemed to resurface. Over the last several months, he and Chenko had established a routine whereby they would meet in the wardroom during their overlapping off-duty hours for a game or two of chess. Shiloh was getting better at it, and he would actually win the occasional game. This time he was losing badly and Chenko seemed to notice.

"You seem distracted, Commander. Your game isn't up to the standard that you've been displaying lately."

Shiloh nodded. "You're right. I'm having difficulty concentrating on the game. This waiting is getting to me more than usual. When we were on defensive patrol at Bradley, we weren't expecting trouble, and we had the occasional simulated battles with the other squadrons to look forward to. Here, it's just us, and we could be in the fight of our lives literally at any minute. What worries me more than anything else is the thought that there may be more than the three ships that 257 detected. I'm confident this squadron can hold its own against more or less even odds, but if we're outnumbered, things could get really nasty. Unfortunately the Powers That Be, in their infinite wisdom, did not give any guidance in the Alpha III plans as to when, and under what circumstances, I'm allowed or required to withdraw the squadron from combat."

Chenko did not respond right away but then said, "Let's hope that situation won't arise, Sir."

"Amen to that, XO."

Chenko made a move. "Checkmate."

Shiloh nodded and tipped over his King.

Chenko said, "Another game?"

"Nope. My mind's not into the game at the moment. Let's hope my strategic skills are sharper when the enemy finally does show up."

Shiloh got up from the table, nodded to Chenko and walked away.

Six hours later, as Shiloh was getting ready to assume the Con for his Bridge shift, Chenko called him.

"Bridge to Commander Shiloh!"

"Shiloh here, go ahead."

"339 has just received a contact report from one of the recon drones. Six unknown ships tentatively identified as hostiles have been detected approaching the furthest gas giant. With the transmission lag from the drone, that news is over ten hours old, but we're just getting it now."

"Okay. Put the Squadron on alert. I'll be on the Bridge directly. Shiloh out."

As Shiloh was about to leave his cabin, he felt a wave of dizziness that was strong enough to force him to sit down. The view of the cabin faded out and was replaced by a vision of a wounded Chenko asking him how he came up with the idea of luring the ships into an ambush by ordering the picket ship to micro-jump closer. The vision faded before he heard his own reply. When the cabin came back into view, the dizziness went away and Shiloh was able to stand again. He ran to the Bridge where Chenko had already vacated the Command Station.

As Shiloh sat down he asked, "What's our status, XO?"

"The Squadron's on alert. No further reports from 339, Sir."

"Very well. XO, you'll con the ship while I handle the Squadron as we did last time. I'm going to send a message to 339 which I want the rest of the Squadron COs to hear as well."

"Yes, Sir."

Chenko snapped her fingers at the Com Tech to make sure he was paying attention. He nodded and began manipulating his controls. Chenko then walked over to the Helm station and tapped Lt. Verlander on the shoulder. He immediately got up and let her take the Helm Station.

When Shiloh received word that the communications setup was ready, he said, "Shiloh to 339. This is what we're going to do. I want 339 to micro-jump to a point 50,000 km in front of the Squadron's path. Those enemy ships will detect your emergence and jump in to intercept. That's when we'll surprise them! While 339 is doing that, the Squadron will deploy a dozen recon drones in a shell around our current location with active scanning and will go to Battle Stations. As soon as the enemy ships jump into combat range, I'll give the command to open fire. We'll concentrate our fire. 344's Weapons Officer will determine the targeting sequence. 339 does not have to acknowledge this message. Your arrival by micro-jump will be reply enough. Shiloh out."

As soon as he finished speaking, he heard Chenko order the ship to Battle Stations. With Chenko looking after the 344, Shiloh motioned for Senior Lieutenant Sykes, the Weapons Officer, to come over to his station.

"Sir?"

"I want you to concentrate the squadron's fire, Lieutenant. Pick three targets and assign three frigates to each of the first two, with the remaining two frigates on the third. As soon as a target is clearly damaged and no longer maneuvering, switch to a new target. Understood?"

"Yes, Sir."

As Sykes went back to his station, Shiloh checked the status of each frigate in the squadron. All were now at Battle Stations. The larger Tactical display showed that a wave of recon drones had been launched and were moving into their prearranged positions. Sensor data from their active scanning was being received but nothing to report so far. With a touch of the simulated button on his Command Station view screen, he opened up the audio channel for squadron communications and heard Falkenburg talking.
"—if they don't take the bait?"

Before anyone else could reply, Shiloh said, "If those enemy ships don't try to ambush a single frigate, I'll be very surprised. But if it does happen, I'll seriously consider going after them directly. Anyone else have any questions?"

Cmdr. Adams replied, "Yes, Sir. Will 339 be joining us in the battle?"

"That's the plan, Felicia. As soon as 339 arrives, she'll be ordered to join the squadron and tie her laser fire into our collective targeting strategy. In the meantime, I want our recon drones to be out in front. Let them take enemy fire. Don't use your ship's active scanners unless you're no longer getting sufficient targeting data from the drones to get hits. If the 344 is knocked out of action, then Commander Sanchez will assume temporary command of the squadron. Rico, if you see my ship unable to maneuver and I'm out of communications, then take over, okay?"

"Okay, Victor. I got that!"

"Speaking of communications, Fletcher!"

The Com Tech looked over.

"Make sure a message drone has the latest data and launch it back to Bradley Base ASAP!"

"Yes, Sir!"

"Okay, everyone. Let's stay on our toes! It'll take another two and a half minutes for my message to reach the 339 and then another few minutes for them to change heading for a micro-jump here. If a ship shows up at about the right time, let's not fire on it until we know for sure it's NOT the 339. I'll keep this channel open, and I want idle chatter kept to a minimum. Standby everyone."

Shiloh checked his ship's status, and saw that it was at Battle Stations and that Chenko seemed to have everything well in hand. His own Bridge crew were speaking in low tones into their microphones in order to be able to hear voice commands from Shiloh or Chenko. The Tactical display was now showing the sensor data from the various recon drones actively scanning the space near the squadron. Shiloh found that he was breathing fast due to adrenaline rush and fought to slow it down. *At least this time they won't catch us by surprise*. He asked himself what else he could do to improve his ship's chances of making it through this battle successfully. If the Bridge took a direct laser hit, most of the senior officers would be killed. Perhaps the XO should be redeployed in Engineering just in case.

"XO."

Chenko looked at him and he waived her over.

"Yes, Sir?"

"Just to be on the safe side in case the Bridge takes a hit, I want you to shift your conning of the ship to Engineering. Verlander can take the Helm Station and the Con temporarily until you get to Engineering."

While the full meaning of this sank in, Chenko said nothing for about two seconds, then nodded and turned away, giving orders to Lt. Verlander and the other Bridge crew about her intention to resume command of the ship after reaching Engineering. Shiloh checked the time display and saw that the 339 would be receiving his message right about now. The next four minutes seemed to take forever.

At that point, the Tactical display pinged to notify Shiloh of a new contact. A single ship emerged from Jumpspace at the extreme edge of the recon drones' scanning range. Its transponder automatically answered the electronic challenge with 339's ID. Before the Weapons Officer could verbally announce the ship's arrival, Shiloh spoke.
"I see her, Lieutenant. Fletcher, add the 339's to the open squadron channel."

"Yes, Sir. Go ahead, Sir."

"Commander Caru, I see that you got my message."

"Yes, Commander. But I'm not really sure if I want the enemy to take the bait or not."

They both chuckled. Shiloh was certain that he would have had some reservations as well if their positions had been reversed. At least, Cmdr. Caru hadn't disputed Shiloh's orders. Technically he wasn't required to obey Shiloh's orders because they were the same rank and the 339 wasn't part of the Squadron. On the other hand, refusing to cooperate in any plan that had a good chance of a significant victory against the enemy would have been difficult to justify to Admiral Howard afterwards.

"Commander, I'd like to add the 339 to the squadron fire control net, and therefore it would be ideal if you brought your ship closer. Okay with you?"

"Yes, that's fine. We'll stand a much better chance of surviving the battle if we're not dangling out here all by ourselves when they show up. I'll have my Weapons Officer get in sync with yours."

"Excellent. Keep your channel open. Good hunting to you and your crew and to the Squadron. I expect we'll see some action very soon."

"Thank you, Sir."

Shiloh could tell that Caru was continuing to talk to his own people because his voice sounded further away as he turned his head away from the microphone. Shiloh figured they had another three to five minutes before the enemy showed up, but they reacted much faster than that. Less than a minute after talking with 339's Caru, the Tactical display pinged again, and this time six ships emerged from Jumpspace. They were almost immediately designated as hostile contacts. In a split second reaction, Shiloh touched the view screen command alerting the Squadron to commence fire. Sen. Lt. Sykes acknowledged instantly.

"We have good targeting data! Opening fire! Two Hits by God! Weapons recharging and ready to fire in three … two … one … firing again!"

Shiloh watched the display as one and then another of the enemy ships staggered from damaged propulsion effects and blew apart. Another enemy ship was clearly damaged, even as Caru's 339's ship symbol started blinking, indicating hull breeches and atmospheric venting. She was the obvious target since not enough time had passed to allow her to merge with the rest of the squadron. Shiloh could dimly hear Caru yelling to his crew about damage control, and then suddenly his voice was cut off. The symbol on the display broke apart and faded away. Shiloh realized he had been holding his breath and forced himself to breathe again. Looking back at the enemy formation, he realized that there were only two enemy ships left, and one was falling behind the other. Just then, power to the Bridge flickered for half a second, and on his Command Station half a dozen status indicators changed color from green to yellow. The ship had been hit, but apparently not too seriously. Before he could say anything, the lead enemy ship jumped away. Seconds later, the lagging ship blew apart.

The battle was over.

Shiloh checked the display's duration of battle indicator and was shocked to see that the entire battle had taken less than 30 seconds! His squadron display showed that 299 and 301 were damaged.

"Shiloh to Squadron. Report damage and casualties as soon as you have that data."

Shiloh noticed that Sen. Lt. Sykes was listening to his earpiece and looking at him at the same time. When it was obvious that Sykes was no longer listening to anything, Shiloh motioned him to come to his Command Station.

"Is there something I should know, Lieutenant?"

"Yes, Sir. I've just been informed that Commander Chenko was slightly wounded when her console in Engineering shorted out from a power overload. She's on the way to Sickbay and I've been informed that I have the Con, Sir."

"Very well Lieutenant. Find out what damage and casualties we've sustained, and then get back to me."

As Sykes returned to his station, Shiloh said in a louder voice, "Lieutenant Sykes has the Con."

The other Bridge personnel nodded their acknowledgement. By the time Shiloh received all of the After-Action damage and casualty reports, he realized that the 144th had been very fortunate. Only two crew killed and half a dozen injured. Both 299 and 301 were still space worthy and, in fact, had all their weapons functional as well. Upon further reflection, Shiloh admitted to himself that the Squadron's luck was due to Cmdr. Caru and 339's misfortune to suffer the brunt of the enemy's attack. After thirty minutes had passed without any further sign on enemy activity, Shiloh ordered the Squadron to stand down from Battle Stations. He left the Bridge to go to Sickbay and ran into Chenko in a corridor on the way there. The right side of her head was covered with the sprayed on bioplastic material that functioned as a bandage.

"Glad to see you're up and around, XO. What happened in Engineering?"

Chenko nodded and took a breath. "As best we can tell, the ship took a laser hit. The hull armor mitigated most of the energy, but enough got through to cause a power surge in some of the equipment, which I happened to be standing next to, Sir. How did we make out?"

"Only two other frigates took any significant damage, but they're still operational. The enemy lost five ships outright and the sixth might be damaged to some degree too, but it managed to bug out. We lost the 339 though. By concentrating exclusively on her, the enemy gave us time to inflict serious damage on them, and that shifted the odds decisively in our favor."

"Then congratulations are in order, Sir. You've achieved a tactical victory. Can I ask how you came up with the idea of using 339 as bait to lure the enemy here, Sir?"

Shiloh hesitated. After all this time, he dearly wanted to tell someone about his visions, but he had this nagging feeling that now was not the best time.

"Well, let's just say that I had a flash of inspiration."

Before Chenko could say anything else, he continued. "Are you up to finishing your shift on the Bridge?"

"Yes, Sir. The medics told me the anesthetic would last that long. After that I'll be too dopey from the painkillers I'll have to take."

Shiloh nodded and smiled. "Fine. Let's get back to the Bridge then. I'll stay on as Squadron Leader until your shift ends, and then I'll take the Con for the next four hours."

When they got back to the Bridge, Shiloh ordered two message drones sent to Tango Delta 8 and 9, informing the squadrons there of the battle and outcome. He then called the COs of frigates 299 and 301.

"Felicia, Marcus. Your ships have taken the most serious damage and crew casualties. I'm going to detach both your ships from the Squadron, with orders to return to Bradley with my After-Action report. You can let Korolev know that the rest of us will stay in this system while we await further orders."

Both frigate COs acknowledged the order and soon were on their way back to Bradley Base. With plenty of fuel to spare, both ships accelerated to a very high rate of speed before entering Jumpspace and arrived back in the Base star system in less than twelve hours.

It was almost 36 hours later when a message drone arrived with orders for the 144th squadron to return to Bradley Base. By this time, Shiloh had ordered his ships to collect as much of the alien wreckage as they could. Some pieces were too large to fit into the cargo hold of a frigate, and those were tagged with locator beacons for future retrieval. None of the smaller pieces held bodies or parts of bodies, much to Shiloh's relief. If they had, he would have seriously considered leaving them behind as well, rather than risk contamination with alien viruses or bacteria. His ships, however, did find some of the larger pieces of wreckage of the 339, and those DID contain bodies. They were recovered and brought back to the Base. It reminded Shiloh of all the dead Space Force crews lost in the original battle, and at Zebra 9, who were probably now floating in the depths of space, and who would be for all eternity.

When the Squadron arrived back at the Base, Shiloh met with Sen. Cmdr. Korolev, the Base Commander. As

Shiloh entered her office, she got up and walked around her desk to offer her hand, along with congratulations.

"Welcome back, Commander. Congratulations on an outstanding victory!"

Shiloh shook her hand and said, "Thank you, Sir. I just wish that Commander Caru and his people could be here to share in it."

Korolev nodded solemnly and said, "Yes indeed. Their bravery and sacrifice will be recognized and remembered. Too damn many of us have met the same fate! But at least we're starting to give as good as we get!"

"Yes, Sir."

Korolev gestured to the comfortable chair opposite her desk. "Have a seat, Commander. Let's talk."

Shiloh sat down and waited.

When Korolev had settled back in her own chair, she said, "In case you hadn't heard, the 55th and 77th did not find any sign of enemy activity. I've ordered them back here too. Since the 144th was about due to rotate back to Sol when we got the picket alert, your squadron will be released from sentry duties here in a day or so. You may as well take back the alien debris with you. We don't really have the appropriate facilities to analyze them here. I'm going to ask you to take back the bodies of our fallen comrades-in-arms as well."

"Of course, Sir."

"Good. Now I've read your After-Action report but I want to hear what happened from you, in your own words. Go ahead."

Shiloh took a deep breath.

"Well, Sir, there's really not much to tell that wasn't in my report. We arrived at Tango Delta 6, and made contact with the 339. When her recon drones detected enemy activity, I got the idea of using their jump emergence technology against them, and ordered 339 to micro-jump to our position. She did so, and the enemy followed a few minutes later. We were ready for them, and by concentrating our fire on just three of their ships, we took them out before they could fire back. From that point on, our numerical superiority overwhelmed them. Unfortunately, the 339 was closer to them than we were, and so they concentrated their fire on her. I would have been happier if we'd gotten them all, but as you know, one got away."

Korolev frowned. "Yes, that was unfortunate, but I don't see how you could have prevented it. It means they'll know that moving in the direction of Tango Delta 6 will bring them closer to us, but that's just something we'll have to live with. They were bound to find out that information sooner or later. I'll be VERY glad when the new combat frigates start showing up here in substantial numbers. Then maybe we can actually push them back into their territory for a change."

"Yes, Sir!"

"You may also be interested to know that the R&D boys are finally getting somewhere with detection of ships emerging from Jumpspace. They've figured out how, now they just have to figure out how to do it accurately enough to be of some tactical use to us. I heard that you had some considerable input to the recommendations from the Strategic Planning Group. Was the

Autonomous Fighting Platform one of your ideas, Commander?"

"Well Sir, you know how it is with brainstorming sessions. The ideas get thrown around back and forth so fast that it's hard to keep track of who come up with what idea. So I really can't say."

"Hm. Well whoever came up with it had a great idea. I hear that the AFP and gunboat projects have been combined. The result is going to be a larger vehicle of about 5500 metric tons that can be configured as either an unmanned unit under AI control or as a manned vehicle using interchangeable modules. The thinking seems to be that the unmanned version can be deployed for longer periods of time, while the manned versions will be retained for operations that are shorter in duration and require flexibility in strategic and tactical thinking. In some circumstances, both kinds of units may operate together. In terms of long-term defense of this base, that's what seems to be coming down the pike. Squadrons of unmanned units will be on permanent patrol, while manned squadrons will be on standby alert status for quick deployment as needed. When we get to that point, this base will have more protection, with less strain on our ability to support them logistically. Personally, I can't wait."

Chapter 11 The Better Part of Valor

SFE144 was ordered back to Sol. On its way inward after emerging from Jumpspace, Shiloh noticed how much more industrial and shipbuilding infrastructure there was since the last time the 144th was in Sol system. Dozens of combat frigates and other ships were under construction. Orbital traffic around Earth and the Moon were both noticeably higher. With the squadron's frigates installed in parking orbits around the Moon, the crews were ferried down to the Moon's naval base and then transferred via shuttle to Earth. By the time the shuttle landed, and Shiloh stepped out onto the spaceport tarmac, it was night. The tarmac was still wet from the rain that had ended only minutes before. Shiloh took a deep breath and savored the fresh smell of clean, moist air. This last tour of duty had been the longest of his entire military career. With a guaranteed stand down for the Squadron of at least four weeks, Shiloh was looking forward to some serious R&R, but first things first. There would be the usual debriefing, as well as memorial ceremonies for Cmdr. Caru and his crew. With a sigh of resignation, Shiloh followed the robotic luggage caddy that carried his and his officers' luggage to the Space Force bus that would take them to temporary quarters where they would get some sleep. The debriefings were now only seven hours away.

The debriefings were routine except for the fact that several very senior officers, including Admiral Howard himself, were in the room as observers. A large screen on the wall showed the recorded tactical data from the battle, while Shiloh narrated the battle's progress, followed by a question and answer session involving all of his squadron's Commanding Officers. Shiloh expected to be called to Howard's office when it was over, but that didn't happen. With the debriefing out of the way, Shiloh and the other officers made their way back to their quarters and gathered in the Officers Club for dinner, drinks, and some games of pool and darts. Shiloh was just about to doze off with a beer in his hand while sitting in a comfortable chair by the roaring fireplace, when Chenko sat down in the chair next to him and nudged him on the arm.

"What's up, XO?"

"I just wanted to share with you a rumor I heard from one of our debriefing officers during the afternoon break, Sir."

"Oh?"

"Yes. It seems that the scuttlebutt has it that all squadron CO's are to be awarded the Outstanding Combat Medal, and that 339's crew will be awarded a unit citation."

Shiloh paused to consider that and then said, "That's very interesting, XO. Caru and his people definitely deserve the citation. I'm not sure I see the justification for awarding the OCM. It was an ambush after all. The enemy really didn't stand a chance, so it's not like we persevered in spite of overwhelming odds or anything like that."

Chenko nodded, hesitated for a second or two, and then said, "I also heard that you're going to be given the Sentinel, Sir."

Shiloh was wide awake now. He was about to reply when the room disappeared, and he was in Admiral Howard's office. He barely had time to realize that he was having another vision when a clearly older Howard said, 'When you turned down command of the Sentinel, I thought you had lost your nerve. However with the benefit of hindsight, I now realize that you made the right decision. I shudder to think of where we'd be today if you hadn't stuck to your guns when I tried to pressure you to accept that command.'

The vision faded and Shiloh found himself looking at Chenko, who said, "Are you okay, Commander?"

Shiloh tried to laugh it off.

"Yes, of course, XO. Why do you ask?"

"Well, you were staring off into space for a few seconds there."

Shiloh thought fast. "Yeah, sorry about that. I guess I'm kind 'a tired."

Chenko nodded. "It's been a long day, Sir."

"Yes it has, XO. Goodnight."

"Goodnight, Sir."

Shiloh got up and walked to his quarters pondering the meaning of this latest vision. The next morning he received word that he and his people were free to start their leave. After saying the usual goodbyes, the officers and crew dispersed to their homes and various other destinations. Within 24 hours Shiloh was sunning himself on a white beach, looking forward to some scuba diving later that day.

Two weeks later, he received a message to report back to Space Force HQ for reassignment. After checking-in his things to his temporary quarters, he arrived at Admiral Howard's office as ordered. They exchanged salutes, and Howard gestured for Shiloh to sit down in the comfortable chair facing his desk. While they chitchatted about Shiloh's leave, Shiloh accepted the offered cigar and lit it. When both men had taken a good puff of their respective cigars, Howard got to the point.

"It's unfortunate that I had to call you back in when your leave was only half over. If it's any consolation, you're not the only one who's been called back early. In your case, I wanted you back here now because we've waited as long as we can to name a CO for the first of the new combat frigates. It's almost ready for its shakedown cruise. That ship is the Sentinel, and she's yours if you want her. As CO of the Sentinel, you'll also be Squadron Leader of a new squadron. It will be fleshed out with upgraded exploration frigates, but only until they can be replaced with the combat frigates that will be sliding out of the shipyards at a rate of about two a month before much longer. That new squadron will be where we will assign all of our most capable and aggressive officers, and I guarantee that promotion will be fast. You'll be a Senior Commander before you know it. Well, what do you say?"

Shiloh hesitated. He realized that he was sweating and breathing faster than normal. If he hadn't had that vision, he would have said an yes without hesitation, but after having three visions pan out perfectly, he felt he should heed this one too. He took a deep breath before speaking.

"If you're giving me a choice, then I'm going to respectfully decline the offer, Sir."

Howard was clearly surprised, and just as clearly annoyed.

"You can't possibly be serious, Shiloh! I know officers who would literally give their right arms for this command. Why don't you want it?"

Shiloh sighed. "Personal reasons that I'd prefer not to elaborate on, Sir."

Howard said nothing for a few seconds and then replied. "Are you absolutely certain about this? You do realize I trust that this will generate a hell of a dark cloud over your career for years to come!"

Shiloh nodded. "Yes, Sir. I'm aware of the repercussions, and yes I am certain that I do not want this command, Sir."

Howard shook his head as he took another puff from his cigar.

"I don't understand this, Commander. You've always struck me as someone who's cool under fire and not afraid of a fight. Did something happen at Tango Delta 6 that's making you gun-shy?"

Shiloh replied without hesitating. "No, Sir."

"Well then, what is it that has you spooked about this command? I insist that you tell me!"

Shiloh wondered for the nth time if he should tell the Admiral about his visions. If that was the right thing to do, why didn't he hear Howard mention it in his vision? Keeping the secret to himself had seemed to work so far, and he decided to stay the course, but he had to tell Howard something.

After some more thought he said, "Well, Sir, the thing is this. I don't think I'm as good a combat strategist as you and the other senior officers of the Space Force think I am. My past success has, in my opinion, been due to a combination of luck and gut hunches. This is not something that I would want the fate of Humanity to hinge on if I were eventually to be in command during a key battle that decided the outcome of this war."

Howard's response was immediate and unexpected.

"Bullshit!" He paused then blurted out, "I think you've lost your nerve!"

Shiloh said nothing. He tried to remain calm, but his stomach was tied up in knots.

Howard took his cigar and stubbed it out, then leaned back in his chair. "I'm tempted to order you to take that command, but if in fact you really have lost your nerve, then that's the last place you should be!" He paused again. "Alright! I'll find someone else to take command of the Sentinel. You're dismissed. As far as the rest of your leave is concerned, that's over. Stay close to your quarters so that we'll know where to reach you when we've decided what to do with you. By the way, you were going to be awarded the Combat Medal, but I've just decided to rescind that award! Now get out of my sight!"

Shiloh jumped to attention, saluted and left the office quickly. The ride back to his quarters aboard the Space Force shuttle bus seemed to take forever. Shiloh wondered if he had done the right thing. His head said yes, but it didn't feel right. When he got back to his quarters, he stayed in his room for the rest of the day. After a night of fitful sleep, he felt a little better after a shower and headed down to the Officers Mess for breakfast. While he was eating, a steward brought an envelope to him that had been delivered by courier. It was from HQ. He opened it and began reading.

From: Admiral Dietrich, Chief of Personnel
To: Commander Victor Shiloh.

As of 0800 hours today you are relieved of the post of Squadron Leader of SFE 144. You are also notified that you are relieved of command of FE 344. You are ordered to report to the Alpha Weapons Development and Test Base as soon as transportation can be arranged.

The loss of his ship was like a blow to the gut. He started feeling a slight queasiness in his stomach and wondered if he was going to throw up. After another minute or so he decided he wasn't and looked at the message again. He had never heard of the Alpha Weapons Development and Test Base, nor did he know where it was or how to get there, but that wasn't much of a problem. One call to Space Force Transport Command should clear up the mystery. What they wouldn't be able to tell him was what he'd be doing once he got there. Unable to finish his breakfast, Shiloh returned to his room, called the SFTC, and soon found out that the AWDT base was a newly established station in the Epsilon Eridani star system. The next transport ship scheduled to head that way left orbit in 36 hours. Shiloh made arrangements to be on the last shuttle carrying cargo and passengers to the transport ship.

With that out of the way, he checked to see if any of his crew were still nearby and was surprised to find that Chenko was at Space Force HQ. He arranged for her to get a message asking her to meet him over lunch.

When Chenko arrived at his table in the Officers Dining Room, the first thing she said was, "I heard they relieved you of command of the 344! Why did they do that?"

Shiloh shook his head. "They offered me the Sentinel, just like you heard, and I turned it down. That's why."

Chenko reacted with uncharacteristic shock. "You did what?"

"Yup. I turned it down. I'm not the right man for that command. Howard and everyone else seem to think I'm some kind of tactical genius, and I'm not."

Now Chenko was clearly angry.

"Well you're certainly better at it than most of us. Now they'll assign someone to the Sentinel who isn't half as good, and he or she will probably screw up royally! For God's sake, Shiloh, how can you be so selfish?"

Chenko's use of his name instead of his rank surprised him. She was clearly upset.
"I'm sorry you feel that way, Svetlana. You've learned to trust my judgment during our deployment on the 344. I'm asking you to trust my judgment one more time."

Chenko said nothing and looked away, clearly still unhappy. After a few seconds, Shiloh tried to change the subject.

"Do you know who will take over command of the 344?"

Chenko sighed. "Yes, I will. Temporary promotion to Commander until further notice. Unofficially I've been told that if I don't screw up during the next deployment, the promotion will become permanent."

Shiloh nodded. "Good for you, Svetlana! You'll make a fine CO."

She gave him a small smile in acknowledgement of his compliment. "Thank you, Sir. Do you know where you'll be assigned?"

Shiloh told her about the AWDT Base. She nodded.

"Well, I suppose if you're not going to be commanding a combat ship, then helping with weapons development is the next best thing. Good luck with that, Sir."

"You too, Svetlana." She nodded once again, then turned and walked away.

Shiloh spent the next 36 hours doing things to make the time go faster. He had difficulty sleeping that night, wondering if he had made the right choice. He was no closer to figuring out an answer to the mystery of his visions than he had been before. What really began to bother him was that his visions were only showing him confirmation of decisions when they would have been different if he *hadn't* had the visions. Which came first, the actions or the visions? It seemed as though the visions were coming first, but that made no sense because the visions were of future events that depended on him taking the right actions. How could an effect precede the cause? It would have made far more sense if he had the visions AFTER deciding to take those actions because then the visions would be confirmation of something that he was going to do anyway. But in each case, his decision to take the correct action happened after his vision. Thinking about it gave him a headache.

When it was time to board the shuttle that would take him to the transport ship, Shiloh was resigned to his course of action. If he'd made a mistake, then he just had to find a way to make the best of it.

The trip to the Alpha Base in Epsilon Eridani, took almost three days, and transport ships weren't known for their comfortable accommodations. As it turned out, the accommodations at the Base were even worse. Since the Base itself was so new, parts of it were still under construction. Naturally those parts included living quarters for the base personnel. Until they were completed, Shiloh and most of the others assigned there had to sleep wherever they could find space, as well as be content with emergency rations until the kitchen and mess hall were completed. It took a bit of pushing, but Shiloh eventually found out what his assignment was. He was the Weapons Development Board Liaison to the Base, which was a totally unnecessary position as far as he could tell. The WDB didn't need a liaison to the AWDT Base because the Base Commander and the Project Leader both reported directly to the WDB anyway. The Liaison position was clearly intended by Admiral Howard to punish Shiloh for his perceived lack of fighting spirit.

With literally nothing to do, Shiloh made up his mind to make himself useful in any way he could. When enough of the other technical and engineering staff had arrived to allow actual work to begin, Shiloh made sure he sat in on all meetings. One thing became clear very quickly, something that Shiloh hadn't expected. The Alpha Base wasn't going to be doing basic design and prototype construction. That was being done closer to Earth. What the Alpha Base would do was take prototypes already built and test them as much as possible under simulated field conditions to assess equipment reliability. Then they would calculate the most efficient way to mass-produce the resulting production versions. Once that was figured out, other facilities in the Epsilon Eridani system would become the production centers for those weapons.

The first weapon system that the AWDT base would work on was the modified version of the AFP or Autonomous Fighting Platform. Base Commander Korolev had been right. The concept had changed. The original concept was a small AI controlled drone that could be used for long duration patrols and long-range combat operations, supplemented by larger, human piloted gunboats. Then someone had suggested the obvious, which was to build one common platform that was highly modular and could be configured either as an unmanned drone or, with the proper modules attached, as a manned vehicle. While the advantages of using a common basic vehicle were obvious, there were some disadvantages as well. In order to be able to carry a human crew, the vehicle had to be larger than the original drone concept, which meant that the new ships wouldn't be able to carry as many of them as planned. To offset that, it was pointed out that the larger vehicle could not only carry a powerful enough laser to actually be a threat to enemy ships, but could also carry an impressive load of smaller recon, message or attack drones.

It took until almost a month after his arrival for the first prototype to be ready and delivered for testing. The testing program was a compromise between being thorough and fast. A thorough program would have taken up to a year or more, and Space Force Brass decided that was just too long. So the risk of technical glitches was considered acceptable in order to get the thing into the field as fast as possible. That was fine when they were testing the prototype in its autonomous configuration because any technical glitch would not put humans at risk, but eventually they had to test it with humans on board and in control. The test pilots assigned to that duty weren't happy with the simplified testing program, which they considered reckless, and rightly so, in Shiloh's opinion.

When a test of the vehicle's crew module almost resulted in the death of its test pilot due to a failure in the life support system, the test pilots refused to participate in any more tests until the crew module had undergone hundreds of hours of additional simulated field tests. Shiloh had a gut feeling that they couldn't afford that much additional time. It wasn't a vision, just a nagging suspicion that wouldn't go away, and so he volunteered to pilot the prototype during human-controlled tests as originally planned. Those tests and their preparations kept him so busy that time flew by. When the testing program was completed, Shiloh was surprised to learn that he'd been there almost four months. By then the project to mass-produce the upgraded production version was well under way. Normal practice was for the first few production models to be tested, as well to make certain they were being built to the required standard, but just as the first production model Configurable Fighting Platform, as they were now known, came off the production line, Shiloh and the rest of the base personnel heard the bad news.

Chapter 12 One Step Forward, Two Steps Back

The Space Force Command Staff, after regrouping, had decided to try to engineer another ambush using the same tactic that Shiloh had used in Tango Delta 6. The ambush had backfired badly. In fact, it looked as though the aliens had set their own ambush. How they had managed that, no one knew, but the result was that the Space Force had lost two full squadrons of frigates, including the new Sentinel. The message carrying the news didn't identify which other frigates were lost, and Shiloh wondered if the 344 was among them. There was another surprise message in the same data transmission. Admiral Howard wanted to reassign Shiloh. It appeared that his exile was over. He arrived on Earth five days later and found himself back in Howard's office the following morning.

Upon entering, Shiloh saluted, and Howard reciprocated, then gestured to the chair facing his desk. When Shiloh sat down, Howard leaned back and started speaking in a slow voice.

"When you successfully pulled off the makeshift ambush, I was sure that you had the skill and instincts we needed to win this war. Then when you refused command of the Sentinel, I thought you'd lost your nerve. That made me angry. So angry in fact that I made up my mind that I was going to prevent you from ever having a command again. I was going to make sure that you were given one useless assignment after another until you either resigned or retired. I realize now that I was being unfair. By stepping up to pilot the untested manned version of the CFP, your performance at Alpha Base showed me that you hadn't lost your nerve. I still don't understand the real reason why you turned down the Sentinel, but I'm prepared to admit that my negative assessment and treatment of you was unfair and unprofessional of me. For that, I apologize."

Shiloh didn't really know what to say to that, so he just said, "Thank you, Sir."

Howard nodded. "Now that we've got that out of the way, let's talk about giving you a useful assignment. With the time you've spent piloting the CFP prototypes, you've racked up more flight hours than anyone else. That makes you the closest thing to an expert on operational use of CFPs that we have. We'll soon have enough production models available to consider using them in the field. I'd like to hear your thoughts on how you think we should do that."

Shiloh wasn't surprised by the question, and he'd had lots of time to consider the answer on his way back to Earth. "Well, Sir, I have some ideas, but it would help me if I knew where we stand now strategically."

Howard nodded. "Fair enough. You know about the debacle at Tango Delta 5?"

"I heard the results, but no details of the battle itself, Sir."

"Okay. We sent a task force composed of a Command ship, three support ships, six tankers, and four frigate squadrons to TD5. The plan was to send two frigates to the vicinity of a gas giant that previous reconnaissance had determined contained alien surveillance gear. We figured that sooner or later the aliens would show up to check the activity recorded by their robotic station, and they would detect our two frigates while, at the same time, we would detect their presence and order the frigates to microjump back to the vicinity of the Task Force.

"What we didn't count on was that the aliens were already in that star system in force, and they had put their own bait in place. That bait amounted to eight of their ships orbiting the gas giant. Task Force Commander Mbutu took the bait and ordered three frigate squadrons, which included the Sentinel, to microjump to the gas giant. He was aboard her when the Task Force split up. As soon as the microjump was complete, 32 more alien ships also microjumped into the battle area. The odds against him were five enemy ships for every three of his. With that many ships on each side providing radar data, laser fire accuracy was as close to 100% as is realistically possible, but as you know, the enemy has more powerful lasers. Our ships started dying faster than theirs. Sentinel was destroyed within seconds, taking Mbutu with her. His deputy leader had enough presence of mind to order the rest of the force to microjump away, while also ordering the rest of the Task Force to rendezvous back at TD3.

"The microjump by the frigates was only partially successful. Because of the alien's ability to detect ships leaving Jumpspace, they were able to pinpoint where the survivors jumped to, and they followed them. In hindsight, they should have jumped farther away. When the survivors were caught again, the Acting Task Force Leader realized his mistake and ordered another, much longer microjump. That prevented further pursuit. But by then only 6 of the original 24 frigates were still able to microjump away. We have to assume that the rest were destroyed either by the aliens themselves, or by our own crews to avoid capture.

"That defeat has rocked us back on our heels. We've lost so many frigates that our forward bases, particularly Bradley, are now considered at risk. On the plus side, two more Sentinel-class frigates are very close to completion, which means they'll be operational in roughly a month. Six more are also within a couple of months of completion. The first long-range scout ship will also be ready in a month's time. Construction has started on the first two Heavy Cruisers and the first CFP Carrier. And as you probably know already, CFP production will be ramping up gradually to a projected rate of one a day by three months from now. That's where we are now, Commander."

"Thank you, Sir. May I ask what we've learned about the alien debris so far and also about the status of the jump detection project?"

"Unfortunately, the debris analysis hasn't revealed anything really useful. Their technology seems to be more or less on par with ours. None of the debris came from their weapons so we can't analyze those. The jump detection project has made some useful progress. They're testing some equipment they think will give approximate location data on ships that have just emerged from Jumpspace. The effective range is estimated to be three light minutes, but accuracy drops off dramatically the further away the emerging ship is. Arrangements are being made to include the first field versions in the Sentinel class of frigates and long-range scout ships as they're completed. Do you have any other questions, Commander?"

"Just one more, Sir. Have our recon tankers found any more star systems with an alien presence?"

Howard frowned. "No, and the tanker that we sent out after Gnat's successful mission never returned. We have no idea what happened to her. With the loss of most of our tanker fleet at Zebra 9, we couldn't afford to risk any of the remaining tankers. We'll resume long-range scouting as soon as the new long-range scouts come out of the shipyards. Anything else?"

"No Sir. Thank you for that update, Sir."

Shiloh paused to organize his thoughts. The aliens were moving inexorably closer to the Bradley Base and to Earth, and the Space Force knew no more about which star systems the aliens occupied than they did after the ambush at DT6. They seemed to be very aggressive in their efforts to learn as much about Human Space as possible. Keeping them from learning more had to be a high priority, but the new weapons systems, and especially the CFPs, needed to be tested under realistic conditions to see if they performed as expected. So while stopping the aliens' advance pointed to a defensive strategy, gaining operational experience with the new systems required a more aggressive approach.

"Well, Sir, I want to say first that the time I spent observing and testing the CFP prototypes was a useful experience. We learned some things that hadn't been considered yet. For example, if more than one CFP is operating autonomously in an otherwise uninhabited star system, on some kind of sentry patrol let's say, and alien ships shows up, what criteria do the AI's controlling those vehicles use to determine what their reaction should be? Does one AI made a decision on behalf of the group? Or do they react individually depending on their relative positions to each other and to the aliens? One approach will be best under some circumstances, while the other approach would be better under others.

"There are other considerations as well. There wasn't time to do long term field tests. So we don't know how mechanically reliable the production CFPs will be after they've been operating autonomously for months at a time. It's considerations like that, that have me in a quandary. I recognize and understand the need for preventing the aliens from advancing further into our space. We need to deny them as much information about us as possible, while at the same time learn as much about them as possible. Having said that, field testing our new ships, weapons and other systems, might be crucial to victory in the long run. With the CFP carrier at least a year from being operational, our ability to concentrate a large CFP force will be limited, and I can't help thinking that CFPs won't realize their full potential until they are used in large numbers. What I would hate to see is them being used in small groups as a way of stretching our limited number of frigates. I think that would be a grave mistake. With that in mind, I think the best use we could make now of the limited number of CFPs that we're going to have available in the near term, would be to assign them the base defense role at the Bradley Base. I'd recommend using them to accomplish the following objectives.

"First, if the jump detection gear can be made so that it can be loaded as a module, then we can use a small number of CFPS as jump detection pickets to extend coverage, but also to increase accuracy by combining data from multiple platforms.

"Second, they would carry a mixed load of recon and weapon drones so that we'd have the option of tracking the alien ships without giving away the location of our own ships or platforms.

"Third, we'd have to arrange for communications between the Base and the CFPs, so that their AIs can be instructed on the best way to coordinate any response to the alien incursion, without also tipping off the aliens to the presence of the CFPs.

"As far as the CFPs directly attacking the alien ships with modular lasers, I would recommend doing that only as a last resort. The longer we can keep the aliens in the dark about our CFPs, the better. Essentially what I'm suggesting is that the system containing Bradley Base becomes our line in the sand that we keep them from crossing. While we're keeping their attention focused on that line in the sand, our long-range scout ships will be trying to find their bases and inhabited planets. To avoid jump detection, they'll be jumping into unexplored star systems far away from any planets, and then, if necessary, maneuvering deeper into the systems to get better data or to refuel. When we find one of their bases or planets, then we can switch from a defensive strategy to an offensive one and take back the initiative."

Howard didn't say anything for a few seconds. "I'm not sure I like the idea of allowing them to push forward until they find Bradley. My instincts tell me that we should try to stop them where they are now."

"Well, Sir, in order to do that, we'd have to commit large numbers of frigates to multiple star systems to prevent them from flanking the systems where we've already had encounters. Given our recent loses, do we have enough frigates to accomplish that on a sustained basis? Wouldn't we be risking further loses that we really can't afford?"

"I see your point, Commander. But what's to prevent them from bypassing Bradley altogether?"

Shiloh had to think about that one for a bit. "In order to bypass it, they have to know about it. If they just explore every star system in the direction they think we come from, sooner or later they'll arrive at Bradley. Considering that they've inflicted disproportionate losses on us in every battle except one, I'd expect them to have enough confidence in their tactical superiority to make at least one attempt at attacking Bradley base, if only to further assess our defensive capabilities. Isn't that what we'd do if the positions were reversed, Sir?"

"Hmm. Perhaps we would and perhaps we wouldn't, but I take your point. Fortifying Bradley would have some advantages that we wouldn't have if we were trying to hold the line in an otherwise empty system. Refueling would be a lot easier for one thing. So would communications."

Howard paused and Shiloh took the opportunity to comment. "Operating CFPs out of the base would give the CFP commander a lot more flexibility too, Sir. CFPs deployed from combat frigates are going to be stuck with whatever modules and weapons load they were given when the frigates left the nearest base, but if they're operating from Bradley, they can be configured for the most effective payload before being launched from the base and also reloaded quickly if they've fired their drones and the battle is still continuing."

Howard raised his eyebrows at the mention of a CFP Commander. "Do I understand you to mean that any CFPs deployed out of Bradley should have their own commander?"

"Yes, Sir. If Bradley has a mixed force structure that includes frigates and CFPs, then I think each weapon system needs to have someone in charge of it who is familiar with the best way to employ that weapon system. Neither the Base Commander nor the frigate Task Force Commander will be familiar with the potential that CFPs have, Sir."

Howard didn't respond right away. He continued to look at Shiloh with a thoughtful expression. "If we go with your recommendation to make Bradley the line in the sand, then I'll keep your suggestion for a CFP commander in mind. What I'd like you to do now is spend the next 24 hours writing a detailed proposal on how we can make the best use of our limited quantity of CFPs in defending Bradley. When you're finished that, you're free to go on two weeks leave. Just make sure that we know where to reach you. Any questions?"

"No, Sir. I'll have that report submitted by this time tomorrow."

"Very good, Commander. You're dismissed."

Shiloh left and made his way to the Officer's Mess for a late breakfast followed by a leisurely coffee during which he made notes on the back of some napkins. When he returned to his quarters, he settled down in front of a computer terminal and started working on the report. When he had the first draft finished, he looked up and realized that it was now dark outside, and he was hungry. By the time the final draft was finished it was daylight again. He sent the report electronically, and then stumbled over to the bed where he fell face down and slept for ten hours.

When he woke up, it was evening in Geneva, but it felt like morning to him. He decided to start his leave by shifting to a time zone that matched his biological clock. After sending several personal messages to Johansen, Chenko, and a couple of others, as well as letting Howard's staff know where he was going, Shiloh packed his gear and hitched a ride on a Space Force sub-orbital transport to the opposite side of the world. Six hours later he was once again sunbathing on a white beach, with a cold tropical drink in his hand.

To his surprise, Shiloh wasn't called back early from his leave. When he checked into the Temporary Officers quarters again, he found a message from Admiral Howard.

[Your recommendation to make Bradley Base the Line in the Sand has been accepted. You'll be in command of all CFPs assigned there. Overall command of ALL mobile defenses will rest with Vanguard CO. Report to Vanguard within 48 hours. Good hunting!]

Shiloh knew that Vanguard was one of the Sentinel class combat frigates, but he didn't know who its CO was. A quick check made his jaw drop. It was Angela Johansen! Both of them were now Commanders, but she was also Squadron Leader and Acting Task Force Leader. His title was Commander, Autonomous Group or CAG for short. He wondered if their previous comfortable working relationship would work as well with positions reversed. He was a little disappointed that he would be reporting to her because if neither one was taking orders from the other, that made the possibility of a non-professional relationship much more attractive. But no one claimed that a Space Force career was good for developing personal relationships. Besides, Humanity was at War, and that had to be his priority.

Chapter 13 The Iceman Cometh

Shiloh reported aboard Vanguard six hours later. Angela met him at the docking hatch. Even though she was his superior officer, protocol did not require him to salute her because they were technically the same rank. She smiled and offered her hand, which he shook.

"Welcome aboard Vanguard, Victor. It'll be good working together again," she said.

"Glad to be here, Angela and yes, it IS good to be working together again. Congratulations on your new command. I can't wait to take the tour!"

Johansen laughed as she let go of his hand. Was it his imagination, or had she held on to his hand just a bit longer than normal?

"I'll be glad to show you around, but why don't you get settled into your quarters first. It's not much, but at least you'll have a cabin to yourself. When you're settled, you can find me in the Officers' Mess, okay?"

Shiloh nodded. "That's fine, and my quarters are where?"

Johansen turned to nod at a young man standing off to one side that Shiloh hadn't even noticed was there.

"Yeoman Hanson here will lead the way. I'll see you shortly then." She gave him a friendly smile as she turned and walked down the corridor.

Shiloh turned to the young Space Force Yeoman and said, "Alright, Hanson. Lead the way."

It didn't take long to get settled in his small but comfortable cabin, and Johansen was soon showing him her new ship with obvious pride. Shiloh was impressed. The Sentinel class of combat frigates was quite different from the exploration class frigate that he was used to. Exploration frigates were designed for long missions where crew comfort was a high priority. In Combat Frigates, crew comfort was clearly a lesser priority.

Each major system had multiple backups. The laser turrets could be completely retracted to streamline the ship for gas giant skimming. That itself was something new. Tankers carried fuel shuttles that could skim a gas giant's atmosphere, scoop up hydrogen, and filter out the heavy hydrogen. Those same fuel shuttles could then transfer the heavy hydrogen to other ships. Combat Frigates would not rely on smaller craft to refuel. They would dip down into the gas giant's atmosphere themselves, and while the technique had been successfully tested with ships this large, it'd be a new experience for everyone aboard. Johansen told Shiloh that practicing refueling was a major part of the ship's shakedown cruise, scheduled to commence in less than 48 hours.

She saved the best part of the tour for last, the ship's Bridge. It was impressive by itself, and it also included a small section, partially partitioned off from the rest of the Bridge, where drones and CFPs could be monitored and controlled with equipment designed especially for that purpose. That would be Shiloh's station. Its main screen wasn't as large as the main Bridge screen, but it was quite impressive nevertheless. He sat down in the command chair, which immediately readjusted itself to fit his body. The manual controls were all within easy reach to supplement voice commands if necessary. His part of the shakedown cruise would be to test the equipment and also command the drones and CFPs in simulated exercises, with exploration frigates playing the role of enemy vessels. Being able to determine and transmit commands to multiple drones quickly would take practice, but Shiloh was determined to master that skill before the next encounter with the enemy.

With the tour complete, Johansen invited Shiloh to join her later for dinner in the Officers Mess. Most of the crew was not yet aboard, and they had the Officers Mess to themselves, which Shiloh was aware of but Johansen didn't seem to notice. The conversation was mostly about the Vanguard, and Johansen did most of the talking. Shiloh managed to ask her if she knew why the CAG was expected to control the autonomous units from a frigate instead of from the base itself since that was where the drones and CFPs would be maintained and configured for missions. Her reply was that since combat frigates were designed from the outset to be able to control large numbers of drones and CFPs in star systems that didn't have a base, and since Bradley Base didn't yet have the same kind of command and control equipment installed, it just made sense that the CAG would have to be on board one of the combat frigates. Shiloh would have a deputy CAG at the base to look after the day-to-day functions needed to keep drones and CFPs operational. It made sense but only as the best of a series of less than desirable options.

When Vanguard was fully manned, she slipped out of lunar orbit along with the other seven members of the first squadron of frigates designated for a combat role, SFC 007. The squadron included the only other Sentinel-class combat frigate, Sentry, plus six more heavily modified exploration frigates, which would eventually be replaced by Sentinel-class ships as they became available. The squadron headed for Jupiter so that Vanguard and Sentry could practice refueling operations, while the other six frigates practiced keeping a protective watch from high orbit. With no drones of any kind to worry about during the refueling exercises, Shiloh monitored the operation from his command station on the Bridge, and he was glad that he had enough presence of mind to strap himself down tightly. Unlike the high speed dips that the fuel shuttles used, which were done at supersonic speeds, the Sentinel-class frigates had to decelerate until their speed was subsonic and drop down into the gas giant's atmosphere in what Johansen later described as a controlled plunge. At the right altitude, the ship then used its maneuvering engines to pitch the nose up at an angle with just enough forward thrust to counteract the pull of gravity. Shiloh learned that the slow speed was necessary to allow a moderate flow of gases into the hydrogen/heavy hydrogen separation plant that would generate a constant flow of heavy hydrogen into storage tanks. Too much speed would cause the faster inflow of gases to overwhelm the separation system and contaminate the flow of heavy hydrogen, and because the output of heavy hydrogen was measured in liters per minute, it took a minimum of six hours to fill the fuel tanks. The obvious drawback to subsonic speeds was the vulnerability to turbulence, which the artificial gravity wasn't fully able to negate. While most of the turbulence was just a nuisance, there were moments when the ship's motion was so severe that Shiloh would have been thrown from his Command Station chair if he hadn't been strapped in.

When the exercise was finished, and the ship was back in space, Shiloh unstrapped himself and walked over to where Johansen was seated. He could see that her uniform was soaked with sweat, and she looked exhausted from the strain of maintaining a constant watch on the ship's attitude and systems. The rest of the Bridge crew looked like they had been through the wringer too.

"How did we do?" asked Shiloh.

Johansen took a deep breath before answering. "The simulations don't do this maneuver justice. Not by a long shot. We got through this okay. All systems are still functioning, and the crew is able to continue at their posts, but I'm not sure that doing this over and over again out in the field will generate the same results. The ship took a hell of shaking! At some point, enough of that will break something, and if that something is our maneuvering engines, then we might find ourselves plunging down into a gas giant in an uncontrolled crash. And as if that wasn't bad enough, what if enemy ships detect us while we're crawling along at subsonic speeds and can't defend ourselves? This is a bad idea. They should have given the ship enough room to carry a fuel shuttle the way the new long range scout ships will be able to, but the designers didn't ask us ship jockeys for our ideas."

Shiloh said nothing but nodded in sympathy. He would not want to be conning a ship for six hours during this kind of refueling maneuver. He wondered if there was a better way. He decided to access the engineering schematics of the refueling system during his off duty shift to see if he could come up with any ideas.

With Vanguard now refueled, Sentry took her turn, and Vanguard practiced docking with the exploration frigates to simulate the transfer of heavy hydrogen. In essence, Vanguard became a very heavily armored and armed tanker, since the exploration frigates didn't have the same capability to skim gas giants.

After reviewing the engineering data for hours, Shiloh decided to get some sleep. As he started to drift off, he suddenly had an idea that made him wide awake again. Quickly calling up the data, he asked the ship's computer to simulate a specific sequence of actions, then leaned back in satisfaction as he scanned the results. There WAS a better way. It wasn't perfect, and it had its own drawbacks, but it would be much easier on both the ship and the crew. He checked Johansen's duty schedule and saw that she was in the middle of her sleep shift. He left her a message asking to meet over breakfast to discuss an alternative refueling process.

Johansen looked skeptical when she sat down beside him later in the Officers Mess. He waited until she finished ordering breakfast before sliding a data tablet in front of her. As she looked at it, he started explaining.

"The key to this alternative process is the outflow of heavy hydrogen. I'm guessing the designers wanted to have a continuous flow of heavy hydrogen, which requires a continuous supply of atmospheric gases. My approach dispenses with the continuous outflow criteria. Here's how it works. The ship basically takes the same supersonic dip that a smaller fuel shuttle takes. At those speeds, the intake scoops only have to be open for a few seconds for the holding tanks to be filled with gases. Then the scoops are closed. The ship continues to push its way through the atmosphere at supersonic speeds while the contents of the holding tank are processed. When the holding tank is empty, the scoops reopen and fill it up again, and the whole cycle repeats. Now the drawback to all this is that a complete refueling will take a minimum of 12 hours, but on the plus side, the ship won't have to put up with all that turbulence, and since the hull is armored, the hull should be able to stand up to that long supersonic passage quite well. With far less turbulence, wear and tear on the equipment will be much reduced."

He waited while Johansen finished absorbing his verbal explanation and the data displayed on the tablet. When she looked up at him, she said, "Have you run simulations?"

"Yes, and they confirm that it should work."

"I'd like to see another simulation myself," she said quietly.

She handed the tablet back to Shiloh, who accessed the engineering program and reran the simulation. Johansen watched it, and when it was finished, she nodded.

"It looks good, but as we both know, the real thing is quite often different from the simulations. I'm also not that happy with the extra six hours of being vulnerable to enemy fire. At these speeds, our laser turrets would have to be retracted to keep the ship as streamlined as possible."

"Yes but even under the shorter, subsonic profile, you know that any gas giant's atmosphere will cut your lasers' effective range down to just a few kilometers. How likely is it that enemy ships will get that close?"

She thought about that for a few seconds and said, "You have a point there. Okay, I'm tempted to try it, but only if my Engineering Officer has no serious objection to the idea. What made you think of this idea, Victor?"

Shiloh grinned and shrugged. For once he could tell the truth.

"I was on the verge of drifting off to sleep and the idea just popped into my head."

Johansen laughed and shook her head. "Honestly, sometimes I think angels or somebody, are sending you messages telepathically!"

Shiloh laughed with her, but the comment alarmed him even though he knew it was meant in jest.

"If somebody IS sending me messages, I hope they keep it up," he said.

"Amen to that!" said Johansen.

The refueling idea dealt with, they switched their attention to breakfast and light chitchat. Half an hour later both were back on the Bridge, Johansen at her CO station and Shiloh at his CAG station. Vanguard had finished transferring some fuel to each of the six exploration frigates in the squadron quite a while ago, and those frigates had then left Jupiter orbit to prepare for the upcoming wargame exercise. Sentry had finished its subsonic refueling exercise. Sentry's CO had left an emphatic message conveying his dislike of what he referred to as the 'six hours of sheer terror' refueling procedure. There was also a message waiting for the squadron CAG. The five prototype CFPs that Shiloh had helped test at the Alpha base were now back in the Sol system. They were headed for Jupiter to rendezvous with the 007 squadron for the simulated exercise, using unarmed attack drones and the modules equipped with the new jump detection gear. Rendezvous eta was in just over three hours time. With their vector from the Moon known, Shiloh was able to figure out their current position, and he used Vanguard's communications equipment to send them instructions to take up a standard High Guard overwatch patrol of Vanguard when they arrived, scan for any ships emerging from Jumpspace, and await further instructions.

Johansen's Engineering Officer didn't take long to let his CO know that Shiloh's supersonic refueling procedure was feasible and very likely preferable from the point of view of not having his beautiful new ship shaken apart. With that opinion on the record, Johansen decided to try the new procedure. With the CFPs due in just a couple hours time, the refueling attempt would only be a partial test. Just long enough to see how the ship handled at supersonic speeds, plus one brief attempt to scoop gases. While Vanguard slowed its orbital velocity in order to drop into Jupiter's upper atmosphere, the squadron's six exploration frigates were already so far away that they'd be hard to detect if their location wasn't already known, and only Johansen knew where they were now.

Shiloh was gratified to see that the high speed dive into Jupiter went as expected, with virtually no turbulence, and the single, five second opening of the scoops filled the holding tank with enough hydrogen to process a worthwhile amount of the heavy hydrogen. For once, the simulation and reality matched perfectly. Vanguard broke out of Jupiter's atmosphere just as the five CFPs decelerated into orbit. With contact made between Vanguard and the five drones, Shiloh heard Johansen speak to him over the intercom.

"Okay, CAG. Let's see if your drone jockeys can take on my frigates."

Shiloh grinned, even though Johansen couldn't see him, and said, "This should be interesting."

Shiloh didn't know where the frigates were or from what direction they'd be approaching. He did know that at least one, but possibly more, would head out far enough from Jupiter's gravity well to allow for micro-jumps in order to test the jump detection gear.

Shiloh opened the channel to the five drones and said, "This is Commander Victor Shiloh. I'll be your CO for this simulated war exercise. The ship I'm on is to be defended against a simulated hostile force of six ships. CFP0001, you are designated as the Flight Leader.

Deploy your flight, and patrol with passive sensors and jump detection gear only. Recon drones can use active scanning. Intercept unidentified ships with near misses by unarmed attack drones at your discretion. Confirm your understanding of the simulated nature of this exercise, CFP0001."

The response was immediate.

"CFP0001, call sign now Iceman. Simulated nature of this exercise understood. When will we get to fire at real targets, Commander?"

Shiloh laughed hard enough that Johansen and the rest of the Bridge crew probably heard him. CFP A.I.s were much 'smarter' than the limited electronic brains of the typical recon or message drone, but the lab geeks insisted that they weren't sentient. Shiloh was becoming more and more convinced that they were, or were at least in the process of becoming sentient. He had worked with all five of the A.I.s at the Alpha base long enough to detect slight differences in attitude and response time between them. Before he left Alpha Base, CFP0001 had already asked him about the tradition that human pilots had of adopting a call sign. Shiloh had explained it as best he understood it, and that had been the end of the conversation. Now it was clear that 0001 had picked a call sign. Shiloh wondered if the other four had done the same thing. He was willing to bet money they had. The question about getting to the real action was also typical of 0001's … Iceman's increasingly gung ho attitude.

"Patience is a virtue, Iceman. I have it on good authority that you and your fellow … fighter pilots will see the real thing in due course. For purposes of this exercise, my call sign will be CAG. Proceed at your discretion, Iceman. Good hunting."

"Ah roger that, CAG. It's good to be working with you again. We'll make you proud."

Shiloh was stunned by the sentimental nature of the reply. None of the five had shown any inclination to behave that way at the Alpha Base, and the added 'ah' was a deliberate affectation that Iceman must have picked up from listening to the human test pilots. He focused on his Tactical display and saw that the five drones were already maneuvering away at a high rate of acceleration. From this point on, he would sit back and watch. The com channel to Iceman and to the other four was still open, but he knew that any communication between the drones would be a stream of digital signals sent so fast that he couldn't possibly understand them.

Nothing much happened for over 40 minutes, and Shiloh wasn't surprised. The frigates were limited to a much slower acceleration rate than the fighters, and they were starting the exercise from jumping off points that were so far away they couldn't be detected with passive sensors only. Shiloh was certain that Johansen had assigned vectors to her frigates that minimized the chance of the drones detecting reflected sunlight off the frigate hulls. Vanguard and Sentry had special hull coatings that absorbed 99.999% of light, making them very hard to see against the usual background of space. Now, however, they were orbiting Jupiter and would be clearly visible against Jupiter's much brighter background. Shiloh jumped when the first contact report came in.

"This is Hunter. I have detected a light reflection. Deploying recon drones now."

Before Shiloh could respond, Iceman spoke. "Good job, Hunter."

Shiloh took note of the fact that Iceman had bothered to translate that comment into human speech for Shiloh's benefit. He could see the bearing of the detected reflection as a dotted line on his Tactical display. As soon as a second fighter or recon drone also caught a reflection, the two lines would meet, and the point where they crossed would be the detected bogey. Suddenly five red lines appeared, all intersecting at a point that wasn't on the first line. This had to be another ship that had just emerged from a micro-jump.

"A single bogey has just been detected emerging from Jumpspace, CAG. I've ordered Firefox to intercept." said Iceman.

The fighter now moving towards the new bogey had to be Firefox. Shiloh could see that the range between it and its target was almost 35 million kilometers. Jupiter's mass made jumps within a radius of two light minutes impossible. While the defending force knew exactly where the bogey had exited Jumpspace, its course and speed were as yet unknown, but so far the jump detection gear that each fighter carried seemed to have worked perfectly. The frigates could accelerate at 133 Gs – 1.3 kilometers per second squared – while the fighters, which was how Shiloh had decided to refer to the CFPs, could accelerate at just under 400 Gs – 3.92 kps squared. If Firefox and the bogey were accelerating directly towards each other, the range would drop to zero in roughly 78 minutes. Shiloh hoped Iceman would not commit all five of his fighters, or even most of them, to long range interception attempts. The bogey, having just emerged from Jumpspace, was very likely hoping to draw as many fighters away from the vicinity of Jupiter space as possible. The first contact could be just as far away, or it could be a lot closer. There was no way to tell until a second contact bearing could pin down its location.

As more minutes went by, Shiloh noticed that Iceman was keeping itself and the three others relatively close to

Vanguard's location. Firefox's range to its bogey's estimated position was down to 25 million kilometers. By this time, the reflected sunlight contact had disappeared, almost certainly due to the bogey maneuvering with the reflected sunlight now pointing in a different direction. *Launch recon drones and have them go to active scanning*, thought Shiloh. He could have ordered Iceman to pass those orders to the others, but that would have undermined the purpose of this test to see if autonomous units could make the appropriate tactical decisions on their own. Two minutes later, all five fighters launched recon drones. The drones didn't start scanning right away. *Good boy*, though Shiloh. Get the drones far enough away from each other that their active scanning won't tip the enemy off to the approximate location of the fighters themselves. Another 10 minutes passed without new contact reports of any kind. Suddenly all the recon drones commenced active scanning at the same time. The overlapping fields of radar energy bounced off six new contacts. One was much further away and the rest were all within two million kilometers of Vanguard.

"Gotcha!" said Shiloh.

He was expecting to hear Iceman or one of the other fighters say something, but they didn't. Instead, they acted. Firefox swung around to go after a target that was closer to it. Each of the other fighters changed vectors to intercept one of the other four frigates. Shiloh noticed that the recon drones were using intermittent scanning to minimize the enemy's ability to pinpoint their locations and 'destroy' them with low powered simulated laser fire. Even so, one recon drone, and then a second, shut down in response to laser fire from their targets. If Iceman waited too long to fire his attack drones, there wouldn't be enough radar bearings left to give the attack drones a good chance of finding their targets. But if they fired the attack drones too soon, the drones would run out of fuel before reaching their targets. A human pilot wouldn't be able to compute the trade-off between the probability of missing versus the probability of never reaching the target trade-off, but an A.I. could.

Three minutes later, three more recon drones had been 'hit' but each target still had at least two recon drones scanning it. Firefox was the first to fire. Two attack drones streaked away on an intercept vector to its target. Shiloh checked the vector and was pleased to see that Firefox had done the correct thing. Attack drones didn't use radar to see their targets because that would have made the drones themselves vulnerable to enemy laser fire. The drones used a low-powered laser to reflect off the target's hull, thereby creating the same effect as reflected sunlight. Because the low-powered laser was a very narrow beam, it was unlikely to hit any kind of optical sensor on the target's hull, which would have enabled the target to pinpoint the attack drone's location. The attack drone then relayed the target's bearing and distance back to the fighter that launched it, via another low-powered laser, so that the fighter A.I. could keep track of both the attack drone and the target. In order not to give away the fighter's position in case the attack drone was detected, its intercept vector created a shallow detour slightly off to one side. If the target assumed that the drone's launch platform was directly behind it and fired at that point, they'd miss the fighter by a wide margin.

When a second fighter launched one attack drone at its target, Shiloh wondered how much longer the frigates would hold off from active scanning themselves. He didn't have long to wait before finding out. All five of the closer frigates went to active scanning in an attempt to get accurate bearings on the remaining recon drones. It almost worked. The fighter A.I.s realized what was happening and were able to react fast enough to prevent most of the recon drones from being 'hit' by return fire, by shutting down the recon drones' active scanning. With only their own radars to aim their lasers, the frigates still had a tough time hitting the much smaller recon drones. As soon as the recon drones stopped actively scanning, the frigates attempted to maneuver to a new vector. The position and vectors of two frigates were still known because they hadn't been able to shake off the low-powered lasers from the attack drones. That left three more frigates, aside from the one at long range. Shiloh knew immediately what Iceman was attempting to do. The A.I.s could easily compute the expanding circle that represented each frigate's furthest possible position over time. The three fighters that hadn't fired yet continued to close the range to the general vicinity of their targets. As soon as they got close enough to ensure that the attack drones would reach their targets no matter what the frigates tried to do, they ordered their remaining recon drones to go back to active scanning just long enough to enable their attack drones to acquire the targets and launch towards them.

As soon as all five of the nearer frigates were being tracked by low-powered laser light, Iceman played his Ace-in-the-Hole. Each fighter launched two more attack drones. These drones could also have fired their low-powered lasers at their targets, but that wasn't necessary. They could see the reflected laser light from the other attack drones and homed in on that. It didn't take long for the Acting Squadron Leader of the aggressor force to figure out that his frigates had to resume active scanning, even though their positions would be clearly visible, if they wanted any chance at all of surviving the drone attack. The problem was that attack drones were designed to be as difficult to detect by radar as possible, with many flat surfaces that bounced radar signals away from the radar source. They weren't completely invisible to radar, but the reflections were so small that the frigates' lasers had difficulty hitting them.

In a real battle, the attack drones would have rammed their targets, and the kiloton fission warheads would have exploded on contact. In the simulated exercise, each attack drone that made it through the defending laser fire deliberately missed the target by a kilometer and transmitted a signal on the monitored frequency to indicate a successful intercept. Four of the five frigates were successfully 'intercepted'. The fifth was not. Under the criteria of the exercise, it was deemed to have penetrated the defending force. The sixth frigate attempted to get through, but with all five fighters gunning for it, it didn't stand a chance. With the simulation over, all of the recon and attack drones shut down their engines and activated their homing beacons to be recovered by the fighters that had fired them.

"Five of six bogeys intercepted. Sorry we let one get through, CAG," said Iceman.

Shiloh waited a few seconds before responding. "What did you learn from this simulation, Iceman?"

"The fifth bogey could have been intercepted if Hunter and Maverick had maneuvered close enough for converging fire," said Iceman immediately.

Shiloh had to stop to analyze that answer. *My God, he's right*, he thought. With attack drones coming from two completely different directions, the frigate's counter-fire would have been far less effective. There was no way that a human pilot could reach that conclusion without the assistance of some kind of computer.

"Since the objective of these simulated battles is to learn from our mistakes, I would say that this exercise was a success from that point of view. Your team has performed well, Iceman. Were there any equipment issues that I should be aware of?"

"No, CAG. These birds performed perfectly. What are your orders after we recover our drones?"

Shiloh grinned. He had the answer to that already figured out. "After all drones have been recovered, I want your flight to re-assemble and take up station behind Vanguard, in a V formation. Maintain the V formation as precisely as you can. Let's show the Squadron Leader and the other COs what you fighters can do."

"Ah, roger that, CAG. We'll put on a good show for you."

Shiloh couldn't help chuckling. Iceman was sounding more and more human by the minute. "Very good, Iceman. Unless you have something else to convey, you're free to carry out your orders."

"Iceman clear."

With the lengthy recovery process now underway, Shiloh felt free to get up from his Command Station and walk over to Johansen's station.

She looked at him as he came close and said, "My frigates came out on top."

Shiloh gave her a small smile and said, "One out of six frigates got through the outer layer of defense. That's true. But are you going to congratulate your frigate COs when you debrief them, considering that they lost 83% of their combined strength, or are you going to berate them?"

Johansen took a deep breath and said in a somewhat chastised voice, "I'll be honest. I'm inclined to chew them out. I really thought more of them would get through. Then again, they are only exploration frigates, after all."

Shiloh said nothing.

When it became clear that he wasn't going to say anything more, Johansen said, "How long will it take your CFPs to recover their drones?"

Shiloh knew the answer to that. Iceman had already figured it out and had transmitted the information digitally to Shiloh's consol.

"Eleven hours and thirty-five minutes is the estimate from Iceman."

Johansen raised her eyebrows. "Iceman?"

Shiloh forgot that she hadn't been listening to his com channel chatter.

"CFP0001's call sign. He picked it himself."

"He? You're referring to an A.I. as a male? Why not she? We refer to our ships as 'she' don't we?"

"Well, if the picked call sign had been IceWOMAN, then I'd probably refer to it as a she. It's hard to think of IceMAN as a she."

Johansen didn't have a snappy comeback for that one.

Chapter 14 Stepping Over The Line In The Sand

The squadron remained near Jupiter for several more days. Two more exercises showed that the five fighter A.I.s were getting better as time went along. As a result, Johansen was getting more and more irritated with her frigate COs, which Shiloh thought was unfair. Their combat training was minimal, and their ships weren't really designed for multiple ship combat. With the exercises finally over, the squadron received orders to return to lunar orbit to pick up the rest of the Task Force that Johansen would take to Bradley Base. When the eight ships and five fighters slipped into lunar orbit, Shiloh saw that Admiral Howard wasn't wasting any time. Two tankers were ready to take the five fighters onboard and ferry them to their destination star system.

Until the new carriers were ready, fighters had to be transported by tankers in place of some of the fuel shuttles that they usually carried. Shiloh suspected that as the fleet gradually transitioned to ships that could refuel themselves, tankers would eventually be used primarily as fighter transports. In addition to the two tankers, there was also a supply ship carrying new equipment, plus lots of recon and attack drones. After all ships were topped up with fuel, Johansen gave the order for the Task Force to head out for the trip to Bradley Base. The trip seemed long to Shiloh, even though he'd made the it multiple times. He wondered how the A.I.s were handling the wait. To the lightning fast minds of Artificial Intelligences, days of doing nothing must seem like eternities. Shiloh had briefed Iceman, Hunter and the others before they boarded the tankers, and they knew what to expect.

Upon their arrival at the star system containing Bradley Base, Shiloh was relieved to learn that no sign of alien ships had been detected, although the base didn't have any of the new jump detection gear prior to the Task Force's arrival. If the aliens had carried out reconnaissance here, they had done it very carefully. By prior arrangement, all five fighters had their unarmed practice attack drones replaced with the real thing. As soon as the Task Force emerged from Jumpspace, the tankers deployed the fighters, which then accelerated at 400Gs to take up their assigned patrol stations. Bradley Base was under a steel dome built on a moon orbiting the system's only gas giant. Johansen's squadron joined the two squadrons composed solely of exploration frigates, and Senior Commander Korolev assumed command of the combined force as the designated Task Force Leader. That opened up some interesting possibilities now that Johansen and Shiloh were equals in both rank AND position, but Shiloh wasn't sure if Johansen had any interest in something other than a professional relationship. She had never given even a hint that she might be receptive to something more. Shiloh decided to wait and see. He suspected that, whatever else, Johansen probably would not want to risk having rumors spread among her crew, even though a more intimate relationship wouldn't be breaking any regulations. Off duty between missions might be okay, but not while a mission was in progress.

After a few days, Shiloh settled down into a routine. Korolev insisted on some kind of tactical exercise every 24 hours, which kept the fighters happy but made everyone else grumble. Shiloh was pleased when the duplicate autonomous units control station was assembled in the Base itself. That meant that the drones and fighters would not be left hanging if something happened to Vanguard. The Lt. Cmdr. assigned as Shiloh's Deputy CAG was one of the test pilots he had worked with at the Alpha Base. What Sejanus lacked in tactical skills was more than made up for by his easy and natural interaction with the fighter A.I.s. He recognized them as more than just soulless machines.

When almost two months had passed without any signs of the aliens, Shiloh allowed himself to be less anxious. With additional frigates, supplies, drones, and – more importantly to Shiloh – more fighters arriving on a regular basis, his worry about the Line in the Sand not being sufficiently defended started to abate. When the second batch of fighters arrived, Shiloh and Sejanus discovered something very interesting about the fighter A.I.s. The new CFPs were controlled by A.I.s far less developed in terms of their own identities. He had queried Iceman about that, and the A.I. explained that the 'rookies' just needed time to develop new neural pathways that would be unique to them. At Iceman's suggestion, each rookie fighter was 'paired' up with one of what Shiloh was starting to think of as 'the veterans'. Even though they weren't operating physically close together, low-powered laser communication meant they could communicate with each other far faster than with a human mentor. Within several days of the arrival of the rookies, all five of them had chosen their own call signs and were beginning to display their own unique speech patterns, much to the obvious delight of Iceman, Hunter and the others.

The days turned into weeks, and the weeks started to turn into months. With absolutely no sign of any alien incursion or even a quick recon mission, Korolev was beginning to wonder out loud if the whole Line-in-the-Sand strategy was a failure. Maybe the aliens had reconsidered their aggressive posture and were holding back, or maybe they were flanking the Base system altogether to bypass its defenses.

It was on the 55th day that the aliens made their presence felt. Shiloh happened to be on the Base itself when word arrived by messenger drone that a convoy of supply ships and tankers had come under laser fire from a dozen alien ships. The convoy was too deep into the gravity zone of a gas giant to be able to microjump away. With Vanguard orbiting the Base, Shiloh decided to assume control of the fighters from the ground in order to save time. As he arrived at the Base's Control Center he heard Korolev speaking.

"Commander Johansen will take her squadron and the 88th to search the ambush system for survivors, and to engage any enemy ships that might still be lurking there. Any questions?"

He was speaking to all five squadron leaders whose video images were on the main display. Shiloh could see that Johansen wasn't happy with those orders, and he thought he knew why. Sending two of five squadrons away from this system would weaken it considerably and was in contravention of the stated goal of beefing up Bradley's defenses. When it became clear that Johansen wasn't going to say anything, Shiloh decided that he would.

"If this attack is a diversion meant to pull some of our forces away from Bradley, then we'd be doing the wrong thing."

Korolev was clearly surprised by Shiloh's presence and challenge.

"What would you suggest instead, Commander? Should I just ignore the fate of hundreds of our fellow comrades who may be injured, and who may die if they don't get assistance?"

"No, Sir. I suggest sending a much smaller contingent. Specifically, a combat frigate carrying one fi—CFP, accompanied by a support ship, to emerge at the edge of that system where the CFP can be used to recon the ambush site. If there are survivors and no signs of the enemy, then the frigate and support ship can move in to render assistance."

Korolev didn't blink an eye.

"And what if the recon shows that there are enemy ships still in the vicinity, using the survivors as bait for another ambush the way they did in your first encounter, Commander? The relief force will then be outnumbered, and more time will be wasted while they send a drone back asking for reinforcements. No! With two squadrons deployed, we'll still have 24 frigates plus your 20 CFPs to defend this Base. I'll take the risk of an attack here. I think the aliens know we're too strong here, and they've decided to bypass the base altogether. My order stands, Commander."

Turning to look at Johansen's image, he said, "Do you wish to object to my order for the record, Commander Johansen?"

Shiloh's heart sank when she said, "No, Sir. I'll take the 88th and my squadron to search for survivors immediately, Sir."

"Very good, Commander. Carry on. Task Force Leader clear."

Korolev turned to Shiloh and said, "With Vanguard no longer available for you to use to control your drones, you'll no doubt want to take your station on the ground here, Commander."

The statement was so self-evident, that Shiloh could only interpret it as a command for him to attend to his duties and to leave the strategizing to wiser heads. He nodded his assent to Korolev and turned to relieve Sejanus at the autonomous units control station.

"I'll take over, Marcus," said Shiloh.

As his deputy got up, he said in a quiet voice that Korolev wouldn't hear. "For what it's worth, Boss, I agree with you."

Shiloh nodded, but he said nothing.

When he was settled in, Shiloh reviewed the status of his 20 fighters. Four of them were in the Base hanger bay getting refueled plus a quick maintenance check. As Sejanus was about to leave, Shiloh turned to him.

"I want you to go down to the hanger bay and get those fighters ready to launch as soon as possible. Light a fire under the maintenance crews if you have too."

"You got it, Boss," said Sejanus.

When he was gone, Shiloh looked at his Tactical display. The 15 fighters currently on patrol were slowly orbiting the gas giant at a distance of a million kilometers so that their jump detection gear would overlap as much as possible. This would allow for triangulation of the exact position of any ships emerging from Jumpspace. Johansen's 007 squadron and the 88th squadron were accelerating while coming to a new heading for their eventual entry into Jumpspace. Shiloh was surprised to see that the projected course would be exactly parallel to a line that ran from this system's sun, through the gas giant that Bradley's moon was orbiting, to the ambush star system. The alignment was so precise that Shiloh couldn't help thinking it wasn't a coincidence, although he couldn't come up with any reason for it.

A quick check of the Tactical display showed that it would take almost an hour and a half for Johansen's squadrons to get far enough away from the gas giant's gravity zone to be able to enter Jumpspace safely. With an acceleration of 133Gs, their velocity would be over 7,220 kilometers per second by the time they reached that point. Shiloh opened a com channel to Vanguard and spoke in a voice low enough that Korolev wouldn't hear him.

"Vanguard, this is the CAG. I'd like to speak with CO Johansen." The reply was almost immediate.

"This is Vanguard. Standby, CAG."

Johansen came on the line after several seconds.

"What's on your mind, Victor?" she said.

"I have a bad feeling about this, Angela. It smells like a trap to me. How are you planning on proceeding when you emerge from Jumpspace?" There was a pause.

"I haven't got that far in my thinking yet. Any suggestions?"

"Yes. Drop out of Jumpspace well away from the refueling point, and I mean WELL away! If the aliens are waiting for you, they'll try to pick up your emergence point. Since we don't know what the range of their detection gear is, I'd rather you err on the side of caution."

"The problem with that, Victor, is that the further away we enter the system, the longer it'll take to reach any survivors."

"Granted, but you can make up for that by emerging with a higher velocity. You've got enough fuel to do that, right?"

"Hold on. I'll check that," said Johansen after a short pause.

As Shiloh waited for her to confer with her Astrogator, he noticed that the status lights of one of the fighters in the hanger bay had changed from yellow, indicating not available, to the green that meant available for launch. He checked which fighter it was and saw it was Hunter, the veteran leader of this flight of four. The other three would be rookies. Shiloh would have been tempted to listen in to any human chatter from those fighters if he hadn't been waiting to hear back from his former XO.

"Victor? We've got enough fuel to emerge zero point seven five AUs from where the convoy would normally be, and still get there at a reasonable time. Any further away than that, and we wouldn't be able to make up the time."

Three quarters of a standard Astronomical Unit was almost twice the distance that the gravity zone of the target gas giant would require. *I'd double that if I were in command, and to hell with the added time*, thought Shiloh. *Easy to say,* he then thought. *You're not the Mission Commander.*

"Let's hope that's far enough," said Shiloh. He thought for a couple of seconds before adding, "Listen. Keep your ships out of the target gravity zone or at least most of them. Let your recon drones go in first while you're still decelerating. If it is an ambush, and you stay out of the gravity zone, you can always microjump away."

"That's a good idea, Victor. I'll definitely keep that in mind, depending upon what the recon drones find."

She paused, and something told Shiloh to wait before saying anything else. When she spoke again, her voice had a sad quality to it. "I'm glad you're not on board Vanguard now, Victor."

Shiloh couldn't help thinking that she meant she didn't want him to suffer the same fate she faced. Friends sometimes said that kind of thing to each other in situations like this, but so would lovers. *If she gets back alive, I'm going to ask her how she feels about the two of us*, he thought.

"Message received and understood," said Shiloh, not wanting to say more when he knew that all transmissions were recorded. There was a long pause that started to become awkward. Finally she spoke.

"I'll keep this com channel open in case you have any other thoughts or suggestions, but right now I have other things that need my attention. Thanks for the advice, Victor."

"You're welcome, Angela. I'll be standing by if you need me."

The sound coming from Vanguard disappeared, but a quick check revealed that the com channel was still open. Shiloh understood that Johansen had muted her microphone so that she could talk to her crew privately. Shiloh did the same thing. He didn't want to distract her with his chatter to his fighters or to anyone else at the Base. A second fighter in the hanger bay was now ready for launch. Shiloh switched his earphones to the channel reserved for the hanger bay's launch operations.

"—it easy, Hunter. Our people are working to get you and your team ready as fast as possible," said Sejanus.

"You tell them that if my team isn't ready for action in two more minutes, I'm going to complain to the CAG himself!"

Wow, thought Shiloh. *He's actually shouting. Don't tell me there's no sentient consciousness behind that voice.*

"Okay, Hunter. I'll tell them."

Sejanus' voice was heavy with amusement. The two minutes went fast and Shiloh noticed that all four fighters were ready by the deadline. He switched on his microphone.

"Hunter, this is CAG."

"Go ahead, CAG," said Hunter.

"I suspect that the attack on our supply convoy is intended to divert our defenses in order to attack us in detail there AND here. Your flight will be held in reserve until we see if they attack us here. I know I can count on you and your team to accept that as the professionals you are. Are you getting the tactical feed okay?"

"Yea, we're getting that. We'll calm down and be ready when you need us. Thanks CAG."

"Very good, Hunter. CAG clear."

The next hour and twenty minutes were eerily uneventful. No further message drones from the convoy, which by itself was worrying. No signs of any alien presence in this system. Suddenly Shiloh's earphones were filled with the sounds of a ship going to Battle Stations. At first he thought Korolev was sending the Base to its Battle Stations, but then he heard Johansen's startled voice.

"Victor! We're under laser attack! Not sure from where! Vanguard's already taken one hit! We're evading! Going to active scanning now! Oh God! There's 34 of them! They must have seen us from the reflected sunlight off our hulls! We didn't see them because they're in the gas giant's shadow! We can't microjump yet! Gotta fight it out. I've already lost fo—"

Shiloh saw that the com channel was broken off at Vanguard's end. He hoped it was just due to damage of their com system and not the destruction of the ship itself. He was about to hit the alarm when he heard the Battle Stations warning Siren going off. Clearly Korolev was aware that the relief mission was under attack. Shiloh then heard the Task Force Leader and Hunter talking at the same time. He concentrated on Hunter first.

"—give us the word, CAG!"

Switching his microphone to the right channel, Shiloh said, "Wait one, Hunter." He then switched back to the Base intercom channel while focusing on Korolev's words.

"—re-deploy your squadrons between the attacking force and the Base. Stay in the GGs shadow when you get around to the other side. You'll have CFPs in support. Did you copy that, CAG?"

Shiloh had heard enough to understand that Korolev was taking a huge risk.

"Copy that. Fighters will support frigate squadrons, however I respectfully suggest that we keep our remaining strength close to the Base! This may—"

Korolev wouldn't let Shiloh finish the sentence.

"I'm not letting them get close enough to fire on the Base directly, CAG! Now order your fighters to launch, dammit!"

Shiloh reopened the com channel to the fighters, while keeping the intercom channel open so that Korolev would hear him.

"CAG to Hunter. Your team is cleared for immediate launch. Form up on our remaining frigates and coordinate your actions with the Squadron Leader in charge. Acknowledge your orders."

"Orders acknowledged, CAG. What about Cyrano and Bulldog? Recommend they shadow enemy force."

Shiloh looked at the Tactical display closely and saw that the fighters with those two call signs were on jump detection patrol closest to the battle. Why hadn't they detected the enemy's emergence from Jumpspace? The answer could only be that they had emerged from beyond the fighters' detection range. THAT was disturbing because it implied they knew what that detection range was. The cluster of dots that represented Johansen's 16 frigates were all flashing yellow, signifying hull breaches and major systems failures, and Shiloh didn't need to count them to know that there were no longer 16 ships there. He also noticed that their velocity was so high now that neither of the two nearest fighters had any hope of catching up with them in time to join the battle. As he continued to watch, the Tactical display showed a much larger cluster of red dots intermittently flashing due to interrupted radar scanning data feeds from at least one of Johansen's frigates. The red dots were moving much more slowly, and it wouldn't be long before the ambushed frigates would be past the enemy force and moving further away. Hunter's suggestion was the right one. Cyrano and Bulldog couldn't join the fight, but they could attempt to track and follow the enemy formation with their recon drones.

"Your recommendation is approved, Hunter. Contact Cyrano and Bulldog. Advise them of their new orders. Maintain an open channel to me. Good hunting."

"Yeah. Let's hope the bogeys cooperate and stay where they are, but I doubt they will, CAG. Hunter clear."

By now Johansen's frigates, what was left of them, were at their closest point to the enemy formation. The number of dots was shrinking. Shiloh queried his tactical computer if any of the remaining dots was Vanguard. The answer was no. He felt as if he'd been hit in the gut. He had to remember that the absence of a dot didn't necessarily mean that Vanguard was destroyed. With Johansen's force on the opposite side of the gas giant, there was no way that the Base's ground-based radars could try to get a fix on both friendly and enemy ships. What little data they were getting was relayed from Johansen's ships, via a satellite in orbit around the gas giant, and then on to the Base. Without active scanning, the tactical computers had to rely on transmissions from a particular ship to confirm its status, or indirect data from the radars of other ships. Vanguard might still be intact but unable to communicate. Once the reinforcement frigates moved around the gas giant enough to establish line-of-sight, they could use their own radars to pinpoint enemy and friendly ships. Shiloh hoped the frigate squadron leader wouldn't order his supporting fighters to reveal their existence by actively scanning the battle area. That was contrary to Shiloh's standing orders and the Line-in-the-Sand plan's doctrine. The CFPs were meant to be one of Mankind's Aces-in-the-Hole and the longer the aliens didn't know about them, the better.

Then Shiloh noticed something quite strange happening. The number of yellow dots representing friendly frigates stopped shrinking. Shiloh eventually realized that the enemy ships had to have stopped firing on the frigates. They were still close enough that some of them should have been hit, if the aliens were still firing at all.

When all of the alien ships disappeared from the Tactical display, Shiloh queried the computer for the reason. The answer was lack of radar data from any of Johansen's frigates. Some were still able to communicate with the Base but either weren't capable of scanning the enemy fleet any longer or chose not to do so. So now the question was what would the aliens do next if they weren't firing on Johansen's frigates any longer?

Shiloh manipulated his Tactical display to get a better sense of the overall picture. If the gas giant was the center of a clock, the aliens were in the direction of 12 o'clock. The moon containing the Base and the system's sun, which was much further away, were exactly lined up in the direction of six o'clock. The sun, moon, gas giant and alien formation all lined up in a straight line. That couldn't be just coincidence. What was it that Johansen had said? The aliens had approached while hidden in the gas giant's shadow to avoid detection by reflected sunlight. All human ships, on the other hand, had to come at them from around the side of the gas giant, thereby making detection by reflected sunlight a distinct possibility. It looked to Shiloh like a very carefully planned trap, one that could only have been planned that way if the aliens already knew about Bradley Base and the relative positions of the gas giant and its moons. And that meant that the attack on the supply convoy was in fact a diversion to pull ships away from the Base so that they could be attacked separately, thereby weakening the Base's defenses. The obvious next step was to attack the Base itself. Korolev was making that possible by sending all her remaining frigates to the aid of Johansen's survivors, which the aliens had carefully refrained from wiping out completely. If it looked like there were no survivors at all, then sending reinforcements might be deemed unnecessary, and that would leave the Base more heavily defended then the aliens would want.

Zooming in on the Base's moon, Shiloh saw that all the remaining frigates were forming up while accelerating in a curving trajectory that would take them around the gas giant. He tried to put himself in the alien Commander's seat. *What would I do next*, he asked himself.

Chapter 15 All Of Us Understand The Situation

There were only two ways to get close enough to the Base to attack it directly. Accelerate towards the gas giant from the 12 o'clock position and swing around to attack the Base from the rear OR microjump to the opposite – six o'clock – side of the gas giant, which would put them in 'front' of the Base, and accelerate into attack range from there. If the enemy formation moved into the gas giant's gravity zone, then microjumping was no longer an option, and it would be a head on clash between the reinforcement frigates and the enemy formation. *That would be risky*, Shiloh thought. 24 exploration frigates supported by five fighters against possibly as many as 34 enemy ships. If the alien objective was to destroy as many human ships as possible, then they'd let the reinforcement formation get within combat range. But if the primary objective was to destroy the Base, the aliens might not want to risk having their fleet depleted by battles that could be avoided. With the Base destroyed, the remaining frigates would have no choice but to retreat to friendly space, assuming they had enough tankers to refuel them on the way back. Shiloh then had a horrifying thought. If the aliens succeeded in destroying the Base AND those tankers now in orbit, then the remaining frigate crews were doomed to die from lack of air and food when their ships ran out of fuel. *We can't let the tankers be caught in orbit if the Base is attacked.*

Shiloh thought about the implications of that for a few seconds and then said, "CAG to TF Leader."

Korolev's voice was calm once again as she answered. "What is it, CAG?"

"Sir, I strongly recommend that you order our tankers to disperse out beyond the GG's gravity zone, just in case the enemy formation decides to microjump to our side after our reinforcements are too far away to make it back in time. Even if the Base itself is destroyed, our ships can still get home as long as they have at least one tanker to let them refuel on the way. The tankers can microjump to a rendezvous point that's far enough away to avoid jump detection."

Shiloh was expecting his suggestion to be dismissed out of hand, but to his surprise, Korolev reacted differently.

After a long pause, she said, "Yes I see what you're thinking. Use the relief force as bait to lure our remaining strength out of position and then attack the Base. You may be overestimating their cunning, CAG, but it's a scenario that deserves to be taken seriously. If I order our frigates to stay close to the gas giant, then Johansen's force will be completely on its own. The aliens might decide to finish off any survivors if they come to the conclusion that we're not taking the bait. Your recommendation about the tankers is a good one. I'll do that in any case, but I'd also like to hear your suggestions on what else we should do now."

Shiloh thought fast. What they needed was time. Time for Johansen's surviving ships to use their built up velocity to get far enough away from the enemy formation to be safe from additional laser fire. That meant that the aliens had to continue to believe that the bait was working. If they saw ships moving towards them from around the gas giant, then that should make them believe their plan was working, but at some point, the reinforcement frigates would be too far away to come to the Base's aid if the aliens microjumped to the other side. Then he had an idea.

"Okay, Sir. I do have one idea. Since we have an approximate location on the alien fleet, we can use our recon drones as decoys. When our reinforcement forces have moved far enough around the gas giant and are in the right spot, they launch all the recon drones they have and order the drones to hold their acceleration down to match what our ships can do. The drones will also be ordered to orient themselves in such a way as to maximize the possibility of reflected sunlight reaching the alien fleet. Our frigates will try to minimize the likelihood of revealing their positions from reflected sunlight. They'll stay in the gas giant's orbit and, if possible, stay in its shadow while our decoys head for the alien fleet. Meanwhile, I have two other fight—CFPs maneuvering to use their recon drones to track the enemy fleet so that we know what they're doing. As long as the enemy thinks our ships are headed towards them, they'll continue to leave the relief force survivors alone. Once enough time has passed, what's left of the relief force will be too far away for the enemy to pick off. Sooner or later the enemy will catch on to our decoy maneuver, and then we'll see if they commit to an attack on the Base. However they come at us, we'll have time to bring back all our CFPs to help defend the Base alongside our frigates. That should be enough to tip the battle in our favor, Sir."

There was another pause followed by, "CAG, come over to my station."

Shiloh got up and walked quickly over to the center of the large Command Center where the Base Commander's station was. Korolev watched him come and leaned towards him. She clearly wanted to speak to Shiloh in a voice low enough that none of the other personnel would hear her. When Shiloh was just a few centimeters away, Korolev quietly spoke.

"I like your idea but I'm concerned about Johansen's relief force. Once the enemy knows we've fooled them with our decoys, what's to stop them from microjumping in front of the relief force survivors and wiping them out?"

She waited while Shiloh pondered the question. Unfortunately, he couldn't come up with a solution to the problem.

"I wish I had a solution for you, Sir, but I don't see any way that we can protect the survivors as long as there's a substantial enemy presence in the system."

"So how do we get them out of this system?"

Just as Shiloh was about to say that he didn't know, Korolev's face disappeared, and was replaced by a vision of Shiloh standing next to a medical bay bed where a heavily bandaged Johansen lay.

She looked up at him and said, "God, that was tricky of them to microjump to the opposite side so that the sun was directly behind them! If we had launched attack drones from in front, the reflected laser light would have been lost in the sun's glare. Having your fighters attack them from the rear not only eliminated the glare problem, but you caught them by surprise too!"

The vision faded and Korolev's concerned face was back.

"Are you okay, Commander? You seemed to blank out there for a few seconds."

Shiloh was too overcome by relief that Johansen wasn't dead to respond right away, but he nodded so that Korolev could tell he was listening again.

"I'm okay, Sir. I was just lost in thought. I think I may have a solution. I'm convinced now that they intend to microjump to our side and attack the Base as soon as they think it's no longer well defended. And while they could microjump just about anywhere along the gas giant's gravity zone perimeter, I'll bet a year's pay that they'll jump to the exact opposite side so that the sun's directly behind them. That will make optical detection impossible, and our attack drones will not be able to distinguish the reflections from their targeting lasers from the sun's background glare. That is, unless we shift our CFPs around so that they'll be able to attack the enemy fleet from THEIR rear. Then the sun's glare will benefit our side instead. With a little luck, my fighters might be able to catch them completely by surprise."

Korolev frowned. "What if they stay where they are long enough to figure out that we've used decoys?"

Shiloh took a deep breath and said, "That's definitely a risk, Sir. But if we forget about the decoy idea, and our reinforcement frigates really do go after the relief force survivors, then they're more likely to fall for OUR trap. And if the enemy microjumps as expected, the reinforcement frigates can then continue to go to Johansen's survivors' aid."

"So now you're recommending we abandon the decoy idea that you suggested a few minutes ago?"

"That's right, Sir. I hadn't fully thought through all the ramifications when I suggested it."

Korolev looked away while she drummed her fingers on the armrest. After a brief pause, she said, "If we go with your CFP ambush idea, can they get into position before the enemy jumps?"

"If we need more time, we can slow down the reinforcement force and make it look like they're advancing cautiously. If I were the enemy fleet Commander, I'd wait until the approaching ships were at least half way between the gas giant and my fleet before ordering the microjump. With the CFPs acceleration, they should be able to get into position long before we reach that point, Sir."

Korolev took a deep breath and said, "Okay. We'll go with your ambush plan, but those five CFPs escorting the frigates stay with that force. If the enemy intends to fight them first, those frigates will need all the help they can get. The other 15 CFPs are at your discretion, Commander. As soon as you know how much time they'll need to get into ambush position, let me know, and I'll order the frigates to adjust their accelerations accordingly. Any questions, Shiloh?"

"No questions, Sir. This will work."

Korolev nodded, and Shiloh headed back to his station. It only took a second to open the com channel to Iceman.

"CAG to Iceman." There was a seven second lag due to the distance.

"Iceman here. Go ahead, CAG."

"We think the enemy will wait until our frigates are out of range, then microjump to the base side of the GG and attack the base. All gravity zone perimeter fighters including Cyrano and Bulldog will proceed at maximum acceleration to a rendezvous point that will enable you to attack the enemy fleet from their rear after they microjump. Once they microjump, let them get within the gravity zone before you fire on them. The location of the rendezvous point and attack vectors is at your discretion. Once you figure that out, transmit the information to Base asap. Hunter's wing will stay with the reinforcement force. Repeat my orders to confirm, Iceman."

The A.I. repeated the orders and then added. "Very clever idea, CAG. Who knew you were that sneaky?"

Shiloh didn't laugh or even smile. He wasn't finished giving orders.

"Iceman, when you fighters are ready to fire, I want all of you to fire all of your attack drones. All 15 of you are then ordered to accelerate at maximum with the objective of ramming any enemy ships that have not been destroyed or crippled by the drone attack. We have to get them all, Iceman, otherwise the survivors will attack the Base before our frigates can get back. I need to know that I can count on all of you to carry out that order if the circumstances require it."

Even with the light speed lag, Shiloh thought there was the barest hint of a pause before Iceman responded.

"All of us understand the situation, CAG. We'll do whatever's necessary to stop them. Is there anything else?"

Shiloh felt a lump in his throat. Over the weeks of waiting for the attack, he had come to like all twenty of his fighter A.I.s. Each one was a unique individual with its own quirks and eccentricities. Losing any of them would be like losing someone from his own former crew.

"Yes, there is. Once you're in the ambush position, cut off communication with the Base the instant that the enemy jumps. Maintain communication silence until the battle's over. Any questions?"

"No questions, CAG."

"Very good, Iceman. I'll be available if you need me until you break communications. Good luck and good hunting to all of you."

"Ah, roger that, CAG. Iceman clear for now."

It took less than a minute for Shiloh to receive the data concerning the rendezvous point and the estimated time to get there. He passed that on to Korolev. Within a couple more minutes, all the frigates and fighters were responding to the new plan. Cyrano and Bulldog had the furthest to go, and even at 400Gs acceleration, it would take them almost 30 minutes to go from the edge of the gas giant's gravity zone on one side all the way over to the opposite side. The tricky part was arriving at the rendezvous point facing the right direction and at the right speed, which in this case meant facing towards the Base's moon and traveling slow enough not to overrun the enemy's emergence point. Korolev's frigates, with Hunter's wing as escort, were accelerating at only 66Gs,and the frigates were doing their best to be obvious about it.

Shiloh wondered if they should send a message drone back to the nearest contact point, but then realized that the drone would get dangerously close to the enemy formation before it could enter Jumpspace. As he watched the display, he noticed that the tankers, which had been orbiting the moon, were now heading for orbit around the gas giant. From there, they could avoid detection by keeping the gas giant between them and the enemy fleet.

The next 45 minutes were the longest of Shiloh's life. He couldn't help thinking about Johansen. She was still alive. Of that he was certain, but she was also apparently severely injured, and it would be many hours yet before the reinforcement ships could catch up with the damaged frigates. The reinforcement force was almost half way between the gas giant and the enemy fleet that had been tracked for several hours by long range radar from the frigates. The enemy fleet had moved away from the gas giant in order to get outside the gravity zone, but now it disappeared into Jumpspace. Within seconds, the com channels to the fighters in Iceman's squadron shut down. That was the tipoff that the enemy had jumped to the opposite side. Shiloh and Korolev didn't know precisely where the enemy was, but it was clear that Iceman did. With the communications blackout, Iceman was in charge of the ambush. Shiloh called Korolev.

"The CFPs have broken off communications, which means the enemy has jumped into their vicinity, Sir."

Korolev's reply was immediate. "Understood, Commander. I'm ordering the tankers to swing around to the far side of the GG, and the reinforcement force Commander will launch message drones back up the supply chain to let HQ know what's happening now that the enemy fleet's no longer in the way."

Shiloh said nothing. There wasn't anything else to say. Iceman and his team would be accelerating at maximum to get to the optimum firing range, which only they knew. So there was nothing to do now but wait some more.

It was half an hour later that the passive detection gear on the Base picked up the action. Thirty-three radar sources suddenly started to scan in all directions. They were approximately five million kilometers inside the gravity zone. At that distance, any radar energy reflected off any of Iceman's fighters would be too weak for the Base's detection gear to pick up. The Tactical display only showed the enemy fleet which was moving towards the Base and now maneuvering in what appeared to be an attempt to evade. Shiloh held his breath. Suddenly there were multiple and simultaneous detonations of what had to be the attack drones' nuclear warheads. At this distance, the Base's optics couldn't tell how many individual explosions. The combined EM pulse of those explosions drowned out the radar emissions so there was no way to tell how many enemy ships were still scanning.

The tsunami of EM and other radiation quickly died down. Shiloh refrained from attempting to communicate with his fighters because of his previous order to Iceman to maintain communications silence until the battle was over. So until he heard from Iceman or one of the other fighters, the battle was still going on. Finally, about 20 minutes later, optical sensors picked up two momentary flashes followed seconds later by the re-establishment of the com channel with Iceman.

"CAG, this is Iceman."

CAG here. Go ahead, Iceman."

"Thirty-three enemy ships were destroyed. Thirty-one by attack drone warheads. Two were rammed by Bulldog and Firefox. Five fighters confirmed destroyed by enemy laser fire. Three fighters are adrift and do not respond to communications. They appear to have suffered damage. Extent of damage unknown. Request that SAR shuttles be dispatched. What should we do now, CAG?" Shiloh had a lot to think about but he needed more information first.

"How's the fuel situation, Iceman?"

"The five of us that are left have sufficient fuel to stay on patrol for another 36 hours, CAG."

"Okay. Well done, Iceman. Pass that on to the rest of your team, too. I need to confer with the Base Commander. Maintain your present vector for the time being."

Shiloh was about to end the conversation so that he could discuss strategy and options with Korolev when he had a thought. "Iceman, what's your evaluation of the situation now?"

"While the destruction of 33 enemy ships is a tactical victory, this battle has to be considered a strategic defeat, CAG. Relayed radar data from the opposite side of the GG showed 34 enemy ships. Only 33 microjumped to this side. That means one ship went somewhere else, beyond our detection range. My calculations reveal an 89% probability that the missing ship returned to its nearest base. Therefore reinforcements may be on their way here. In addition to that, the fact that the enemy knew where to ambush the supply convoy, as well as that they knew enough about this star system to wait for a favorable configuration of sun, gas giant and the ambush star system, indicates that they have detailed astrogational information on star systems they haven't surveyed themselves. The only way they could have that information is if they've captured at least one of our ships intact and extracted its navigation data. That being the case, we have to assume that they know where all our bases are and where Earth is. We therefore can't expect to stop their advance here. They've already demonstrated their ability to go around Bradley Base."

My God, he's right, thought Shiloh. *Why didn't I see that myself? If they know where Earth is and all the explored systems between Earth and their territory, they could launch a massive attack on Earth by using uninhabited star systems that contain gas giants to refuel. There are dozens ... hundreds of those kinds of systems that we couldn't possibly fortify or even monitor effectively! This information has to get back to HQ ASAP!*

"I think you're analysis is correct, Iceman. Standby while I confer with the Task Force Leader."

After the normal delay, he heard Iceman say, "Ah, roger that, CAG. We'll be here."

Shiloh switched his com channel to Korolev.

"Sir, this is Shiloh. I've just spoken with my CFPs. Here's the situation. Of the 34 bogeys detected by Johansen's force, 33 microjumped, as expected, to the opposite side. The 34th has apparently jumped back to its nearest base because there's no sign of it in this system. Drone warheads destroyed thirty-one bogeys. Two had to be rammed by CFPs. Additional CFP losses include five destroyed and three disabled by enemy laser fire. Our SAR teams should recover those last three because their AIs are worth saving due to their experience. As important as that summary is, Sir, what I really need to share with you is my assessment that this whole battle, including the convoy ambush, couldn't have been set up the way it was unless the enemy had precise astrogational and operational data. And they could only have gotten that by capturing one of our ships. That means they almost certainly know where Earth is and how to get there. We have to warn HQ that Earth or any other colony star system could be subject to enemy attack. The one that got away may trigger another wave of ships."

Shiloh heard Korolev groan, then curse in a low voice. "Wait a minute, Shiloh! I need to understand the reasoning behind your conclusions better. Why would they need captured data in order to set up this ambush?"

Shiloh forced himself to remain calm as he spoke. "They had to know about the precise positions of this gas giant and our moon in order to be able to hide in the gas giant's shadow and still be in firing range of Johansen's relief force on its way to investigate the convoy ambush. That meant that the course her ships would take to eventually jump to the ambush system had to be exactly parallel to the shadow cast by the GG. Since we have no indications at all that any enemy ship has surveyed this system, the only way they would know about that precise alignment AND the fact that our supply convoys refuel in that particular star system, is if they got the data from one of our ships. The mere fact that they knew where to ambush the convoy is pretty damning evidence of captured data all by itself, wouldn't you say?"

Korolev took his time answering. "Well, when you put it that way, I'm forced to agree. There's no way that they would send 34 ships to one star system unless they had a pretty good idea of what they'd find there. Damn! We have to get this back to HQ fast! I'll send several message drones to Omaha Base just to make sure that at least one of them gets through. Is it your assessment that there is no longer any enemy presence in this system right now?"

"Yes, Sir. It is."

"Then I'm inclined to split the reinforcement force into their separate squadrons and send one to render assistance to Johansen's survivors, another to investigate the convoy ambush situation, and keep the third squadron back here. I'd be interested in your thoughts on that plan, Shiloh."

Shiloh paused to think that over. The bogey that got away left before the fighters destroyed the other 33 ships, and therefore wouldn't know the results of the battle. They wouldn't suspect a negative outcome of the battle until their 33 ships were overdue in reporting back. That meant the Space Force had some time.

"The enemy Command Structure won't know about the outcome of the battle for some time, so I agree that we can safely split up our remaining forces. Johansen's survivors and their rescue squadron will probably be back here within 24 hours. I'd expect that the squadron investigating the convoy ambush will find nothing, and it'll be back here within 36-48 hours, too. I'd like to get my CFPs back to the Hangar Bay to reload, and I'd also like to recall the five units escorting the reinforcement squadrons for jump detection patrol, Sir."

Korolev nodded. "Yes, go ahead and do that. Okay, I'll redeploy the three frigate squadrons, bring the tankers back and send out the warning drones. Now what was it you said about SAR teams recovering the disabled CFP A.I.s? Is that really necessary, Shiloh? Even if the A.I.s are still intact, we won't have any CFPs for them to pilot. Why not just write them off?"

Because they're intelligent beings you stupid ass! thought Shiloh. He took a second to get his voice under control.

"Well, first of all, CFP A.I.s are especially good at learning, and they can transfer their 'wisdom', for lack of a better word, to other A.I.s. So recovering them will only make our future CFP force more capable by adding to its experience pool. Secondly, even though the tech weenies swear up and down that the A.I.s aren't sentient, they certainly ACT that way and that includes behavior that seems to be motivated by pride in being part of the Space Force Brotherhood. If we expect them to continue to be willing to sacrifice themselves as necessary to protect us, then we need to demonstrate to them that their survival matters, too."

He heard Korolev take a deep breath. "I'm not sure I accept your second point, but the first one makes sense. I'll arrange for Search and Rescue teams to recover those A.I.s if they're still intact. Anything else, Shiloh?"

Shiloh was about to say no when a new thought popped into his head.

"Well, Sir, something's just occurred to me. Sending message drones back down the chain will mean that HQ won't get our warning for… six days at the earliest. I'd have to check if this is feasible, but I wonder if one of my CFPs can accelerate to a high enough speed to launch a message drone that could jump directly to Sol without any intermediate stops. If the drone doesn't have to use any of its own fuel to accelerate to jump speed, it might be able to make it all the way."

"Now that is worth looking into. If you think it'll work, go ahead and do it. I'll still send other drones back the normal way just to be sure and also to let our other bases know to be on alert. Anything else?"

"No, Sir. Nothing else."

"Very good, CAG. Carry on."

Shiloh immediately switched back to Iceman's channel.

"Iceman, this is CAG. I've spoken with TF Leader. Your team is to return to the Hangar Bay asap to rearm and refuel. Contact Hunter and advise him that his fighters are to return to Base orbit and establish a jump detection patrol. SAR teams will be dispatched shortly to recover the disabled fighter A.I.s. I also have a mission that you can evaluate for me. Can a fighter reach sufficient speed to enable a launched message drone to make it back to the Sol system in one jump? If the answer is yes, then determine which of the remaining operational fighters, including Hunter's group, has the necessary fuel reserves to launch the message drone and still be able to return to Base. Transmit that data to me as soon as you have the answers. Any questions, Iceman?"

Shiloh wasn't really expecting an answer quickly but he got one.

"Glad to hear about the SAR teams, CAG. We were beginning to wonder if we were considered worth the effort. A single jump by message drone from here to Sol is theoretically possible but not certain. In order not to miss the Sol system altogether, the message drone has to be launched on a trajectory with a higher degree of accuracy than is usually required. There is an additional complication. A fighter can accelerate to the required speed, but a normal fuel load would be insufficient to enable the fighter to return to Base. One option would be to rendezvous with a fuel shuttle either on the outward or inward leg, or both. None of the operational fighters in this system currently has enough fuel to reach launch velocity and return to base."

Iceman's comment about being considered worth the effort to recover sent a chill down Shiloh's spine. *If we break faith with these boys, we'll have a hard time winning it back*, he thought. *I have to be honest with them.*

"Iceman, it pains me to admit this, but not everyone here understands that you and your fellow fighter pilots are sentient beings who should be treated with the same respect and loyalty as any human member of Space Force. It'll take time to change their minds. Sejanus and I are working on that. Continuing to perform reliably is the best thing that all of you can do to speed up that process."

This time there definitely WAS a longer pause than just the light speed lag.

"Thanks for being straight with us, CAG. We know we can always count on you to watch our backs. One more thing regarding the single-jump-to-Sol problem. Bradley base has one of the new Mark 4 fuel shuttles, which has the capability to be piloted by one of us instead of a human crew. Any of us that are successfully recovered from the cripples can pilot the shuttle, which will therefore have a higher acceleration profile, and that will make it easier to refuel the fighter."

"Understood. Very good, Iceman. Excellent idea! I'll see you all personally when you're back in the Hangar Bay. CAG clear."

Shiloh called Sejanus and told him to relieve him at the Command Station. When he'd been relieved, Shiloh headed down to the cavernous Hangar Bay and confirmed that there was a Mark 4 fuel shuttle and that it did have the capability to be piloted by the advanced A.I. units.

Chapter 16 I Need Two Volunteers

None of the A.I. units piloting the disabled CFPs had been recovered by the time Iceman and his team landed in the Hangar Bay, although the SAR teams were on their way. As soon as the maintenance techs started working on refueling and rearming Iceman, Shiloh walked over to stand in front of Iceman's fighter, where the optical scanning unit could see him. Using his implanted com equipment, Shiloh spoke to Iceman.

"Iceman, can you see me?" asked Shiloh as he waived to the optical unit.

"I see you, CAG."

"Good. As you know from the tactical feed, the SAR teams haven't reached those three cripples yet. The Task Force Leader and I agree that Earth should be warned as soon as possible. I need two volunteers from your team. One to pilot the Mark 4 fuel shuttle and the other to boost and launch the message drone to the Sol system."

He got an immediate response.

"I'll launch the drone. Maverick will pilot the shuttle, CAG."

"Very good, Iceman. I'll supervise Maverick's transfer myself personally."

Shiloh gave Iceman another wave and walked over to the officer in charge of the bay. He told the officer what he needed, and several minutes later Shiloh was standing beside a Maintenance Tech on top of Maverick's fighter. The technician had opened the hull where Maverick's modular electronic brain resided. Under Shiloh's careful gaze, a crane lifted the 44 kilogram spherical unit out of its bracket. Shiloh knew that Maverick was still receiving audio and video transmissions from his fighter and from the video unit on the crane. He could see himself being transferred to the fuel shuttle. Shiloh followed the crane over to the fuel shuttle and watched as Maverick was gently lowered into its electronic interface port.

As the sphere settled into the shuttle, Shiloh said, "CAG to Maverick. Status report."

"Maverick to CAG. All systems within normal parameters. Fuel is topped up and I'm good to go, Boss!"

Shiloh was about to ask Iceman the same question, but he beat him to it.

"Iceman is fueled. Message drone is loaded. I'm good to go too, CAG. Let's do this before I change my mind."

Shiloh chuckled. He knew that Iceman was sufficiently gung ho that having doubts about this mission was not likely, assuming that A.I.s were capable of having doubts at all.

"Standby both of you while I check in with TF Leader. CAG to Task Force Leader."

After a few seconds delay, he heard Korolev's voice.

"Go ahead, Shiloh."

"Sir, unless you tell me otherwise, we're ready to initiate the direct to Earth drone mission."

"That's fine, Commander. You may proceed. Korolev clear."

Shiloh turned to look at Iceman's machine and said, "Okay, Iceman and Maverick. Taxi over to the launch pads. I, or Sejanus, will be monitoring the mission all the way. I'd say good luck but I know you don't need it. You're both too good to need luck."

"Thanks, CAG. Okay, Maverick. Let's go make some history," said Iceman.

"Lead the way, Iceman!" said Maverick.

Shiloh grinned again. The history comment and Maverick's reply could have been done between the two of them digitally, but they used human language so that Shiloh could hear it, too. He watched as the two machines carefully taxied over to the launch pad. Once inside, the inner bulkhead panels closed to protect the integrity of the bay's atmosphere, while the smaller launch pad chamber had its air evacuated prior to the outer doors opening to allow both vehicles to launch. By the time that Shiloh got back to his Command Station and took over from Sejanus, Iceman and Maverick were on their way in a curving trajectory to get clear of the gas giant before settling down on a vector that was aimed at the Sol system.

As he settled down in his chair, Shiloh watched his Tactical display, which showed not only the current position, course and speed of both craft, but also the projected vectors. The plan was simple in concept but tricky in execution. Even with an A.I. at the controls, the fuel shuttle's maximum acceleration was still only about half that of Iceman's fighter. Iceman kept pace with Maverick until Iceman's fighter had used up enough fuel to give it an acceptable reserve after being topped up by

Maverick's shuttle. After the fuel transfer, Iceman would go to maximum acceleration and leave Maverick behind to coast. That was the easy part. The tricky part involved Maverick waiting until the correct time to decelerate to zero and then re-accelerate in the exact opposite direction until the required speed was reached. Meanwhile, Iceman would continue to accelerate to the necessary minimum speed of 77% of the speed of light to launch the drone, while being careful to line up as precisely as possible to the target co-ordinates. Then, after launching the message drone, Iceman would decelerate to zero before re-accelerating to the necessary speed in the opposite direction, and hope that the two of them could match velocities before Iceman ran out of fuel. Maverick would then transfer enough additional fuel so that Iceman could reach the Base with zero velocity. While the danger of running into something was extremely small, it wasn't zero, and at those speeds, even hitting a particle of dust the size of a grain of sand could damage Iceman's fighter, depending on where it hit. Waiting to see if the mission was successful would be hard on Shiloh too, due to its duration. It would take Iceman almost 18 hours to reach 77% of light speed, plus another 55 hours to decelerate to zero and then get back to a rendezvous with Maverick's fuel shuttle.

During the next three days, Shiloh and Sejanus took turns monitoring Iceman and Maverick's progress. When it was Shiloh's turn at the Command Station, he used the time to write his After Action report. The details of the actual battle were quickly recorded. What was harder to write, were his recommendations. The Line-in-the-sand strategy was now obsolete. The aliens didn't need to push past Bradley Base in order to continue exploring Human Space. They apparently already knew what was beyond Bradley. Therefore there was no longer any line to hold here. The Base was still valuable as logistical support for any future offensive actions by the Space

Force, but Shiloh strongly suspected that the enemy would bypass it in order to strike deeper into Human territory.

With that conclusion, the obvious question was what should the Space Force do instead? He spent long hours looking at star maps of colonized and uninhabited but explored star systems between Sol and those systems known to be used by the enemy. Since the alien ships also used fusion power fueled by heavy hydrogen, star systems with gas giants would be just as useful to them as they were to humans. Shiloh came up with a plan to station a flight of five fighters in each uninhabited star system that contained at least one gas giant. Systems with more than one gas giant would need more than one flight of fighters. Each flight would have one fighter outfitted with modular fuel skimming equipment so that the flight could refuel itself as needed. While the fighters would carry some attack drones, in case they needed to defend themselves, their main payload would be message and recon drones to detect enemy activity and report it back to the nearest Base. With this early warning system in place, HQ could deploy frigates and other combat units along the most likely paths of advance and attempt to interdict the enemy strike force. It sounded good in theory, but space was vast, and timely communication was the key. The enemy could move along a broad axis of advance. Concentrations of defending ships had to have enough time to move to where they were needed the most, and Shiloh was afraid that the standard message drones didn't have the fuel capacity to reach the speeds necessary for quick jumps over long distances. He added a recommendation to develop a very fast and therefore long ranged version of the message drone, knowing full well that it probably wouldn't be ready in time for the next alien attack.

Before finishing his report, Shiloh learned what the reinforcement squadron found when it matched velocities with Johansen's survivors. Only six of the original 16 frigates were still intact. Vanguard was one of the six. Her sister ship, Sentry, was not. Two of the surviving frigates were so badly damaged that they had to be abandoned and destroyed after the surviving crew were transferred. Vanguard was capable of maneuvering but only at a reduced rate of acceleration. Johansen herself was still alive but seriously wounded. With all wounded crew transferred to the rescue frigates, the remaining crews brought their damaged ships back to orbit around Bradley Base as best they could. The rescue squadron CO decided to detach half his squadron to escort back the damaged ships, while the remaining four frigates used their superior acceleration to get the wounded back to better medical facilities at the Base as quickly as possible.

The launch of the message drone by Iceman went off as planned. Iceman reported that he was certain the launch vector was accurate enough for the drone to arrive in the Sol system. Shiloh's report was finished just in time to be transmitted to Iceman for downloading to the message drone before it was launched. Six hours later, two things happened almost simultaneously. Johansen arrived at the Base along with other injured crew, and a message drone arrived from the squadron searching for the ambushed convoy. No survivors of the convoy were found, only debris. When Shiloh added the loss of the convoy ships to the damaged and destroyed frigates and fighters, and compared that to the destruction of 33 enemy ships, he came to the conclusion that in terms of material losses, the battle was almost a draw.

It was two hours later before the medics finished dealing with Johansen's injuries and allowed Shiloh to see her. She was heavily bandaged and barely conscious from the residual effects of the medication and painkillers. Shiloh nodded to her and leaned over so that the other patients wouldn't hear their conversation.

"You had me worried, Angela. When Vanguard dropped off the tactical display, I thought the worst."

When she replied, her voice was gravelly and a little slurred. "Sooo … my first battle as a CO and I manage to get my brand new ship shot out from under me. They'll probably bust me back to Lieutenant Commander and ship me off to be XO on a supply ship."

Shiloh smiled and shook his head. "Not a chance. You were following orders and considering how outnumbered your were, I'd say you did pretty well. Vanguard is still space worthy, although her jumpdrive needs some minor repairs. She may not be able to fight until she's fully repaired back at Sol, but she'll live to fight another day."

Johansen nodded slightly, coughed a bit and said, "Tell me what happened after my force was ambushed."

Shiloh told her the basic details.

She scowled and said, "God, that was tricky of them to microjump to the opposite side so that the sun was directly behind them! If we had launched attack drones from in front, the reflected laser light would have been lost in the sun's glare. Having your fighters attack them from the rear not only eliminated the glare problem but you caught them by surprise too!"

Shiloh didn't realize he'd been anxiously waiting for her to say that, until he felt himself relax. *So another vision has come true*, he thought.

"Yes, we managed to turn a crushing defeat into an expensive tactical victory, but from a strategic point of view, we lost."

"I … I don't understand what you're referring to, Victor."

A clear-headed Johansen would have known what he was referring to, but this Johansen was too fuzzy-headed with painkillers to see it.

He smiled at her. "Let's start with the convoy ambush. How did they know that we used that particular system to refuel ships on their way to Bradley Base? How did they even know that Bradley Base existed? And how did they know that this system's sun and the gas giant would line up precisely with the star system where the convoy was ambushed, so that they could use the GG's shadow to ambush your ships? The only way they'd know all that without having surveyed those systems themselves, which we're as certain as we can be they didn't do, is if they got all that data from one of our lost ships. That means they know where all our colonies and home planet are too."

"Oh my God," she said as the implications sank in.

"Yea," agreed Shiloh.

Neither of them said anything for a minute or so.

"What can we do, Victor?"

Shiloh told her about his recommendations for a buffer zone of systems, monitored by CFPs as an early warning system.

"That's brilliant, Victor. Really brilliant. Can we manufacture and deploy that many fighters fast enough?"

Shiloh shrugged. "We just have to try it and find out," he said.

There was another pause. Shiloh was about to ask her about the nature of her feelings, if any, for him when a nurse came in and told him he had to leave now and let her get rest. He promised Johansen he'd visit her again soon and left. When he came the next day, she was asleep. He left a note to let her know he'd come to visit.

Iceman successfully refueled from Maverick, and by the time both returned to the Base, the third squadron had returned from the convoy ambush system. Shiloh waited until Iceman's fighter was back in the hangar to tell him and the others the bad news. None of the three A.I. brains recovered from the disabled fighters were intact. They all had enough physical damage to destroy their neural pathways. Iceman asked Shiloh to thank the SAR teams for their efforts and said nothing more about it.

Johansen slept a lot over the next several days, and Shiloh was unable to talk with her again. When he did finally catch her awake, he had some news to share with her.

"We got a message drone from Sol. They did the same trick we did with a drone boosted to near luminal velocities, after our drone arrived and showed them how it could be done. Vanguard and the other three damaged frigates are ordered to return to Sol. You and some of the less severely injured crew will come along. Admiral Howard wants to see me, so I've been put in temporary command of Vanguard and the ad hoc squadron as a whole."

"Oh, wonderful! I'll be a passenger on my own ship," she said with a touch of bitterness.

"Yes. Sorry about that, but the brass back home apparently want to lighten the load on the med facilities here. Besides, if you're going to resume command of

Vanguard, you can't do that if you're here and she's back at Sol, right?"

She nodded but said nothing. There was a long pause and Shiloh decided to ask THE question.

"Listen, Angela. When we talked before you took your squadron out of orbit, did you mean to send me signals that you wanted us to have more than a professional relationship?"

Johansen said nothing for what seemed like a long time. When she spoke, she sounded embarrassed.

"Well, at the time I was contemplating something like that I guess, but right now … I don't feel that any more. I'm sorry if you got your hopes up, Victor."

Shiloh sighed. *Damn, I waited too long.*

"Oh well. It's a good thing we got that cleared up."

He tried not to let his expression show how disappointed he was.

Johansen put her hand over his. "Once I get back on my feet, maybe …" She stopped, as if she suddenly realized that holding out the possibility of her changing her mind would only get his hopes up again, with no guarantee that she'd feel differently in the future.

Shiloh suddenly felt uncomfortable with this conversation. He wanted to end it and leave.

"It's just as well. We're both serving officers in the Space Force during a war. Even if both of us did feel that way, we're not likely to be able to do much about it until the war is over, and that could be years … assuming we both survive it. I should be getting back to my post. I've got a lot to do if Vanguard is going to leave in 10 hours. I probably won't see you until after you've been moved to the ship. Bye for now."

He patted her hand with his and turned to go. She said nothing as he walked away.

Shiloh found time to say goodbye to his fighter pilots. This time all of them chimed in with the kind of goodbyes that comrades-in-arms usually give one another. Shiloh was profoundly moved by the whole exchange. Saying goodbye to Sejanus was easier, but not by much. Sejanus promised he would promote the view that CFP A.I.s were sentient beings and deserved to be treated as such. When Vanguard, escorted by the other damaged frigates, was just about to reach its jump velocity, the Sensor Tech told Shiloh that all of the fighters on jump detection patrol were flashing their running lights. Shiloh understood the gesture immediately, and he ordered Vanguard to flash hers in reply.

Chapter 17 Enter The Defiant

The trip back took longer than usual because two of the frigates were unable to accelerate as fast as normal due to combat damage. Shiloh visited Johansen about every other day, but the visits were short, and they kept the conversations on safe topics like her recovery, the ship's status, etc.

When the four ship squadron finally arrived back at Sol, they were ordered to the asteroid shipyards. Transport ships brought the crews and the injured directly to Earth orbit. Shiloh managed to say a quick goodbye to Johansen before she was transferred to a special medical shuttle for the trip down to the Space Force medical facility. He and the other crews took the usual personnel shuttles down to HQ in Geneva.

This time they landed in the middle of the day. The sky was a slate grey with overcast clouds, but it wasn't raining. They were met at the spaceport by a clutch of officers including a Lt. Commander who told Shiloh that Admiral Howard wanted to see him right away, and that his gear would be taken to the Temporary Officers Quarters for him. *God! I can't even get settled into my quarters first?* But there was no point is expressing his dismay. Orders were orders. Howard's messenger accompanied Shiloh to HQ in a separate vehicle. When he entered Howard's office, he was shocked at how much the Admiral seemed to have aged in the few months since Shiloh had last seen him. *The strain of this war is really getting to him*, he thought. After the usual exchange of salutes, Howard gestured to the chair facing his desk, and Shiloh sat down. Howard got right down to it. *No cigars this time.*

"I'm guessing that you're wondering why you were called back."

Shiloh nodded.

"Well I had several reasons. The first is your report. By the way, before I get any further, boosting that message drone by CFP so that it could reach Sol in a single jump was a brilliant idea, and yes, we are going to take your recommendation and develop a version that can boost itself up to the necessary speeds. Now back to your report. You and Korolev both sent reports. Her report was written from the point of view of a Base Commander and of a Task Force Leader, and her recommendations reflect that. Your report, on the other hand, not only covered recommendations from a Commander of the Autonomous Group, but also included recommendations for the much larger strategic situation, which I personally found very useful. So naturally I wanted to discuss that with you in person. But we would have recalled you soon anyway because the first light carrier is just about complete, and you'll be her first Commanding Officer. Her name's Defiant, and since you're the only officer who has both ship command and CFP command experience, you were the obvious choice. The final reason is that, even if you don't think so, it's everyone else's opinion that you're just too good of a tactical thinker to remain at Bradley indefinitely. Congratulations on that tactical victory, Commander. When you turned down command of the Sentinel, I thought you had lost your nerve. However with the benefit of hindsight, I now realize that you made the right decision. I shudder to think of where we'd be today if you hadn't stuck to your guns when I tried to pressure you to accept that command."

Shiloh said nothing but nodded. That vision had just come true too.

Howard continued, "So let's talk about your strategic ideas. Stationing CFPs in buffer zone systems containing gas giants is a good idea, but five CFPs for each gas giant is just too many. It'll take us too long to build the 300+ units we'd need to do that. What we're going to do instead is deploy two CFPs per gas giant until the buffer zone is completely covered, and then we'll add more to each system as they become available. And as a matter of fact, that'll be Defiant's first mission."

When it was clear that Howard was pausing, Shiloh spoke up. "So that means that Defiant won't be used for hit and run attacks on enemy systems?"

"I know that was the intention when we started building her, and as soon as we get the buffer zone early warning network set up, we'll certainly give that option serious consideration, but for now we have to be able to intercept any alien incursion into our space with as much warning as possible. Don't you agree? It was your idea after all."

"Yes, Sir. I do agree. I guess since we're short of CFP transport capability, the Defiant will have to do double duty. It's just that it'd be nice if we could strike back at their systems and force them on the defensive for a change."

"It would be DAMN nice, I agree. You'll be happy to know that the first two long range recon frigates are seeking out the enemy systems even as we speak. Now let's discuss your other recommendations. You think we should give CFPs the ability to travel through Jumpspace. Were you aware of the controversy over exactly this issue when the CFP concept was being developed?"

"No, Sir."

"I thought not. The reason the idea was not pursued was the fear that armed ships, capable of jumping and controlled solely by artificial intelligences that were capable of learning and programming themselves, might pose a threat to us if they were to go rogue. That issue doesn't arise with message drones since they don't carry any weapons and their A.I. units aren't as sophisticated to begin with. So explain to me your thinking about why we should take that risk."

Shiloh couldn't imagine Iceman or any member of his team turning against Humanity, but if A.I.s really did have the capability of becoming sentient, then that independence of thought included the possibility of deciding NOT to fight for Humanity and possibly even fight against it, however remote that possibility might be.

"I wasn't aware of the controversy, but I was aware of the standing orders that CFPs were not allowed to carry live weapon drones while in any system that had a human colony or in the Sol system. I always thought that was in case of accidental launch, but now I see the real reason. The thing is, since our colonies in general, and Earth in particular, are now in danger of a direct enemy attack, don't we need to be able to help defend them with armed CFPs considering that we don't and won't have enough ships to defend every inhabited system at the same time? If we were going to use non jump capable armed CFPs to defend inhabited systems, then what difference would it make if they were jump capable? Either way, that or another star system would be at risk of a rogue CFP. I see one huge advantage to having jump-capable CFPs, and that's from a tactical perspective. Carriers can only be in one place at a time, and star systems are huge in overall volume. Being able to microjump a strike force of CFPs from one part of a star system to another virtually instantaneously would be equivalent to having a lot more carriers. Perhaps the fears of runaway rogue CFPs jumping from one system to another can be addressed by limiting jumps to a maximum total distance of say … one light year. Human intervention would be required to reset the limit, so if a CFP did go rogue, it would only have a limited range."

Howard considered his response carefully before replying. "Hm. I can see the tactical advantage of having CFPs that can microjump within a star system. That could be a huge advantage. Limiting their jumping range would let a lot of people sleep easier at night, me included. Now let's talk about your OTHER CFP recommendation. Namely, giving CFP A.I.s some kind of rank structure. I know that you think they have the capability to become sentient, and I also know that the people who designed and built their electronic brains are adamant that they can't become sentient. What makes you right and all of them wrong?"

Shiloh gave that some thought before answering.

"I can't prove that they are, but they certainly act as if they are. They're choosing call signs for themselves on their own initiative. They're acquiring uniquely individualistic speech patterns, and when the question of deploying human Search and Rescue teams to recover the A.I. brains from disabled CFPs came up, one of my oldest A.I.s told me quite explicitly that he … it and the other A.I.s wondered if humans considered them worthy of being rescued. Would non-sentient calculating machines care about whether others of their kind were rescued? The CFPs under my command at Bradley Base seemed to want to be treated like any human member of the Space Force, not as expendable equipment. Laugh if you want to, Admiral, but I'm absolutely convinced that they're motivated by the same things that motivate us, namely pride, loyalty to comrades-in-arms, friendship, just to name three. My suggestion of ranks that would be unique to Artificially Intelligent members of the Space Force would formalize the chain of command among A. I.s that may be at different levels of development, and also motivate the newer units to perform well in order to advance in rank and experience."

Howard looked dubious.

"If anyone else had suggested this, I'd dismiss it out of hand, but because it's you, I'll give it serious consideration. Your final recommendation is the most interesting. Expand on it for me, Commander."

"Yes, Sir. Well, it starts from the assumption that the enemy has complete information on all our explored star systems, colonies and home world, from one or more captured ships. Our ships' astrogational databases include locations of infrastructure installations such as our asteroid shipyards, the Alpha development base on Epsilon Eridani, the CFP manufacturing facility there, etc. That means they could target every key war-fighting installation we have right now. They're ALL at risk. What I'm suggesting is a contingency plan for the worst case scenario. Set up brand new shipyards, mining, processing, manufacturing facilities, supply depots, training stations, R&D stations in new locations that aren't in any existing ships' database and will never be added to them in the future. Then even if Earth and all our colonies along with their orbiting infrastructure are devastated, we can keep on fighting."

"So how would this approach be different than our current plans to continue to decentralize war production?"

"The difference is this. Under my approach, newly developed star systems would be kept secret even from members of the Space Force who might potentially find themselves captured and tortured. The ships, CFPs, weapon drones, new weapon systems, etc. would all be developed and produced in secret. They would be delivered to Sol or wherever they're needed by a separate division within Space Force, and only those individuals would know the locations of those star systems. Even you wouldn't know where they are."

Howard scowled. "Now that's going TOO far, Shiloh. I'm not in danger of being captured."

Shiloh nodded. "No, Sir. I didn't think you were, but if you knew, you might inadvertently let the information slip to someone who could find themselves in danger of being captured. With the worst case scenario in mind, don't we need to err on the side of caution, Admiral?"

"I'm not against erring on the side of caution, but I foresee practical difficulties in doing what you're suggesting. Anyone assigned to these secret locations is going to want to come back for R&R eventually. How are you going to keep them from letting key information slip?"

"Well, I can think of two ways. The less onerous way is not to tell anyone the precise location of the star system they're assigned to work in. Only the Astrogators of the ships that move personnel and equipment back and forth need to know the exact location. The more onerous way is to only assign volunteers who are single, with minimal family connections, and make the assignment one way for the duration of the war. In other words, once they arrive at the secret location, they stay there indefinitely."

Howard looked skeptical. "If we do that, we'd have to provide at lot better accommodation and recreation facilities for those poor souls, otherwise we might have a mutiny or an epidemic of suicides."

Shiloh nodded but said nothing. The Admiral stared at a point on the opposite wall for a few seconds while he considered what Shiloh had said.

"You've given me a lot to think about, Commander. If you weren't so good at tactical combat, I'd put you on my planning staff, but you are, and we can't afford to lose that skill. Now normally after an extended time on assignment, you'd get at least two weeks for R&R, but Defiant won't wait that long. So the next six days are yours to do with as you wish, but be back here on the seventh ready to take command of the Defiant."

Shiloh waited to see if he had a vision, but there was nothing.

"Thank you, Sir. I'm looking forward to that."

To his surprise, he saw the Admiral heave what looked like a sigh of relief.

"Glad to hear it, Commander. Since we're talking about the Defiant, there is one other issue that has to be addressed. The Space Force has never fielded a carrier before, so we're not sure how the command structure should be set up. Does the CAG report to the CO, or are they equal in status with a more senior person aboard to command both, or what? Your thoughts?"

After thinking about it for a few seconds, Shiloh said, "I think that the CO and CAG should be equal in rank, but if a carrier is going to operate on its own and not as part of a task force, then I think one individual should wear both hats. The XO and the Deputy CAG can handle most of the day-to-day issues and let the CO/CAG deal with strategic and tactical concerns. If the carrier is part of a task force, then I think the two positions should be split up and both report to a Vice-Admiral, Sir."

Howard grunted. "Makes sense to me. Unless you hear otherwise, you can assume that you'll be wearing both hats when you take command of Defiant. Unless you have something that you'd like to ask or say to me, you're free to go, Commander."

"Thank you, Sir. No questions."

Shiloh got up, saluted and left. As he made his way back to his quarters, he decided that he didn't want to spend his R&R on a beach again. He would stay in Geneva and relax as much as possible, visit Angela a couple of times and generally get his thoughts together. The six days went fast. Johansen was pleased with his new command and seemed to be making progress on her own recovery.

When it came time to report for duty, a shuttle took him to the moon base. There he caught a transport ship to the asteroid shipyard where Defiant was being fitted out. Shiloh didn't get a good feel for the size of his new ship until the transport was in the process of docking at the shipyard. Defiant was big compared to any other ship he'd ever seen, including the Vanguard Combat Frigate. At 250,000 metric tons mass, Defiant was five times the mass of Vanguard, and yet she was classified as a light carrier. More light carriers were in various stages of completion, and the first heavy carrier, massing half a million tons, was just starting its two year construction phase. Defiant was built to carry a total of 34 smaller craft. While she was streamlined and capable of skimming gas giants herself, she would also carry four Mark 4 fuel shuttles, five personnel shuttles and 25 fighters. Her crew would total almost 500. Shiloh had already studied her specs, and he was impressed. Her huge fuel capacity could enable her to travel twice as far as a standard exploration frigate. She could carry enough consumables to stay in the field for six months at a time. While she wasn't intended to engage in combat herself, her designers had given her four retractable, double laser turrets just in case the enemy found her. Her jet black hull would minimize detection by reflected sunlight, and she carried an impressive load of recon, message and attack drones both for use by her fighters and by the carrier itself if necessary.

It didn't take him long to get settled into his impressively large and very comfortable quarters on board the ship. Only a few of her crew had already reported for duty. While physical construction was complete, the shipyard workers were testing her systems and were crawling all through the ship's innards. A quick check of the personnel roster showed that his Executive Officer and Deputy CAG had not yet reported aboard. He didn't know his new XO but the DCAG was one of the test pilots from his time at the Alpha Base. A glance at the rest of the senior officers did not reveal any other names he was familiar with. *A lot of new faces to get to know.* When Shiloh checked his personal message inbox, he saw a message from Admiral Howard. He opened it.

[It's not official just yet, but by the time Defiant is ready to leave the shipyard, your promotion to Senior Commander will have made its way through the necessary red tape. I'm pleased to say that you've earned it. Congratulations!]

Senior Commander! One step below the one star flag rank of Vice-Admiral. Shiloh realized that his heart was beating fast, and he was breathing hard. Did he really deserve this promotion when he wasn't the tactical genius that Howard and others thought he was? He was inclined to say no but SOMETHING was causing his visions and he doubted that it was a Guardian Angel.

With the planned launch date just days away, Shiloh found himself more and more busy, and he was very glad when Lt. Cmdr. Sumi Tanaka, his new XO, reported aboard. The fact that his XO was once again a woman made him wonder if the Bureau of Personnel was doing it deliberately for some reason. Women in the Space Force officer ranks made up about 46% of the total, and the odds of getting three female XOs in a row was almost eight to one against. But he had nothing against women officers, and both Johansen and Chenko had proven to be quite capable. Tanaka wasted no time diving into her new duties, and Shiloh saw an immediate decrease in his own workload. With no fighters aboard yet, his duties as CAG consisted of supervising the fighter support teams and their officers in the process of getting organized and familiar with their new duties. He was pleased to see that one of his lesser recommendations had been implemented. To avoid duplication of personnel, the officer in charge of each fighter's support/maintenance team was also qualified to pilot that fighter if a human pilot was deemed necessary, although Shiloh had no intention of taking fighters away from their A.I.s' control. When Brad Falkenberg, the new DCAG, reported aboard, Shiloh had a long and friendly chat with him about fighter A.I.s and their apparent sentience. Falkenberg agreed with Shiloh about the need to treat them as if they were fellow Space Force comrades, and he told Shiloh that he would encourage the support team leaders to form close friendships with their fighter A.I.s.

Chapter 18 It Sure Beats My Idea All To Hell

All of sudden, it was launch day. The ship was fully manned and all systems had checked out. It was time to put her through her paces. The next 48 hours were spent going through a series of performance trials, including microjumps and gas giant refueling both by fuel shuttles and by direct skimming. Shiloh's supersonic, intermittent scoop procedure was now the officially recommended way of skimming. With all trials completed and her fuel tanks full, Defiant set her vector for the Epsilon Eridani star system and the CFP manufacturing facility there in order to pick up her complement of fighters and A.I.s. With fuel to burn and the certainty of being able to refuel there, Shiloh ordered the ship to accelerate to a higher than usual velocity in order to minimize Jumpspace duration. His Astrogator told him they set a new record for the fastest jump from Sol to Epsilon Eridani. Shiloh suspected that his Astrogator was exaggerating but didn't bother to check if it was true or not.

When Defiant arrived at Epsilon Eridani, they found 25 eager fighter A.I.s chomping at the bit to land on the carrier and see some action. After all were safely aboard, and Defiant was on its way to their first destination, Shiloh called a briefing of all senior officers, fighter support team leaders and by electronic means, all A.I. pilots.

As he stepped up to the podium, Shiloh said, "Remember this briefing, people. This is the first operational briefing for this ship, and you'll be able to tell your grandchildren about it some day."

There was general laughter at that, and Shiloh could have sworn that some of the laughter came from the A.I.s.

"As you may or may not know, we're on our way to Bradley Base, but that will be a quick stop to refuel and check the status of enemy activity, if any. Our mission is not what I was hoping for, namely that we'd be sent to launch a counter-strike on enemy star systems. Unfortunately, there's a more urgent task that only we can perform for the time being. HQ is convinced that the aliens have downloaded astrogational data from one of our captured ships, data that pretty much lays out all of human-explored space and the locations of all our colonies, and Earth."

There was a groundswell of murmuring which quickly died down again.

"That means they could penetrate deep into our space using systems containing gas giants to refuel, and then strike at military or civilian targets. Right now we have no early warning system in place. Well, our job is to set one up. We'll be deploying fighters in star systems with gas giants, in a buffer zone between our colonies and where we think the aliens are. This buffer zone will consist of five layers that are each about 10-12 light years wide. The Bradley Base star system is in the second layer. Layers one and two will have fighters deployed in them by tankers. We'll take care of layers three to five. This means multiple jumps, and it will take us an estimated 65 days."

That brought groans from the human personnel. Shiloh held up his hand.

"Yes, I know that doesn't sound very exciting, but we need this early warning system. Each gas giant will have two fighters deployed to monitor any enemy activity near it and to report such activity by message drone. Monitoring fighters will avoid detection and especially combat, whenever possible."

More groans, and this time Shiloh was sure that those were coming from the fighter pilots themselves.

"The intention here is to keep the enemy in the dark about our early warning system. If they find out about it, they're likely to try to punch a hole in it by destroying the sentry fighters, and we want to avoid that. One out of each pair of fighters will be equipped with a refueling module so that it can refuel itself and the other fighter indefinitely, but I can assure you fighter pilots that you won't be expected to stay on station out there forever. When you detect enemy vessels, you'll observe their activity and, if possible, determine which star system they appear to be headed for next. Then you'll send a message drone with that information to the nearest base, using the high speed boost maneuver that Iceman and Maverick perfected if necessary. Thereafter, you'll continue to monitor your gas giant. Systems that have more than one gas giant will have more than one pair of fighters. If you're detected, your orders are to disengage and leave the vicinity of the gas giant, and then send a message drone with that information. Fighters will each carry one and only one attack drone to be used when combat is unavoidable. The rest of the two payloads will be evenly split between message and recon drones. Detailed contingency plans will be downloaded to our fighters at the end of this briefing. That in a nutshell is the mission. Are there any questions?"

Naturally there were, and Shiloh did his best to answer all of them. When there were no more questions, he said, "Alright, then. This briefing is concluded. Let's do this right. Our ship has a reputation that needs building. You're dismissed."

The trip to Bradley Base took just over 241 hours. Shiloh made sure that Defiant had enough fuel to skip past the star system where the convoy had been ambushed. When the ship dropped out of Jumpspace in the Bradley Base star system, which was designated as Omega 4, Shiloh was on the Bridge at his Command Station. The ship emerged at the extreme edge of the system at a distance from its sun that would have been beyond the orbit of Neptune if they had been in the Solar System. The gas giant, where the Base was located, was almost on the opposite side of the sun, which blocked a direct line-of-sight path between the base and Defiant. Even with their exit velocity of 500 kilometers per second, it would take days to reach the base traveling through normal space. That was why the Astrogator was already calculating a series of micro-jumps that would bring Defiant on an approach vector to the Base at a distance that should be just inside the detection range of the Base's patrolling fighters. The three microjumps with vector changes in between took almost another hour. After the third microjump, Defiant sent a tight beam low-powered laser signal to the Base with a message announcing their arrival. The reply came eight minutes later. Defiant was cleared to enter orbit around the Base's moon. No further enemy activity had been detected since the battle. There was no personal message from Base Commander Korolev, but there was from Iceman.

"Welcome back, CAG! Now that you're back, we'll see some action!"

Shiloh chuckled and made a mental note to respond to Iceman when they got closer. The trip into orbit was anticlimactically uneventful, which suited Shiloh just fine. After sending a greeting to Iceman and the other fighters that were on jump detection patrol, Shiloh discovered that Korolev was asleep, but Sejanus was awake. With Tanaka in charge on the Bridge, Shiloh went back to his quarters and had a confidential chat with Sejanus by video.

After the usual salutations, Shiloh said, "Listen, Marcus. I wanted to talk with you about Iceman and the others. You've got what … 25 fighters here now?"

"That's right, Sir. They made good our losses from the battle."

"How evolved are the newcomers at this point? Have they displayed the same level of individuality as the veterans?"

Sejanus pondered that for a bit and then said, "I'm not sure they're at the same level of eccentricities, but they definitely act as if they're sentient."

"The reason I'm asking is that I've got a ship full of rookies, for lack of a better word. They're only just starting to evolve their own identities. I'm thinking of swapping half of your veterans for half of my rookies and pairing up one of each for the deployment we've been ordered to make." He then went on to explain the buffer zone early warning network that Defiant was tasked with setting up.

"Yes, I can see how that would benefit things if the sentry fighters detected enemy activity. I'm not sure Korolev would agree to it, though," said Sejanus.

"I'm not sure she would have any authority to veto it. You're the Base CAG. Those fighters are your responsibility, not hers."

Sejanus didn't look happy. "Yes, but she's not only the Base Commander, she's also the Task Force Commander, too, don't forget, and my squadron of fighters is part of that Task Force."

Damn, thought Shiloh. *I did forget that.*

"Okay, I guess she really does have a veto. I'll talk with her when she's awake and see if I can convince her to sign off on this. Now, on to other things. Has there been any sign at all of enemy activity? Anything?"

Sejanus shook his head. "Not a peep. I almost wish they'd send a few ships to recon the system or something. At least that would break up the boredom a little bit. I can't help wondering if they're planning something big."

Shiloh snorted. "Oh, I'm pretty sure they are. The question is are they going to attack Bradley again or go after a new target. That's why we've got to set this early warning network up pronto. When will Korolev be on duty again?"

"Well as you know, she doesn't take regular shifts at Ops, but according to her normal schedule, I'd expect her to be up in about four to five hours."

Shiloh smiled. "Good! That'll give us time to practice fuel skimming the giant. By the time we're done, we'll be fully refueled, and Korolev will be awake. If she's okay with the fighter swap, we can do that while Defiant is heading out for the jump to our first deployment target. I'll leave her a message to call me when she's available. It was good to see you again, Marcus. Shiloh clear."

With the video call over, Shiloh decided to let Tanaka handle the refueling operation. It would be only her second time in charge of that operation, but she had handled the first one just fine, and he was confident she could handle this one too. He would observe the operation from the back of the Bridge, but let her keep command of the ship.

Switching the intercom channel to the Bridge, Shiloh said, "Bridge, this is Shiloh."

Tanaka answered almost immediately. "Go ahead, Skipper."

"Sumi? Take the ship out of orbit and into GG orbit to conduct a refueling operation."

After a slight pause, she said, "Conduct refueling operations from the gas giant, yes Sir! Any other orders, Sir?"

"Not right now. Let me know when we're about two minutes from contact with the giant's atmosphere, would you?"

"Certainly, Sir."

"Very good, Sumi. Carry on. Shiloh clear."

The refueling operation went off without a hitch, while Shiloh watched. As Defiant, now back in orbit again, came out from the back side of the gas giant, Base Commander Korolev called. Shiloh was in command again since Tanaka's duty shift was over.

When Korolev's face appeared on the main display, Shiloh said, "Hello again, Commander. Thank you for responding to my message. Are you aware of Defiant's mission?"

"Yes, Shiloh. I got the notification with the last resupply convoy. I was told to cooperate as much as possible."

Hoho, thought Shiloh. *That makes a difference. Howard didn't tell me that part.*

"Excellent. Here's what I want to do."

He explained the idea of taking half of the Base's experienced fighters and replacing them with 'rookies' and why. Korolev, to her credit, didn't show any negative emotion.

"I have no objections to that at all. In fact, you'd be doing me a favor if you take Iceman, Maverick and Hunter. Their cheekiness is starting to get annoying."

Shiloh laughed. "I can understand that, and yes, I'll be glad to take those cheeky bastards off your hands. I'd like to start the transfer right now while Defiant swings around to our jump vector. Okay with you?"

"Fine, fine," said Korolev waving her hand. "I'll have Sejanus coordinate that with your people. Anything else you need from me, Commander?"

"No. That'll do nicely for now. We'll see you on our return leg. Shiloh clear."

Shiloh let Falkenberg make the arrangements with Sejanus's deputy CAG and listened in to the exchange between the Base and those veteran fighters selected to transfer to Defiant. Iceman, Hunter and Maverick were borderline ecstatic. The others were pleased, too. Shiloh couldn't help wondering if those three were starting to consider Korolev as annoying, too. It took almost three hours of acceleration before the incoming fighters all landed, transferred their jump detection gear to the rookies, who then launched to take their place in the patrol. Those fighters that stayed behind adjusted their trajectories to cover any temporary holes in the detection grid, until such time as the newcomers could take their stations.

As Defiant settled down on the vector that would allow it to jump to its first destination, Shiloh reviewed the deployment plan. The five layers of star systems were color coded, with red being the closest to the sphere of space inhabited by humans, the next being orange, then yellow, green and finally blue. Defiant would deploy this initial batch of fighters in the blue layer, with the first target system designated as Blue1. The path to Blue2 and the rest looked like random changes of direction, but Shiloh knew it actually represented a carefully calculated path that minimized the total amount of time required to jump between systems.

The deployment of the first pair of fighters in Blue1 went smoothly. Defiant didn't even slow down very much while in the system. The deployed fighters accelerated towards the gas giant, and as soon as it was deemed clear of enemy ships, Defiant pointed her bow to Blue2 and re-entered Jumpspace.

As the ship emerged in the outer reaches of Blue2, Shiloh felt a chill run down his spine. He shrugged it off. Several hours later, Defiant was close enough for her two fighters to streak ahead and verify that this system's gas giant was devoid of alien ships. Maverick and Hammer launched and began their high speed run to the gas giant. While they were on their way, Shiloh's duty shift ended, and he returned to his quarters and went to sleep. It seemed to him that he had just shut his eyes when the Bridge called. Checking his chronometer, he realized that he'd been asleep for almost an hour.

"Shiloh here. What is it, Sumi?"

The XO's voice was tense. "One of Maverick's recon drones has detected what appears to be reflected sunlight off a metal hull. Maverick's requesting permission to order the drone to determine distance with its rangefinder laser."

Shiloh was instantly wide awake. "Only one contact?" he asked.

"Only one so far, yes Sir." replied Tanaka.

Shiloh thought fast. The reflected sunlight, if that's what it was, had been detected by passive optical sensors, but it only gave the drone a direction to the object, not a distance. The low-powered rangefinder laser that the latest version of recon drones had would fire a timed pulse of laser light and measure how long it took for the reflected laser light to return. That would tell them how far away the object was. The risk was that the enemy ship might detect the laser pulse, which would tip them off to the drone's presence and eliminate any advantage Shiloh had for covert surveillance. But if they didn't get a range determination, they'd have no way of knowing where the alien ship was headed or how fast it was going, and THAT information was critically important.

"Tell Maverick he has permission to determine the range. Send the ship to Battle Stations. I'll be on the Bridge shortly. Shiloh clear."

No sooner had he finished speaking then the Battle Stations klaxon sounded. Tanaka must have had her finger hovering over the activation button while they were talking. He put on a fresh uniform and sprinted for the Bridge, which was just down the hall. Tanaka saw him enter and unbuckled herself from the Command Station chair.

As Shiloh walked over to her, he said. "I have the Con, XO."

"Yes, Sir. Maverick has the word. We should get a report back in about … 90 seconds or so."

Shiloh nodded as he sat down in the chair. He buckled himself in while the chair adjusted itself to his body.

"Good," he said.

Tanaka started to turn towards the entrance to head for Engineering where the Executive Officer usually went during Battle Stations, but Shiloh had other ideas.

"Not so fast, XO. I'm wearing two hats on this mission, and if we find ourselves in a shooting match, I don't want to have to con the ship and fight the battle at the same time. So I want you to relieve Rodriguez at the Helm Station, and you'll take back the Con while I concentrate on the bigger picture. Rodriguez can take your place in Engineering."

Tanaka was clearly taken aback. "Well, if you're sure you want to do that, Sir, I'll comply with your orders."

Shiloh smiled and said, "I know what I'm doing, Sumi. I've used this technique before when I was Squadron Leader, only this time I have a squadron of fighters instead of frigates."

"Yes, Sir."

She nodded and stepped over to the Helm Station. Rodriguez had heard the exchange and was already vacating his station.

As soon as Tanaka sat down, Shiloh said. "The XO has the Con."

With the rest of the Bridge personnel now clear as to who was actually running the ship itself, Shiloh turned his attention to the displays that monitored the status of the fighters still in Defiant's Hangar Bay. Most were showing the green light of ready-to-launch status. The

Hangar Bay was in the process of depressurizing. All personnel there had already donned pressure suits.

"Iceman to CAG."

The sudden voice made Shiloh jump.

"Make it fast, Iceman. I'm kinda busy now," said Shiloh.

"Ah, roger that, CAG. If there's more than one bogey out there, we'll have a better chance of finding them if we launch more recon drones. Request permission to take Cobra Flight out for that purpose."

Shiloh wasn't ready to make that call yet. He needed more information first.

"I'll take that under advisement, Iceman. Standby."

The 90 seconds should be just about up by now, thought Shiloh. Sure enough, the data, relayed by Maverick from his drone to Defiant, showed that the bogey was almost six million kilometers away from the drone, and due to the geometry of Defiant's relative position to the drone, the range to Defiant was just over nine million kilometers. The ship's tactical computer took the range data, the drone's position relative to Defiant, and displayed the tactical situation on the main display. Shiloh looked at it carefully. Nine million kilometers sounded like a lot, but compared to the size of your average star system, it was relatively close. It was the vectors that were going to complicate things. Defiant was on a vector that would cross the gas giant's orbit while at the same time angle up from below the system's ecliptic. The bogey was heading 'downward' and off to one side of Defiant's vector. Defiant had enough speed left over from the jump to make it difficult to intercept the bogey or even just slide in behind it on a parallel vector. As Shiloh continued to evaluate his tactical options, he noticed that the contact status indicator beside the bogey's icon on the Tactical display changed from 'constant' to 'intermittent'. A beep from his console drew his attention to a smaller screen where Maverick had transmitted a text message.

[Sunlight reflection gone. Continuing to track bogey with laser. Active scanning?]

If the bogey were adjusting its attitude by rotating on its axis, that would change the angle of the reflected sunlight, and it would explain the loss of that contact. Maverick was asking for permission to order the drone to actively scan with radar, which would give them a clear picture of its course, speed, and any companions but also alert it to the human presence. *Not yet*, thought Shiloh. He transmitted the negative response to Maverick.

Turning to the Astrogation Station, he said, "Astrogator. Can you determine what system they're lining up for, if any?"

The reply came seconds later.

"As far as we can tell with this triangulation, they're most likely heading for Green4, Sir."

Shiloh called up the 3D star charts for the immediate environment. Green4 had two gas giants, and from there the bogey could pick from one of two paths containing star systems that formed what looked like rivers of stars with empty gaps in between. One path led to the Nimitz Base, which was also in the same star system as the Avalon colony. The other path led to more heavily populated colony worlds deeper in Human Space.

"I need a projected course change for a jump to Green4. I also need to see how much fuel we'd have upon arrival for various transit times."

"Okay, Sir. I'll have that for you shortly."

Why Green4, Shiloh thought to himself? *It's not that far away.* The bogey's vector seemed to indicate that it was leaving the vicinity of this system's gas giant, which suggested that it had refueled here. Even an Exploration Frigate had enough fuel to jump to Green4 and then jump again without refueling. Suddenly Shiloh knew the answer. The aliens might have survey data on all human-explored star systems, but they couldn't be sure if they'd encounter any human ships in these systems. So the safe thing to do would be to make a series of small jumps, refuel whenever possible, and if they encountered Human ships, they could always jump back the way they came. Far less risky than making long jumps into enemy held systems and not being able to refuel or jump away. *So then the next question was, is this just one ship, which would suggest a recon mission of some kind, or are we seeing just one of a whole fleet of ships on a strike mission?* The only way to answer that question without tipping his hand would be to arrive at Green4 first, ring both gas giants there with recon drones, and see what showed up. He'd have to wait for the astrogator's data on the jump to Green4 before he could answer that question, but there were other questions, too.

He had to get a warning back, but that was easier said than done, and there were several options. One was to send a message drone back to Bradley Base. They could then boost another drone to high speed for a direct jump back to Omaha Base, which was further back and where Shiloh knew that Admiral Howard was in the process of building up a Task Force of combat frigates. They were to be used to intercept any mass incursion that the early warning network might identify. Another option was to send a high speed message drone directly to Omaha Base from here, or they could send a high speed drone to Sol. Sending a message drone back to Bradley and from there to Sol, would be easy but not quick. High speed drones sent to either Sol or Omaha would be quick IF they could boost the drone fast enough before it entered Jumpspace. That IF depended on multiple factors that Shiloh couldn't even begin to evaluate. Before he could get any further in his thinking, the Astrogator put the requested data on the main display. Just as Shiloh had suspected. It would take so much fuel to bring Defiant's current high speed vector over to the right heading, that they'd arrive at Green4 with dangerously low fuel reserves and with a lead time that might or might not let them refuel safely before the bogey arrived. But if Defiant refueled here, the delay would mean that they'd never be able to beat the bogey to Green4. He needed to get help in identifying options.

"Iceman, I'm going to ask the XO and Astrogator to step over to my station for a strategy conference. I want you to listen in. Feel free to offer suggestions."

"Ah, roger that, CAG."

Both Tanaka and the Astrogator heard him and were already standing nearby.

"Okay, here's the problem. Our number one priority is to track this bogey or bogeys so that we find out where they're likely to penetrate our space. Getting to Green4 far enough ahead of them to refuel first will be highly risky. Refueling here first means there's a good chance we'll lose contact with them by the time we get to Green4. We also have to send a warning to friendly forces as soon as the situation allows. A high speed, boosted message drone directly to either Sol or Omaha Base would be ideal, but would put at risk whatever fighters are tasked with that mission due to potential fuel exhaustion. I'm looking for options."

Before either the XO or Astrogator could speak, Iceman jumped in.

"Green4 has two gas giants which now are almost at right angles to each other relative to the system's sun. If we get there first and station fighter sentries at both giants, they can pinpoint which one the enemy will use to refuel and Defiant can then refuel at the other one, using microjumps to get to it. After refueling, the contact fighter can relay the enemy's new jump vector, and Defiant will have enough fuel to boost to a high enough speed to arrive at the next system with plenty of lead time. While Defiant is boosting away from the Green4 GG, it can deploy a fully fueled fighter, which will then have enough fuel to send a message drone directly to Omaha Base and still make it back to the GG to refuel itself. Here's what that would look like."

Shiloh, the XO and the Astrogator turned to looked at the main display, which now showed a tactical representation of Green4 system with the projected arrival point for Defiant and two alternate paths to the gas giants depending on which one the enemy chose to refuel at. Shiloh turned to his Astrogator.

"What do you think, Martin?"

The Astrogator chuckled. "I think Iceman wants to put me out of a job! Without checking the numbers, I can't be sure of course, but it looks doable, and I'm sure Iceman has calculated it down to the final decimal."

Before Iceman had a chance to reply, Shiloh said, "XO?"

She sighed. "It sure beats my idea all to hell, Sir."

It did look good, thought Shiloh. *Damn good in fact, and Iceman came up with it FAST! Maybe A.I.s should be used as Astrogators.*

There were still unknowns of course. If there was only one bogey, then one of the two gas giants would be free for Defiant's use, but if there was more than one, and Shiloh was willing to bet there was, then it was conceivable that the enemy force might split up when it reached Green4 and refuel at both gas giants. Splitting up your force in potential enemy territory was not something that Shiloh would have done, but these were aliens after all, and who knew for certain how they thought? On the other hand, if the enemy force did split up, then Defiant's remaining fighters stood a good chance of kicking the crap out of one group before the other group could come to its aid. That might convince the other group to abort the mission. They might suspect that these intervening systems were being monitored. Keeping that fact a secret, while nice in theory, was not an absolute priority, and an aborted attack would give Humanity more time to complete the network and beef up defenses. There was one more problem.

"How do we know when they'll be arriving at Green4?" asked Shiloh to no one in particular.

Naturally Iceman spoke up first. "I have the answer, but I'll let the Astrogator field this one if he wants to."

Shiloh's eyebrows went up. *What a tactful way of letting Martin save some face. You continue to astonish me, Iceman.* He could see from Martin's expression that Iceman's gesture wasn't lost on him either.

"Thanks, Iceman. It's actually simple, Sir. We line Defiant up for Green4, all the while keeping track of the bogey's speed. When the bogey jumps, we'll know exactly how fast it entered Jumpspace, and that will tell us when it'll arrive at Green4. We then accelerate to a higher speed which will get us there first, with enough time to deploy sentry fighters and recon drones near both gas giants."

"Very good. That's what we'll do. XO, bring the ship to a jump vector for Green4. Iceman, you contact Maverick and Hunter. Tell them what they need to do to keep tracking the bogey, and also make sure that the DCAG is informed as well. Both fighters will stay in Blue2 after the bogey jumps away, as per the original mission. Any questions?" No one had any. "Good. Carry on then."

It took almost an hour for Defiant to swing around to a heading that it could use to jump to Green4. It and the bogey were now on parallel vectors, and while the bogey was further ahead, Defiant at this point was still traveling faster and was therefore catching up. At its closest point, the distance between them would still be more than a million kilometers. Defiant didn't have to get close in order to beat the bogey to Green4. During that time, the half dozen recon drones controlled by Maverick and Hunter used a rapidly repeating series of rangefinder laser pulses to track the bogey. With Defiant now on the precise vector for the jump to Green4, it resumed acceleration. The bogey disappeared into Jumpspace 89 minutes later, and since Defiant's speed was already greater, it jumped three minutes after that.

Chapter 19 Time To Roll The Dice

That extra speed enabled Defiant to emerge 22 hours later into the Green4 star system, 3 hours ahead of the bogey. Time enough to deploy recon drones and a pair of jump detection equipped fighters around each of the two gas giants, while remaining more or less equidistant from both. The drones would passively search for reflected sunlight contacts, while the fighters would attempt to pinpoint the exact location – and number – of ships emerging from Jumpspace. Deploying only two fighters near each gas giant was a calculated risk. A single fighter's detection gear could only cover a limited area, and if the bogey happened to emerge from Jumpspace outside that detection range, the equipment wouldn't see them. The space around each gas giant was so large that even if Shiloh had deployed all of his fighters among the two gas giants, it still wouldn't have guaranteed detection, AND recovering his fighters from both planets would prevent Defiant from being able to jump ahead of the bogey to their next destination. The time to the bogey's expected arrival in Green4 came and went. Because Defiant's distance from either gas giant was measured in millions of kilometers, ordinary light speed communication by tight beam laser was too slow. The only way for a sentry fighter to get word to Defiant quickly enough was to launch a message drone. It microjumped to the area where Defiant drifted, and less than a minute after the arrival time, the ship picked up a text message from a message drone sent from one of the fighters monitoring the gas giant that Shiloh had designated as Green4A.

[55 ships detected emerging from Jumpspace. No visual contact yet]

The text message was followed by a data stream, containing the precise coordinates. Shiloh was stunned. Fifty-five ships! This was no recon mission. It was clearly a major attack. The lack of reflected sunlight contact was very bad news. Without some idea of where at least one of those ships was, the recon drones would have no way of knowing where to point their laser rangefinders and therefore couldn't determine where those ships were heading, or how fast they were going. Using active radar scanning would tip the aliens off to the fact that humans were aware of their presence. At least the lack of contact reports of any kind from Green4B suggested – but did not prove – that the aliens were not intending to use it to refuel. Whatever else Defiant might do, it had to refuel from Green4B as quickly as possible, otherwise its options would be severely limited.

Shiloh was about to order Tanaka to microjump the ship to Green4B to refuel, when the Bridge faded from his field of vision, and he saw himself standing in front of Admiral Howard. But this vision was different. Instead of the usual crystal clear image, this image was blurry, almost as if he were looking at the scene through distorted lens. Howard's voice sounded strange too. The pitch was not quite right, and the words didn't seem to be synchronized with Howard's mouth.

"I congratulate you on your decision to remain at the star system where you detected the enemy fleet. If you had continued to track them, you would not have been able to detect the much larger force that was following in their wake, and we wouldn't have been able to gather enough strength in time to stop it. For your brilliant strategy, I'm promoting you to the next higher level of rank."

As Shiloh listened to Howard's words, which were said in a calm, almost monotone voice, he noticed that Howard was repeatedly jabbing his pointed right hand in Shiloh's direction and the expression on Howard's face did not look particularly pleased. If he'd been watching this scene without any sound at all, he would have interpreted Howard's body language as indicating anger. The dissonance between the visual and auditory impressions was striking.

What is going on, he asked himself. He looked around to see if anyone was looking at him. No one was. Tanaka was conning the ship from the Helm Station again. Falkenberg was down in the Hangar Bay supervising the fighters and their support teams. There was something not right about this vision, but Shiloh couldn't put his finger on it, and he didn't have time to analyze it further. Decisions had to be made. The fighter at Green4A would be following previously given instructions and maneuvering his drones under the assumption that the fleet would head for the nearest gas giant. Even if the drones didn't detect any reflected sunlight from any of the alien ships before they reached the gas giant, those ships would agitate the planet's atmosphere enough with friction and turbulence that their presence would be detected if the drones were close enough. The drones would then attempt to pinpoint the enemy's exact locations and vectors using the range finding lasers as the ships emerged from the planet's atmosphere. In theory it should work, but it had never been tried before, so no one really knew.

What Shiloh had to decide now was whether Defiant would proceed to Green4B, as planned, to refuel so that it could boost a high speed message drone, and also beat the enemy fleet to their next destination. But if the vision were correct about an even larger follow-on fleet, then staying right where they were would be the best option. On the other hand, if the vision were wrong somehow, then perhaps there was a third option that he hadn't considered yet. His visions so far had all involved a change of plans from what he otherwise would have done. If he applied that parameter to this situation, he would proceed to refuel at Green4B. The mere fact that he was having some kind of vision to begin with, strongly suggested that refueling to boost to the next destination was NOT the optimal strategy, but staying in Green4 and doing nothing just didn't sit well with him. The only other strategy he could think of was to attack that fleet before they could jump away. He needed to confer with his senior officers and to his mind that included Iceman as well. Falkenberg could join the discussion by video intercom, as could Iceman. Tanaka and Rodriguez could step over to his station as they had done before.

When all four were present, either electronically or physically, Shiloh said, "Valkyrie has detected 55 ships emerging from Jumpspace near Green4A. He'll try to pick up their precise locations and vectors as they refuel. I now have to decide what our response will be. For reasons that I do not want to go into now, I'm having doubts that our plan to refuel at Green4B and then jump ahead of the enemy fleet is still our best option. I want to hear assessments from all of you on an alternative strategy to attack the fleet here in this system, and if you have a completely different idea, I'd like to hear that too. You first, Brad."

The Deputy CAG took a deep breath and said, "Well, we have 19 fighters still aboard and we have enough attack drones to give them five each, which should be plenty, but the challenge will be to get targeting lasers on each enemy ship, unless we want to use active scanning. Without one or the other, the attack drones won't know where to aim. Right now, Valkyrie doesn't have enough recon drones to target more than half a dozen ships at one time, assuming that they can find their targets to begin with. If they were in fact intending to refuel at Green4A, then the ideal time to hit them would be while they're still deep in the gas giant's atmosphere. Their ability to see us will be limited, but we'd have to get drones and/or fighters in close to be able to precisely locate their ships from the wakes they leave behind as they plow through the gas."

Shiloh nodded and turned from the video screen with Falkenberg's image to his Astrogator.

"Can we get our fighters that close before the enemy re-emerges from the atmosphere, Astrogator?"

"There's no way to know for certain. We don't have any data on how fast they can refuel, Sir. But if their refueling time is similar to ours, then the answer is yes. Defiant would have to jump as close as possible to the opposite side of the gas giant from where the enemy fleet is, so that their jump detection gear wouldn't pick us up. We'd launch our fighters, which would accelerate at maximum in order to make a close, high speed pass, and then fire their attack drones when they had visual contact with the enemy ships."

He was about to say more when Tanaka interrupted. "What if they keep some of their fleet in orbit to stand guard while the rest refuel? If I were their fleet commander, I wouldn't risk exactly that kind of ambush by refueling all ships at the same time. How would we deal with that?"

There was a short pause, and then Iceman spoke. "We launch our fighters and use the gas giant's atmosphere against them. Our recon drones will monitor their position and speed as they refuel. The fighters will enter the atmosphere far enough away that the enemy won't spot them. When the distance has dropped to less than 100 kilometers, our fighters will swing around so that they're behind the alien ships still refueling and then move back up to the edge of the atmosphere. The enemy won't be looking down at the planet for signs of human activity. They'll be watching the space around and above them. When all 55 ships have finished refueling, our recon drones will relay that data to our fighters, which will emerge from the atmosphere, stay behind the enemy fleet at close range and launch attack drones. At precisely that same time, our recon drones will go to active scanning, use that data to triangulate each enemy ship's exact position, and relay that data to our attack drones. The enemy will react to the radar scanning from above and fire at our recon drones while our attack drones get within one kilometer of their targets. They can then use their own radars for terminal guidance, and that fraction of a second before impact won't be enough time for the enemy to retarget their lasers."

No one said anything for almost five seconds.

Finally Shiloh said, "That plan will require split second coordination to work, but other than that, I don't see any flaws with it. Does anyone else?"

The responses were uniformly 'no'.

"Iceman, have you calculated all of the vectors and signal times needed to make this work?" asked Shiloh.

"Ah, roger that, CAG," was the immediate response.

Shiloh took note of the fact that Iceman referred to him as the CAG and not as the ship's CO.

"Very good. In that case, I want Iceman to coordinate this attack. He will issue the necessary orders to Defiant's Helm and all the fighters involved, as well as monitor the attack as it proceeds, and react as needed if things don't go as planned. Iceman, make sure you keep the Defiant's tactical computer updated on all vector changes and transmissions. XO? You'll monitor but not interfere with Iceman's Helm directives."

As Tanaka nodded, Shiloh continued, "Iceman, how soon do we need to begin the attack plan?"

"The longer we wait, the less chance of pulling this off, CAG. I would not recommend waiting more than five more minutes. The sooner, the better."

"Understood. Does anyone have any questions?" No one spoke up. "In that case, return to your stations."

When everyone was back at their assigned stations, Shiloh took a deep breath. *I hope I'm doing the right thing*, he thought to himself.

"Okay, Iceman. The mission objectives are the total destruction of that alien fleet. With that as your goal, you have my permission to commence that attack plan."

"I won't let you down, CAG."

Almost immediately, Defiant's engines started pushing her onto a new vector. The main display showed a countdown to a microjump. Shiloh's station started showing increased activity in the Hangar Bay as the support teams began to load more attack drones onto each fighter. The moment that Shiloh had been dreading, being in command of a major battle WITHOUT any reliable vision to guide him, was now upon him. If this plan went wrong, and he survived the battle, Howard would be within his rights to court martial Shiloh.

It was time to roll the dice.

To Be Continued

Author's Comments:

If you look up my other books on Amazon or Smashwords, you'll see that I've written three sequels to books by H. Beam Piper. The Synchronicity War Part 1 is my first original novel and series. Part 2 and 3 are now available.

The Synchronicity War Part 2

Self-publishing on Amazon is a tough game. Every author is trying to push his or her books into the top 100 of a particular category in order to be seen by more potential readers. Many readers won't even look at a book description if it has an average rating of less than 4 out of 5 stars. If you like The Synchronicity War Part 1, and you think it deserves 5 stars, then please take the time to post a 5 star review. It really does help and constructive criticisms will help me become a better writer. You can be notified by email of when I publish new books by going to my Author's page on Amazon and looking for the subscription link in the top right corner.

I haven't plotted out ALL of the details yet, but I can assure you that Victor Shiloh and Iceman are in for one hell of a ride.

You can follow me on twitter at @DwehrSFwriter.

Made in the USA
San Bernardino, CA
25 June 2014